City of a Million Dots

Pete Maguire

For Dot, everything beautiful begins with you

This novel is a work of fiction, yours, any resemblance to any persons living or dead is entirely coincidental.

Published 2014 in the UK in conjunction with Completely Novel

Copyright © Pete Maguire

ISBN 9781849145206

Cover design by Dan Johnson anotherfinemesh@gmail.com

Interior design and typesetting by Pete Maguire

pete@cityofamilliondots.co.uk
www.cityofamilliondots.co.uk

Dear Victor,

In 18 minutes time I will go and lie on the railway track at Garelt. I will wait for the 00:13 D-train to come around the Garelt bend and 12 seconds after sighting it, it will reach my head. You don't know it yet, but I'm doing this for you, my son. I'm committing your suicide. Of course, it is because of me that you wanted to commit suicide, but that is a small thing, Victor. There is nothing bigger than freedom of choice.

This is my greatest gamble, Victor, the planning has been excruciating, the execution is just that, but the outcome... I daren't even imagine it, for they watch, they are everywhere. You have already encountered them, for it was their minions that killed Emily. I understand that you loved her, but I hope in the future you will be able to count that as an acceptable loss. The heart is an attractive playground, but battles are won and lost at a cellular level. Karl will help you with this.

Before I die, I will be you. I will feel everything that you are. I look forward to knowing you as I could not in life. I cannot send this as it would change too much, I will burn it and perhaps, from the particles that enter the air, you will know that I say, goodbye.

Albert Scram

Body Parts

1

If poor people are the blood of the city, then the Diner is the liver, and in the cold metallic corridor of Crow Street, the humming Diner sign said, come in and I will spit you out a better person.

Victor pushed the door and entered.

In the gloomy interior, the bobbing heads of city misfits stared down as they murmured low vowels at each other. Victor seated himself on one of the cherry drop stools that curved around the counter and carefully placed his coat on the one next to him. A waitress leaning against the back counter glanced up, revealing a red, star-like blemish on the sclera of her left eye. Victor picked up a menu, but ignored all the writing.

'Coffee,'—checking the name tag on the waitress—'please, Linda.' He smiled. 'This place seen better days.'

She seemed little interested but cocked her right eyebrow.

Somewhere clocks ticked, masses of them piled on top of each other, they ticked like his heart. *Let me out.*

On the back counter under glass covers, were a collection of foods looking like pickled body parts. The clock under said 12:45am. Victor had been awake since 3 am previous, stolen from his sleep by the relentless Neon demanding another model.

1

Linda slid a coffee in front of him, the shiny white cup mocking the faded pallor of the Formica. On the counter was a local newspaper with the lead headline *Train Runs Over Sleeping Drunk At Garelt*. Ants and roaches crawled past without a second glance and flies rose lazily out of the sugar bowl. Victor thought of the enzymes and digestive juices oozing from fly proboscis onto the sugar granules. He decided against sugar, splashed some milk in and picked up his cup. For a moment he was alone, coffee swilling into his mouth, giving a dry pleasure.

The flies on the sugar bowl watched him with suspicion. Shit... he'd been working too close with Dr Neon. Dr fucking Neon, the guy was a joke. Yet Victor didn't believe that, he *thought* it, let his mind have the freedom, but it was a futile attempt to escape. Point was, he was hooked. Time and time again he harked back to the night when he'd stumbled upon the Elgance Gallery over on Carden Street. At that point in his life, he had been languishing, passively waiting for something to happen. Then in an instant, reality struck like a wall thudding down in front of him. Something, from gutter to sky, held him on the sidewalk outside the gallery. He had shuddered within his frame, his muscular structure struggling with quick release adrenals, while his curiosity held him rooted. Having been a test pilot, he understood accelerated force and movement, but he had never felt anything like the force that compelled him to turn to the painting in the window of the gallery.

Look at me! It screamed.

And look he had, and still did, every time he closed his eyes. At first glance he'd been overloaded, his brain struggling to comprehend. It was like staring into the turbine of a jet engine.

The picture lurked, grinning like a devil. *The person who did this, I left them there, and now I am here with you.*

'More coffee?'

Victor looked up. 'What? Yeah, thanks.' He watched Linda's arm as she poured the coffee. Sketchpad white, hairs charcoaled in—Melanoma Island just above the wrist. Her hand dipped swanlike in an elegant pour, coffee pot held firm. A smell of lemonade and roses reached his nostrils—her essence.

That was what he'd seen when he'd looked at the painting— the essence of a human. But it wasn't humans as he knew them. It was a mutation, some amalgamation of bodies that Neon had formed. It spoke to Victor's core, tripping a visual floodgate and loosening his grip on sanity. The picture was a promised land. He'd been shocked. Made to stand and watch in awe. There was pleasure, yet somehow it was like being included in a group, only because they wanted to nail you to the floor.

'Want anything to eat?'

Victor looked at the body parts on the back shelf. 'Got anything other than that?'

'You can look at the menu.'

'I don't like looking at menus.' For a moment they stared at each other. 'You recommend anything?'

She smiled, sardonically. 'Many things. None of them available here though.' She shook her head, long brunette hair dropping around her shoulders.

Victor noted the perfect C of her cheekbone. 'Don't worry, coffee's good.'

'Is it?'

'Well actually, it's crap. But that's fine with me.' She was more alive than Victor expected. Neon said to watch for the ones with *Genetic bloom*. Perhaps she would do as a model.

'What you staring at?'

'Nothing, just thinking.'

'Dangerous stuff that.' Linda's face transformed into an emaciated husk and then back to normal.

'Sure is.' He stuck the grotesque image into a head drawer. He had a whole circular cabinet around the inside of his skull — drawers for images of Emily, drawers for the shit Neon set off, drawers for what the Soul Bugs unleashed. The drawers made his skull more solid and everything quieter. Briefly anyway.

He and Linda chatted amiably for a while. Linda laughed about the night weirdos; tight and morose. Victor tried to observe Linda's periphery through Neon's eyes. How when she talked she gesticulated with her hands as if she was mimicking waves. How her cheekbones had as much bounce as her hair and how, under tired eyelids, alert eyes darted. He watched her ghosts and sentries, millions of invisible factions and divisions that revealed more than she would ever tell about herself.

'... so this one guy,' Linda leaned on the counter, shrinking the vacuum of their personal space, 'came in and sat over there.' She waved at a seat over by the window. 'Had a coffee like you, then spent ages folding up his coat. Kept unfolding and refolding it, tutting to himself and starting again. Anyways, eventually he started setting some paper on fire, so we threw him out. Yesterday we heard that he'd folded the coat to make a pillow for his head, cause he'd gone and laid down on the tracks by Garelt. Train went right over him. That's something worth thinking about.'

'Was he drunk?'

'No, not at all. He was here for hours, drinking coffee.'

Victor smiled. 'I'll take it easy on the coffee then.'

'Nah, you go do it if you like, don't mind me.'

Victor looked around. It seemed something here was waiting for him. It couldn't be good. 'Listen, what time you knock off?'

Linda straightened up, eyes squinting. 'I don't date customers. Serving you lot is bad enough.'

Jesus, I'm like a goddamned pimp. 'No, don't get me wrong, it's just, my friend.'

'Blind date, don't think so.'

'Easy. Look, he's an artist.' Victor looked down at his coffee cup, the future looked murky. 'He's always looking for models, muses, you know, call it what you want.'

'And you pick me. Why?'

'I dunno, you got something. Something makes you stand out.'

'Nice. You think I just work here? Don't have other things to do?'

'It's not my concern. Just telling you of an opportunity. I'm thinking more of my friend, actually.' Victor wanted to get out. This girl was alright, perhaps she didn't need to be involved with Neon. The fuck he was doing anyway? Sometimes Victor could swear that models left with something missing, not physical, more subtle.

Victor tried to refocus on Linda but his eyes were pulled behind her to a cake which rotted and then reformed. He shook

5

his head. The fucking *Illumination of Thought*. That was Neon's term for it. Neon said it was an exposure to the real, to the potential in every object for transformation. What it meant to Victor, was that he was on the edge of madness unless he kept his senses under constant control.

When he had first seen Neon's paintings he had looked without hesitation. Each had made an impression on him and he let it happen. Now he realised it was an invasion. Each painting was intense, ripping his perception inward with its colours and contours. When he looked back at the world after staring at a painting, things were a little different—sharper smells, menacing shadows, the incessant clatter of Bugs' feet... when he thought of Neon, he saw haunted hills littered with beacons; signposts left by an author long gone. The first painting was an unveiling of uncharted territory. It was mastery, a molecular alchemy of the soul. The rest —

'Who's your friend?' asked Linda.

'Dr Neon.'

'What the fuck! *The* Dr Neon?'

'Yes, *the* Dr Neon.'

'He's some painter,' said Linda.

'He's not a painter, he's a sick-fuck madman.'

'Good friend of yours then?'

Illumination began to unpeel the corners of reality. Snakes twirled in Victor's coffee cup and rats gnawed at the soles of his shoes. He ignored them and drank more coffee. That was what he did, he kept tight and overrode what Neon was putting out there. There were moments when he felt he was part of the molecular police sent undercover to limit the damage of which

Neon was capable. On other days he thought, Jesus fucking Christ, what the hell is happening, how far is this fucking thing gonna go? He still worked with him though, a part of him feeling that it was worthwhile, that Neon had to be where he was.

'What *do* you *do,* outside of here, Linda?'

'I...' she started up, but then stared past his shoulder, her pupils stirring something deep.

He let her have her moment and looked into the mirror behind the food. His face looked alien to him. A thought buzzed around his head like a fly. Damn pests... then he stopped and looked back at Linda. Jesus Christ, she had the same fucking eyes as Neon.

'I do some—'

'You paint.'

'Yeah, well, a little, my own stuff.'

Light raced over her shoulder. In the details were eddies and torrents, an exotic blend of capability and restlessness above a deep dark underside. Which, again, reminded him of Neon.

'One moment,' said Linda, as someone attracted her attention from down the counter and she moved off, her body undulating under a gray shapeless dress.

He watched her intently. It was very possible, if not likely, that she was capable of using him more than he was capable of using her. He took a breath and locked into her world.

He heard the patter of roach feet and the whish of evaporating water on the counter. The white rubber of Linda's gray plimsoll shoes longed to squeak but was muted by grease on the floor. The polyester of her tights swished while her cotton dress swashed. Folds of skin in her elbows moistly popped while her armpits grated their deodorised stubble. Behind him, the metal blind on the door was still infinitesimally rattling since his entrance. Over on a table by the window, a man cracked a newspaper, each page gave *its* sound; headlines shouted, small print whispered, advertisements blared and pictures sung, thudded and boomed. Salt shakers, long ago put down, settled in microscopic avalanches. Ketchup and mustard pots sludged and the grunge under tables snapped as it dried.

'You need more coffee?' Linda's words dropped in amongst the countless sounds.

Victor looked up. It was funny that in a city of a million sensations, not even considering the myriad others Neon had unleashed, someone would think to offer him a stimulant.

'Yeah, that's a good idea.'

Linda straightened up in front of him. She presented herself like a symphony of potential; eyes that could dance, sing or scorn, a full mouth brimming with mischief, cheeks swelling with self-belief and hair shining from no light in this stinking place. He could see that she didn't realise the immense possibilities that she contained. She had a purity that Neon wasn't capable of, or maybe her chaos was yet to come.

'So what is it *you* do?' asked Linda.

'I'm a little like Frankenstein's assistant. I collect body parts.'

Linda raised an eyebrow. 'That's nice.' Her mouth turned up slightly on the left.

Someone shouted from down the counter.

Victor sighed. Shit.

'Christ, I just gave him coffee.'

8

'Ignore him.'

'I can't do that.'

'Ignore him, trust me.'

'Look, I don't know you and I wanna keep my job.'

Victor took a deep breath, 'Linda—'

The voice from down the counter shouted again.

Yep, thought Victor, definite Bug in that grunt. Victor mused on the fact that they liked coffee too. 'Did you notice the voice?'

'Yeah. He shouted.'

'No.' Victor leaned closer to Linda. 'That, down there, is a Soul Bug.'

Linda's face creased into laughter. 'You're one weird, night time man. A Soul Bug?'

Victor smiled. 'A Soul Bug, yeah. Bugs from the deathlands who hijack human souls through unfulfilled vicious thoughts.'

Linda put her hands up in front of her and shook her head. She stared at him for a moment, then moved off down the counter.

Victor didn't care too much if she believed him. He sniffed the air. It was important to know which bastard he was going to be faced with. A dry musty smell lent towards an Armadillidum, the Wood Louse—not too dangerous, but dogged in their advance.

Linda returned. He liked that. Her face brightened by what she presumed was funny. In that instant there was a scraping noise and Victor rolled back off his stool. The shouting man advanced, emitting a high pitched whelp. He glared at Victor, but rushed past to where the crapper was.

Victor sat down. That was strange. No attack. He looked up. Linda was staring at him.

'That was weird,' she said.

'*Him*?'

'No, you.'

Victor kept his awareness over near the toilet. He had never known one of them to use anything other than instinct. Surely there was no way he was mistaken. Maybe he was too tired.

Shit... he needed to finish up and get out of here. The dullness of the Diner was starting to depress him. 'Look, do you want to work with Neon?'

'Well, you're a weird man.'

'Yes, I'm a weird man, I've always been a weird man. But in the world I live now, there are *weird* men, and when you meet the *weird* men, you'll be happy to know a man who is as sane as me.'

'Is that so?'

'Linda. I don't know you, but you know what? You're alright. You're surrounded by shit, but it doesn't stick. You might have access to potentials of human life that up until recently I didn't even know were possible.'

Linda put her hands to either side of her face, but she did not move away.

'And your eyes. You know, you have eyes just like Neon. Eyes that see further; that see differently. I don't know too much about the science of it, but I know where it is, that's what I do. I can be your friend, or I may even be your enemy. I don't know so much. But I don't put much down to chance. Sure as hell, something dragged me here. Come meet Neon, he's a man who's there. You've seen his paintings. They're not weird, they're true. *This* is the weird.'

Linda stared at him, her lips pursed. The dark of the Diner backed away from her.

It was over to her now. He watched another fly land on the sugar. *Well, if you can't beat them.* He dipped his spoon in and slowly poured the sugar into his coffee. The Soul Bug came out of the toilet. Without turning, Victor watched him in the mirror. The Bug walked close behind. Victor tensed, inhaling the mouldy Wood Louse smell. He could almost hear the plates of its body rustling together as it moved. It passed behind him and quickly left the cafe. The metal shutter clashed and clanked. All that was left was a faint smell of burning plastic. *Why the fuck hadn't it attacked?* Victor let his weight drop onto the round, red faux leather stool. Weariness stomped across his shoulders and the tops of his eyes. He realised he hadn't fully relaxed since he had met Neon, two months ago.

'Your Soul Bug has gone,' said Linda. 'You got some more out there?'

Victor turned and saw a gang of kids, late teens, staring in the window. 'Kage Kids.'

'Kaa-gay kids?'

'Yeah, Kage, means shadow. Techno heads obsessed with virtual worlds. Don't often see them out since people say they killed the internet. Good fucking job if you ask me.'

'Why's that, don't you like progress?'

'Progress?' Victor scoffed. 'New technology, same old human nature.'

'I see. Well, the non-progress is coming to visit you.'

A kid came in and stood next to him; too close. Victor sensed he was staring, so turned to face him. The kid's expression was like he was hanging off a speeding truck. Skin, moonlike. Hair, blonde streaked, slicked over with the grime of this and many other nights. His eyes were tuned into a frequency far higher than the undrugged population. He extended his hand to Victor.

'Bones, Tommy.'

'What?'

'The name. Tommy Bones.'

Victor took the hand, slightly greasy, but a decent hand. He liked the offer of it, but wasn't much in the mood, knowing it was going to end up in a proposition.

'I seen you around,' Tommy Bones said.

'Have you now.'

'You working with Neon?'

'Neon who?'

The kid laughed, short and quick. 'You working with Neon, he's the man, wooo.'

The kid was catterballing, his mind bouncing all over the place. 'What you want, kid?' Victor said, noticing that Linda was watching.

'Me and the droogs, we been clocking in with him.'

'Clocking in?'

'Listen, man.' The kid placed his hand on Victor's shoulder.

'Take your fucking hand off me!' Victor growled.

The kid moved his hand back.

'What the hell you want, kid?'

'I just,' the kid looked around, lowering his voice. 'We been clocking, we got Neon set up in a church.'

'Good for you, go say some prayers.'

'We got rid of the Bug for you, man.'

Victor pulled his shoulders back. 'What you know of Soul Bugs?'

The kid looked uneasily towards Linda.

'Don't worry,' Victor said, 'Linda knows all about the Soul Bugs.'

She flashed a smile at them.

Bones looked down quickly, then back at Victor. 'We see them man, we see them in our machines. Viruses, scrams, sweet truckers.'

'Scrams? What the hell are you calling Scrams?'

'Scrams? Emergency shut-downs, viruses that get in, krang! Whole system goes down, ka-chaa.'

'I like that. So kid, what's this to do with Soul Bugs?'

Bones chewed on his lip. 'Well, in the old days, man, virus comes in: identify, quarantine, remove. Easy shit. But now, juices don't flow as they should, even with the virus removed, there are Bugs in the electrics, in the places they *would've* gone, least expecting it, bam! Curly whirling.'

Linda was watching Tommy Bones intently. The kid's eyes looked like acid had been poured into the iris. He was babbling with his virtual slang-stream. Victor could see the point though, the parallel. 'Slow down, so you're saying the viruses, Bugs in your systems, are not disappearing, they're hanging on as post-emptive ghosts. I see the connection, but how do you hook that up with the real world?'

The kid carried on, not having blinked for two minutes.

'Well, it was Neon. We set him up in a church, put waves all over the dude, mega-homage. Then we seen the Bug trails leading to him. Man, they just swarmed all over, wild, like some charge of joy, and crazy still, viral fucking frenzy feeding on the blocks of paintings. The desire to remove, is the desire to improve.'

'Hold on, what the fuck?'

The kid's eyeballs bulged. 'Well, the act of destroying, was their creation. Fucking Bugs start re-building on screen. Wham bowzer, within three days we saw a physical manifestation of one of them. Johnny Ease had known it was coming, man, built the Bug Box: identify, quarantine, remove. Outta the system, outta the fucking room, man.'

'So you're able to take care of Bugs?'

'We got our ways, we can fuckin' do what is needed.'

'Simmer down, Tommy Bones. I'm sure you got your moves.'

The Diner door rattled behind Victor. He smelt the air—Jesus! A wasp Soul Bug, very fucking dangerous.

Tommy Bones started beeping. 'Shit.'

He and Victor turned around at the same time. Victor reached back and pulled his gun out of his coat—Colt Cobra, snub nosed revolver, six shot, swing out cylinder with a two inch barrel and chequered walnut grip. It was old, but damn he loved the feel in his hand.

Bones pulled out a black beeping box with a red digital read out.

'What the fuck you doing, kid?'

The man who had entered stood facing them. He was

framed by the dull gloom of the Diner reflecting off the steel shutter. At first glance he was a regular guy. Everything was in place; jacket, cream, elasticised waist, not too expensive, no brand identification. Trousers, cream chinos, nicely creased. Shoes, black, non-scuffed and shiny. His face though, seemed hollow, a protruding nose making the eyes appear pulled back. The eyes were small, black and trained on them.

For an instant there was quiet.

Victor figured the Bugs didn't like the human form as it stole most of their arsenal. But they came anyway, that was their way, attack and learn. What they attempted to do was to override your senses, using Bug hyper-pheromones to seduce the glandular system to panic.

Victor liked them to move first, but this one was happy to wait.

'Hey,' Linda shouted. 'I don't want any trouble here.'

Victor grinned. When it came to the Bugs, he would smash up his mother's house to get to them. The Bug's shoulders twitched. Victor raised his gun. The acrid pheromone smell hit the air. Victor felt anger and hate trying to crawl into his mood. He stayed focused. It was important to learn their ways, to see what new methods they were attempting. Tommy Bones slapped down on his box. The Soul Bug jerked, its eyes pulled open. There was a burning plastic smell, and he seemed to shrink in on himself. He turned quickly, yanked the door open and, emitting a squeal, ran off.

'What the?'

Tommy Bones turned to him. 'Soul Bug removed!'

'Tommy Bones, that's a useful piece 'a kit you got there.'

Bones grinned manically. 'And yours, man. Didn't get the name?'

'The name's Victor Scram.'

'Ha! Scram. That's why you was asking. You're the Emergency Shutdown man.'

'Don't you forget it.'

Some kids banged on the window outside.

'Chatter you later, man.' Tommy turned and scarpered.

Linda shook her head. 'You guys are waaay weird.'

'You're pretty weird yourself, Linda. Listen, I gotta get going, you have a think about working with Neon. I'll check back another time.'

'Yeah, you do that. Take care of yourself, Victor Scram.'

Menace in the Flower Garden

2

They walked fast, but Victor stopped as they entered each new street to check it out. His strut reminded Linda of her brother, Tony. They had the same tough way of being at the centre of everything. Tony was four years older than her. She had really looked up to him until he hit his late teens and left her behind. *Not this time Linds...*

For the first time in months there had been messages at the Diner from Tony, telling her to get in touch. She hadn't, she wanted to make something of herself first, didn't want to hear the *told you so*. Which was part of the reason she'd let Victor persuade her to come and meet Neon. But now, as they walked in the darks of Mariner Street, she realised she hadn't fully thought about what she was getting into.

Signs hung over shops; *Laundry, Gold-Cash-Gold, Same Day Loans,* but the shabby interiors didn't look like they could live up to their promises. The gangly, poorly illuminating street lights reminded her of Tommy Bones. Tommy had been coming to the Diner a lot over the last few weeks. He was a nice combination of peroxide blonde, techno-neural physicist, meshed together with a goofy, shy kid who was stoned all the time. Where the hell did she fit in though? She believed in herself, but this was one different world she was walking in.

They crossed the road. Mariner Street was quiet, warehouses

all shut up for the night, meshed behind black metal.

Victor looked up and down again and seemed annoyed by an ambulance parked about twenty feet away.

'That's where we're going,' he said, nodding to the warehouse beside the ambulance.

She'd been to a party there about a year ago. Back then, it had been occupied by artists and musicians, buzzing. Now it was sullen and dark.

'Neon sick?'

'He's sick alright, but what the fuck that is doing there, I don't know.'

They moved up quickly. Victor striding towards the ambulance, shoulders pulled back, arms out by his side.

The ambulance was a box plopped on the back of a truck, mainly white with a red bottom quarter. It was grimy, very settled into the night.

As they got closer, pressure built in her head like she was being pushed underwater.

Victor's face visibly tightened. 'What the?' his voice was gravelly. He reached an arm out and touched the corner of the ambulance.

Linda thought of graveyards, coffin lids and jagged spiky fences. She thought of naked limbs pale against dark soil and tree branches biting downward. A high pitched whine cut inside her head.

Written in the grime on the back of the ambulance was *Ambulance of Unforgiven Screams.*

'Victor?' The whine increased in her ears.

There was a bang from the warehouse where they were

going.

'Shit!' Victor moved back. 'Come on.' He rubbed at his face then turned quickly and yanked the door of the warehouse open.

They stepped inside, the piercing whine stopping as soon as the door clanked behind them.

A small square entrance booth led into a long corridor intermittently lit up by blinking strip lights. To the left was a windowless exterior wall. On the right, about fifteen feet ahead, were windowed rooms, giving the corridor a key shape. The corridor was littered with broken glass, aerosol cans, beer bottles, cigarette packets, computer monitors, condoms, paint cans and paint brushes.

'This way.' Victor placed his hand on Linda's lower back moving her forward.

Linda felt lighter for every step away from the ambulance.

Victor stopped every so often and listened.

There was a clanking, which seemed to be coming from rusty pipes that ran alongside and above them. But there was another sound like footsteps. It was hard to place where, but it seemed close.

'What is it? Soul Bugs?'

Victor shook his head, held up a hand and moved forward.

She followed, stepping quietly over the debris. Most of the separating walls between the corridor and side rooms were pulled apart, fluffy insides spilling out. The doors were all kicked off and windows smashed. The rooms were dark and trashed; tables turned upside down, chairs lying about with snapped off legs, posters had been ripped down and flung around. Linda peered into the darkness but couldn't see anyone and moved on, trying to stay close to Victor.

'Hey?' said Victor.

There was a man just ahead in the corridor, half hidden in the shadows. He stepped out into the light, kicking some cans out of the way like he was squaring up. He was about Victor's size, maybe fifty, with a hard worn face. His slicked back hair was strange—even in the dreary interior it seemed to have a metallic sheen to it like it was cast from iron.

'What you doing here?' said Victor.

'Any of your business?' Iron Head's voice was slow and calm.

'All my fucking business.' Victor stood big. 'You wanna get the fuck out?'

'Maybe I gotta see somebody.'

'Got an appointment?'

'Nope.'

Linda noticed the man glance up. She turned and saw another big man in a red chequered shirt moving quietly up the corridor behind her. 'Victor!'

Victor turned and leapt behind Iron Head, hooking his arm around his throat.

Linda had hardly seen him move.

Iron Head's calm face briefly registered surprise, but he didn't struggle. Almost as quick the new man rushed past Linda and dived towards Victor, fists flying. Dull thuds sounded as he hit Victor's face.

Frantically Linda looked around for a weapon.

Victor shook his head and with a roar raised up his arms

throwing Iron Head to one side. He thumped the new man, who staggered back against the wall. It was like the building had been shaken. Victor looked immense, fists balled and a grin on his face.

'Stop. STOP,' said Iron Head picking himself off the floor. 'Leave it, Arthur.'

The new man, Arthur, looked as capable as Victor. 'He touched the fucking ambulance. I thought it was going to explode in there. Who the fuck are you, man?'

'The name's Victor Scram.'

'Jesus,' said Iron Head. 'Victor fucking Scram. Well, that explains it.' He brushed himself off.

Linda watched Arthur staring at Victor in awe. There was something about the Arthur that horrified Linda, not him as a person, he had a nice enough face—bit scarred and worn—but he looked like he'd seen terrible things.

'Explains what?' said Victor. 'What is that ambulance? You don't look like paramedics.'

'It's a sealed box,' said Arthur. 'Nothing gets in and nothing is talked about.'

'What does the *Ambulance of Unforgiven Screams* mean?' Linda asked.

Arthur looked at her.

A high pitched whine pierced into her head and her breath was pulled to the back of her throat. Arthur looked away and it stopped.

'It don't seem right to me,' said Victor, 'but it don't interest me that much either.'

'Don't be so sure of that,' said Arthur.

21

A light blinked, like the building had taken a snapshot of the moment.

Victor held Arthur's stare. 'You got business with Neon?'

'Think we'll just leave it,' said Iron Head. 'Maybe catch him another time.' They turned and walked past Linda. Iron Head nodded at her and raised his eyebrow at the piece of wood in her hand. With a clank they were gone.

'Weird.' said Linda.

'Ain't that the truth.'

'You okay?'

'Course.'

'But he hit you *hard*? Didn't that hurt?'

'If you speed things up it hurts, if you slow it down, there are only little changes and little changes don't hurt.'

'Little changes?' Linda looked around at the mess. 'There are a lot of them going on.'

'That's the world, Linda. Come on, let's move.'

They reached a spiral staircase at the end of a corridor, went up a couple of flights and entered another corridor. Victor stopped and turned to face her. Behind him, the grimy glass of a window gave the city lights a sepia tinge.

He seemed enormous.

'You okay?' he asked.

'Fine.'

'Look, I know it's a lot of stuff to take on, and when you meet Neon... shit, he's full on. But, listen, you gotta believe in yourself. You understand that? Don't let go of what you are. I've seen too many models come out lacking something.'

'*Something*? What *something*?'

'There's nothing else to be said, it doesn't lend itself to words. I'm not going into the hoodoo bullcrap. Let's put it this way, Neon's brain works fast, too fast.'

Linda wondered if Victor ever slept. He had dark caverns under his eyes. But deep within, were the eyes of an elephant, a gentleness to his belligerent, gun toting self.

And then she noticed a distortion around his shoulder. She thought it was behind in the glass of the window, but it seemed in the air itself. As she looked, her vision sharpened and she seemed to be viewing Victor as if she was hovering above him. Then she was back in front of him, viewing him up close. Her vision jarred, eyes taking in more detail than she had ever seen. Victor was no longer just a person. There was a person underneath, like a Russian doll, and underneath was another and another. He was layered, each layer more symbolic and significant. She let her mind flower open. Victor *was* one person, but that was like saying the city was one building. She saw a million configurations and connections; roads, traffic lights, cars moving in a chaotic cohesion, she saw shops and houses, uptown, downtown, parks and rivers, buildings, factories, skyscrapers, roofs strung together by electrical lines, satellites and communication systems invading everything.

Then Linda took a breath and was standing in front of Victor.

'You see something there, Linda?'

'No, I—' She wasn't going to do it, she couldn't. On one hand there was nothing but a man in a black coat, tough set shoulders, hard face. But then there were millions of connecting fibres, strings that made him so much more.

'You see it, Linda. That's the potential.'

Fucking hell. She didn't want to think of it. The vastness. She thought of the Diner, of people shouting 'Where's my order?' 'Excuse me, Miss.' 'Alright, cutie...' Faces grimacing, mouths crudely chewing, words being spat out with bits of food. She thought of who she was, her life as a person amongst people, normal people. Now her brain seemed clenched like her jaw. Maybe she was going to have a fit.

'All people can realise potential,' Victor said quietly. 'People see what they wish, what they are ready for. But me I'm just secondary, you get this close to Neon, things start accelerating.'

Linda looked down the corridor. On the wall to her left there were some marks like footprints. Beyond these was a door. She thought of the journey to here, footsteps through the streets, right, left, right, left, right, down the key shape of the corridor, up the spring of the spiral stairs—the key to spring the lock.

The door burst open.

'Ah ha! Victor, *my* Victor, so good you could come.'

The man's face was a blank sheet, then details started filling in. Eyes, at first black, then really bright. Skin vast, like the face was enormous, but it wasn't, it was hard, worn and furious. The cheekbones were like boulders. The nose long, poignant, and the mouth, a black crevice.

The man paid her no heed, keeping his gaze on Victor.

'How's things going, Neon?' asked Victor, looking over Neon's shoulder into the studio.

'Just perfect, Victor. Come in.' Neon stood back and gestured into his room, nodding at Linda as she entered.

24

She smiled but he was back to watching Victor. She moved into the studio, her eyes taking a moment to adjust to the brightness coming from three huge steel pan lights. The room smelt nutty like a damp oil painting.

Victor walked across the large studio and began leafing through some drawings on a large teak bookshelf. Linda followed, not really sure what to do.

'So tell me, Victor, what's sweet on the street?' said Neon still standing by the door.

Victor turned and walked over but Linda stayed looking at the piles of images. They were all of hands—painted, sketched and charcoaled. By her feet were more images—torn, shredded and burnt. To the left was a shelf of metal sculptures—twisted, shaped, jagged, rounded and rusted hands. Below these, bones were shaped into hands—broken, carved, wrapped in tapestry, paper, cloth, wax and string. All of the same hands...

An obsession.

Neon and Victor stood talking by the closed entrance to the room. Neon wore a t-shirt that might once have been white, but was now covered in mould. His trousers were shapeless, paint splattered to the extreme. There was nothing faded about the person though. His moniker of Neon fitted him well. His whole body was animated—arms raised, hands gesturing, fingers wriggling, head tilting and snaking, mouth and jaw working, and the eyes occasionally turning their fierce glare on her.

Victor raised his head to her, then he and Neon went through an opening to another room to the left of where she and Victor had entered.

Linda felt like laughing. The pictures of hands made her own feel restless. She wanted to touch everything, to be invasive and naughty.

She trailed her hand over the dry wood of the cupboards under a bench which ran along the outer wall. On top of the bench were a number of large oil paintings. There was a real buzz about Neon's paintings. She was dying to look but turned away, savouring the moment. On the other side of the studio, an enclosed cube shaped room was elevated on thick posts with a wooden ladder leading up to it. Checking first to see if Neon and Victor were coming back, she poked her head up to see a mattress and rumpled sheets. She ran her hands over the cold sheets and then jumped down. The studio walls had at some stage been white, but they were now filthy with grime and it looked like wet paintings had been dragged across them, smearing them with lurid colours.

She turned slowly towards the centre painting on top of the cupboards. At first glance, it consisted of slashes of colour. The background was a hollow black and a large sticky swath of entwining oil paint dropped down the centre like a dangling feather. The swath to the left was white; brilliant white, and on the right it was red; raw red. On closer examination she could see a small figure at the bottom, an exquisitely painted ballerina. A scrawled card lying in front said *The Blood of Human Nature.*

Neon was at her shoulder.

'It's where people go when no one is watching.' He smiled. 'We haven't been introduced, my name was Karl Long.'

'I see, and now?'

'Depends what I am doing. And your name?'

Linda noticed a play in his eyes, nothing innocent—the dance of the dark lord. She flashed a smile, and moved on to the next painting, answering over her shoulder. 'Linda. Linda Kalom.'

'What a nice name.'

'Is it?'

'Interesting...'

Linda felt pressure on her head as if someone was pushing on her temples. She sensed that Neon was attempting to read her thoughts, but how? She looked at the next painting, *The Hollow Tome*. Even before she could register the image, she felt butterflies fluttering around her chest.

She thought of what had happened in the hall with Victor. She liked Victor. He was kind, like a friend. But this one—Neon nodded at her—this one was something else. She moved on. He moved just behind her. He was irritating, invasive, like an insect buzzing around her ear. She felt like telling him to stop, but the paintings were so exquisite.

'So,' said Neon. 'You would like to work as a model?'

'Perhaps.' She was aware of him rubbing his hands together. 'Actually I'm an artist myself.'

'Oh, you are.'

Linda looked at his face. His eyes seemed inside her, like he was looking from *her* eyes and she from his. It made her feel nauseous.

'It could all change here, Linda.'

She moved onto the next painting *Menace in the Flower Garden*. A large white flower, like a sunflower, stood dominant amongst random slashes of green, brown, red, yellow and orange. The flower was white with rough strokes of black and gray. It was, on one level, just a flower, but the way it had been painted, the visible stroke lines of the paintbrush, were so delightful it pulled her into a daydream.

'Who,' —he put his hand on her shoulder —'are we truly?'

His touch pushed her deeper inward.

She was in her Aunt's garden as a child. She wandered away from her mum moaning about another failed relationship. The sun shone as she walked down a piece of lawn surrounded on both sides by flowerbeds. A bumble bee crossed her path and she followed it. Sunshine warmed her bare arms and heated the fabric of her dress. Her dress was too tight, uncomfortable, but the heat made it seem part of her. The bee turned and went into some flowers. She stopped and watched it; heavy, ponderous little bomber. It touched on a striped, red and white flower head like it was ringing a bell and moved off. Then Linda felt a sharp sting on her bare foot and cried out, realising the bee had stung her. In that instant she became intensely aware of herself. Time ceased. Sudden, everything was sudden. The bushes smelt of fresh baked buns and fizzy sweets, the grass smelt of fried onions, and the flowers smelt of lemonade and squash. The sound of the bee and other insects tickled and vibrated inside her ears and she could see that the flower head, touched by the bee, sending shockwaves into the air around it. The heat of the sun made the pain of the sting pulse around her body and up into her head. She felt dizzy and nauseous, but delightfully alive.

A crash. Victor appeared in the room, dragging various

pieces of wire cable.

'Give us a hand here, Linda.' He handed her some cables about half as thick as her arm and covered in black plastic. They had a dead weight—malleable but forceful. On the end of each cable were large bulldog clips. Linda placed the cables on a long dining table in the centre of the room. Next, Victor dragged in a computer monitor and box, placing them next to the cables and knocking paint tubes onto the floor.

Neon tutted. 'So archaic, Victor.' He stood beneath his wall of paintings.

Victor smiled and Linda felt the tension drop. She sat down in a dining chair.

'You heard of the Kage Kids, Neon?' asked Victor.

'I have. Are you joining them?'

'No. But they got an interesting take on the Soul Bugs. You had any here?'

'Here? No, no. Don't like to come in, you see. I hear them, scurry, scurry, round the outside. Know what I mean, Victor?'

'Can't say I do. The Kage Kids say computer viruses have the same ghostly returns as Soul Bugs.'

'Why,' Linda turned to Neon, 'do you say that computers are archaic?'

Victor stood near her. She liked his protective stance, finding the heady mix of Neon's paintings and forceful stare hard to deal with.

'Do you—' Neon directed his first words at her and then turned to Victor. 'Does she understand the process of intensification?'

'Not fully.'

29

Linda started. 'Do you mind?' She felt like a little girl.

'I don't think,' Victor said, 'there is any rush.'

'And I don't think,' Neon's eyes narrowed, 'there is any reason to wait.'

Linda stood up, shooting her chair behind her. 'And I don't think you have the right to be discussing me like a child. I think I know what intensity is.'

Neon rounded on her. 'Oh I see, so you know how it all happens? Do you? Been dancing with the bumble bees, have you? Let loose in the city with the key to the night?'

'What the fuck?' said Linda, stepping back. The seat of her chair knocked against the back of her knees.

Victor faced Neon. 'Leave it, Neon.'

Neon's eyes burned. 'Leave it! Gone native have you, Victor, forgotten how to be?'

'Neon, settle the fuck down. Just take it easy, that's all.'

'Victor, Victor, thoughts in the mind, like a boa constrictor. Victor, I apologise. I do forget my selves, I have so many to remember, you know... It's chaos inside my head.' Neon flicked himself on the sides of his head. 'Makes it so hard to deal with the world. But we must, at all times, be *illuminated*, no?'

Linda noticed the room getting darker, yet the steel pan lights above them had not dimmed. Neon was directly below and the light seemed to be sucked into shadows under his eyes and cheeks.

Victor stood facing Neon.

Linda moved around the table so she was facing the side of both Victor and Neon. They were like two halves of a keyhole and through them she could envisage—not with her eyes, but somehow—a vast kingdom. She thought of when she was a kid, how her mother had told her that thunder was the devil setting his table and she remembered the feeling of awe, believing that there were vast beings in existence; beings whose lives really mattered.

Neon turned to face her. Victor no longer moved to protect her. It was as if she was going to lose her virginity.

'What happens, Linda, when the stars reach the viewer who stares at them too long?' He walked around the table and stood before her.

'Just words...' But it was a question she was posing to herself, because somehow Neon's words seemed to form in the air like undulating heat—strange little transparent sculptures revolving in front of his face.

She closed her eyes and saw a flash of light in her eyelids. Neon's word sculptures arrived into the light and continuing inside her head.

'Concentrate on a sense,' Victor said. 'Take it one sense at a time.'

Linda took a breath and concentrated on smell. It was incredible, there was a whole universe of smells at her beck and call. She could smell every millimetre of the studio. She delved into the smell of oil paints. At first it was a general smell, but within she found that there were layers and layers. She turned towards Neon's paintings and found that each one emitted a different smell—musty, sweet, sour and piercing.

She turned to *The Blood of Human Nature*. Opening her eyes, she could once again see the image of the red and white swathes of paint pushing against each other, but her sense of smell was so intense and exaggerated that the visual image seemed one dimensional.

The white swathe of paint was a rich globulous cream, she could smell the paintbrush that had laid the colour down, the musk of its pig hair bristles. But where the brush hairs were dead, the colour was alive. Linda closed her eyes again and soared away, dropping into an odour inspired daydream. The white paint *was* globulous, but the secret of it was thin, smelling of lake water and reeds; she envisaged a lake—stretched gray sky above, cold black waters below—at the lakeside were softly swaying reeds; intimate scrolls of nature. The reeds were woody, but going beyond the overall smell and into each individual fibre, she broke into a code of triggers, experiences that formed the smell; the remnants of fresh wind, the movement of mist and the cry of birds. It was as if colour couldn't be colour without a smell, but the smell couldn't be a smell without the triggers of experiences.

With sudden arrival, the sticky odours of red paint invaded, transporting her to a cave-like room. In low black and tan lighting, she saw dusty floors and rounded sandy walls with glassless windows looking into tunnel corridors. In the room was a bed with tousled, cream coloured sheets. Linda smelt the warmth of the bodies that had laid there. This triggered a hiccup in her thought, throwing her back in time—a wine glass toppling, red wine spilling in slow motion, droplets landing on the dusty floor like bombs. Deep bass heartbeat came from underneath her feet. Looking around the room; the curved walls, valve-like connections to other rooms. It was the inside of a body. Neon had created this bizarre construction, rooms symbolically representing body parts he wanted to isolate. Then by getting characters to act out scenarios he would replicate the flow of body fluids. He would tweak the nervous system and hormones by changing rooms or instigating actions. Once it all was working, once the body was at the exact temperature, he would spill the blood — the perfect red. All that just to get a colour...

The white and red seemed to be tugged, twisted and infuriated by the ballerina at the bottom. The ballerina had a mischievous grace, a magic, and, best of all, she looked just like Linda.

'That's me!'

'You think so?' said Neon.

Victor cursed, throwing a computer cable down.

Linda refocused on the room. Neon was in front of her. She stared at him with wonder, but he was a million miles away, his gaze trained on some distant point.

'You okay there, Linda?' said Victor.

'Okay? What the fuck?'

'Exactly. Don't ask.'

The Neon Neural Embrace

3

Neon could see Linda was undoubtedly attractive. She had a nice connection to gravity, cheeks curved not dropping, shoulders low, head up, eye muscles relaxed, nostrils tense but not stressing. A starry eyed country girl turned urban schemer. But which part was she selling?

At the table Victor grunted, pounding on the keys of the computer and complaining that there was a Bug in the hall outside.

Chemical details shot over Neon's receptors. He hunted through them, sifting the important from the banal, the active from the passive. The Linda was nervous but not fearful, had many, many layers indeed.

He had enough to get on with though. Information was one thing, but it was distraction. What he wanted, the one scent that obsessed him, was the scent of the city that Victor and Linda had brought in with them. Every city had a smell, a unique combination of rivers, buildings, parks, industry, geographic setting—but within those smells, another smell was emitted— the underlying current, mood feed, a static metallic twang that worked behind sense and synapse.

Elongating his vision, he pushed out and shot back into his head. Inside was a peaceful storm of delightful, electrical trickery. The Little Neons formed a guard of honour to be inspected. Yes, all his little ones, at least those that were left, 323 at last count.

'Neon 23, how are we faring?'

'All present, we are destroying all the memories in here, sir.'

'Good. And what of our guest? The girl, Linda?'

'An interesting one sir, she has an erratic bloom, seems contingent.'

'On what?'

'Well, she has a lot of emotion, but it is very tight to her reality. Her experience is immediate, she doesn't leave any gaps to get in. Soon as we try to access her, she moves and we're left tied up in symbolic reference. Neon 36 has got lost trying to reach her, bloody layers of the stuff.'

'Very interesting. And Victor?'

'Immense, but a disaster.'

'The way we like him. Right, carry on with the memory destruction. We're not going to hit full speed till we have destroyed everything.'

'Destroy everything?'

'Memory serves no purpose, we can review some pieces first, meeting Victor and dealing with Albert. The rest is sentimental. Destroy the lot.'

'Will do.'

Neon watched the little Neons shoot off across the plains of his mind.

'Shit.' Victor said, knocking over one of Neon's paintings.

'Can't you just take care of the Bug, Victor?' asked Neon. 'Maybe not ruin the fucking place?'

Victor gave him a glare, and placed the painting back on the easel.

Ghostlike hands rose out from the painting. Those hands, even in their captured image life sprung from them. They maddened him, long creamy fingers, tickling, teasing, threatening.

'23, what is it with those hands?'

'Destiny conductors.'

'To a gruesome end?'

'We fear it might not be hers alone.'

'Don't fear, 23. Don't ever fear again or you're gone.'

'Yes, sir.'

The hands dropped back into the picture. Nothing got through Victor's defence of leaden gloom. A useful defence in many ways, and maybe something Neon needed. Of course he wouldn't let Victor know that.

Victor frowned at the computer screen.

'What you gonna do, Victor? What's gonna be your method for dealing with the Bugs now that you've destroyed the internet, eh?'

'Neon, shut up, for fucks sake.'

'Of course.'

Neon accelerated into his thoughts and activated a film clip that had been accessed from his memory. It was one of his favourites, *The Meeting with Victor*. Two months ago, wandering down Carden Street was Victor, sullen man with black devious thoughts pouring onto the sidewalk in front of him. He reached The Elgance Gallery, and hanging in the window was *The Neon Neural Embrace* painting, *'Calling you, Victor Scram.'* Bang. There, the vision met the man.

Neon adjusted his view as the film showed Victor turning towards the painting—heavy, dark eyes placed on the edge of human perception. In the single instant when the connection was made, his work had moved from imagination to activation. That was the day, a day that would be written in the annals of the New World, *'On that day, one man, Victor Scram, heard the message, the scared blessing.'* *'He took it, he took it,'* a million dancing girls will scream. *'One man, Victor Scram, sing it again, has seen, and one man seeing, is enough.'*

'Ah, Victor. Remember the night?'

'Every morning, Neon. Got one busy Soul Bug out there, Mantis variety.'

Neon was taken aback by the mention of Mantis. He flipped back inside again.

'Neon 23, Mantis memory...'

'Ah, yes, but destroy everything?'

'Last time.'

A new memory film popped up. First there was an image, a photograph of a man, Karl Long. Neon looked at himself, circa 2012—three years prior. It was taken in the Yucatan jungle, green-black foliage lurking in the background.

The image began to enrich, the foliage swaying and sweating. Neon could smell the fibre of the jungle and feel the sticky humidity. The film switched to Leanne, his then girlfriend—rounded, chocolate ice cream lips, with sour, cherry-caustic tongue. *'How the fuck could you do this to me, Karl, you bastard.'*

The man, that was not Neon at that time, but Karl Long, sighed and waved emotive hands.

'*I wasn't always like this,*' Neon said to no one in particular. '*That man there, the one without cares, him, Karl Long. That man let a Praying Mantis sit on his hand, and out of respect to the ranting lady, did not swipe it away. One swipe was all it would have taken to stop the connection, the electric transfer, which flowed from Mantis jaws into my body.*' Neon looked across and saw 323 little versions of himself. '*But fuck, how we expanded at that moment.*'

And Leanne cries. '*What the fuck has happened to your eyes?*'

Neon remembered the flaming insanity that had ripped throughout his body.

'*Neon 23, tell me of the menagerie that was prescribed on that day by the clawed hand of fate?*'

'*Well sir, it was on that day that a Praying Mantis entered our soul.*'

'*Entered? Claimed.*'

'Hey, Neon,' said Victor. 'What say we bring this Bug in here?'

Neon tuned out. 'Ah yes, Victor, you want to do some research?'

Victor took out his gun.

'You and your gun, Victor Scram.'

'Got a better idea?'

'Paintbrush.' Neon held one up in his hand.

Victor smirked.

From the paintbrush electro-fibres sparked with the intense crackle of life connection as the Mantis began its crawl inwards. Neon willed it on. The same will that had wrenched him from those he had known; family and friends soon had enough, girlfriends headed to the exit and models moved on. All the while 'on' moved in him.

'Yeah, you got moves there, Neon? Show us what you got.'

Neon laughed. Victor's words and gestures mirrored those of the city. Neon jumped into them like they were taxis— cruisers in dim-lit streets. He took a ride over the city's neural landscape, a playground of the filthy and the wise. He cruised through West Side with the top down, had some high times in uptown, saw grotesque faces on the corporate parade and took crystal meth with a street maid. Zooming fast, he stalked the streets like a tiger, trailing claws through the sticky syrup of congealed thought. The word was that the city was being won by the darkness of the Bugs.

Neon returned to himself. *'Neon 23, send one of the Neons to the Mantis, he wants to eat and god knows we like him to eat. That should leave 322. Plenty there for more creations.'*

'And now,' Neon said aloud. 'What lies between me and the brush, dies.' He settled onto his stool. 'Linda, could you pour me a coffee, please.' Neon pointed to a coffee pot on the bench top just behind her. 'Black, three sugars.'

'Am I to be a waitress?'

In her lair were bones of bigger beasts than he expected. He watched her chemical ocean ebb and swirl—emotion streaking in different directions, expressions coordinated, waves crashing and storms blowing. He drank the colours of her eyes; green leafy parks with grass made out of razor blades. He would be getting a lot from her.

For now though, Neon let go of his sensory feeds and dropped back into the pre-translation. The raw information was delectable.

In the studio, Victor opened the door.

The Soul Bug stood sneering, its face twisted like melting plastic. It hesitated in the doorway. Narrow face, small eyes and greasy, brown hair. It tilted its head as it looked at Neon.

Victor moved back to the right of the door, his gun loose in his hand. Linda stood to the left and Neon was further back, poised at his easel with a fresh canvas.

Neon felt his glandulars twitch from the Bug pheromones that were being released. Dirty bastard.

'Hey,' Victor said, 'you notice anything different?'

Neon looked. The Bug didn't seem too different—arms sticking out at the side, legs bowed, nose protruding, nostrils enlarged.

'No.'

'Aren't you gonna do something?' said Linda.

'It's the clothes,' said Victor, 'they're different. They always wear the same clothes, the cream, elasticated jackets.'

It was true. This was wearing a blue Mac. 'So what?

'It's a change, an evolution. They're learning. Dumb as fuck, but learning. You gonna let me in on why they're coming?'

Neon looked over at Victor. 'Nothing to do with me.'

Victor laughed a deep belly laugh. 'That's good, Neon. That's very good.'

The Bug emitted a nasal hiss and advanced into the studio one step. It was unsteady and tilting forward.

'Aren't,' Linda started, 'you gonna do *something*!' she stepped back, nearer to Neon.

'Let's see what happens.' Neon closed his eyes and felt the chilling bite of the Mantis on *Neon 46*.

The Soul Bug lunged.

Linda spun backwards and Neon slashed a stripe on the canvas. The Bug recoiled. Its cheek bleeding.

'What the fuck?' said Linda.

'Did you see what she did, 23?'

'Amazing.'

'Crank up the Mantis awareness.'

Out of the blackness, stimuli began to glow, colour spectrum wavelengths increasing to full neonic splendour. Neon peeled back the division between himself and Linda, savaged her movements down to their core cellular intention. Her DNA was shaping chemistries like a psychotic stripper. Her codes were not just fast, they were magic carpets. Neon glued himself to the ride, *brush stoke*—capillary controlled explosion of paint, *brush stroke*—icy piece of death, *brush stroke*—drops of her universe falling into his interior night.

'Neon 23, report.'

'Well there is the Bug situation, but really, that girl is explosive.'

'Tighten the fucking connection, 23. I want details here. Who is this fucking girl and why is she able to do that? Keep it tight, no transmission. For now, presume she's a dark side stalker.'

'Yessir. Why did Victor bring her here?'

'She's blooming, you can see it all over the place. He doesn't know, he possibly doesn't even fucking care. She's got devils on the inside, he's got them on the outside. What a fucking pair. It's a good turn up, 23, but turning up it is. We're going to have to take this on. Full crank now. Where is the fucking bug?'

'There, far left, sir, back in the shadows. The Bug's young, not a strong force. It's weakly broadcasting to Victor but he's not listening

41

to a damn word.'

Soul Bug pulses came out as small, reversed red and yellows. They ate the ultraviolet. It was instinctive to get rid of them. They were here to wreak havoc, but weren't so capable.

The Bug lunged forward again.

Linda jumped, Neon slashed down, paint oozing as the bug was lacerated again. A fine performance indeed.

Victor looked bemused as the bug fell to the floor knocking an easel over. He clapped slowly. 'Very impressive there, Neon.' His hands were like buildings clapping together.

Once Victor fully tuned in, the city was in for a thrill. Neon knew that, the painting to the left of Victor, *City Sunset and the Shotgun Rose*, knew it, the building knew it, the city in object, form and subject, knew it. There was so much *knowing* going on around Victor that Neon almost felt redundant. Of course, this Linda was going to be taking up much of his time for now, so maybe that wasn't a bad thing.

Plague from a Dark Land

4

Victor poked the Bug. It seemed alive but unconscious. On its face the skin had split and peeled back like singed plastic. Underneath was a sticky red jelly. It stank.

'Is it human?' asked Linda.

'Really? Open your fucking nostrils.' The smell of musty rot really choked him. He thought of Emily, her face twisted in pain: Claridge Street, 11:47pm, June 12th.

Victor! Emily had cried as her mind was being assaulted by a Blister Beetle, *family Coleoptera.*

Victor hadn't been ready, thought the Bugs were drunks. It had happened too fast. Emily had lifted her hands up to shield herself, but he'd seen nothing, just pushed the Bug against the wall. It had squealed—hollow eyes, spiteful and mocking—as Emily had screamed out in pain. Later Victor realised she had emotional blisters forming in her mind and the onset of sudden cardiac arrest.

'Hey, Victor,' said Neon. 'Opening the black box again?'

'Shiiit...' Victor stuffed the image back into a head drawer and slammed it shut.

'Did you just kill it?' said Linda. 'Is it right to do things like this?'

Victor liked that she was trying to maintain disbelief. Her eyes showed that she was taking it all in, but hadn't let go of

43

her old thinking.

'It's not dead. Pass me that bulldog clip.'

'Here.' She flashed a smile.

Victor plugged the cable into the monitor.

'Did you destroy the internet?'

'Hey, now that is just hearsay.'

'Neon just said it. The Kage got the blame.'

'Notoriety does a gang wonders. So I blew up a couple of exchanges, who'd have thought it'd be that easy.'

'Why would you do that?'

'There's too much hidden in that electrical mangle. Enemies are better with faces.'

There was a knock on the door.

Victor got up and cracked the seal on the studio. 'Tommy fucking Bones. Johnny Ease.' It was fitting that there were spacemen outside.

'Scram, man. Hope you don't mind,' said Tommy Bones, shuffling from foot to foot in the murky corridor.

'Why would I? Welcome to the inferno.' Victor pulled the door open and gestured inward.

The Kids shuffled in, moving to some inner tune.

'Neon. The Kage Kids.'

Victor watched the Kages' heads slightly bow. He liked them. They moved sideways, even though they didn't know where they were going.

Neon took them off to the adjacent room.

Linda was crouching down on the other side of the Soul Bug with her nose turned up.

She's cute, thought Victor. 'Okay, Linda, clip that onto the

Bug ear, there.'

'Why?'

'I'm working on the Magnetoreception levels of these beasts.'

'What's that?'

'It's the ability to detect a magnetic field, like a Bug sense that we don't use, not consciously anyway. It's what insects, birds, use to navigate. Something Neon said about how they get into the city.'

'So what are you checking?'

'I'm checking the sensory neurons.'

'I didn't take you for the science type.

'Good.'

'Victor, I...'

Her eyes were dark tunnels one moment and innocent delights the next. She wanted to understand why one foot went in front of the other. It had been easier for him, maybe because of where he was at the time, or maybe just who he was. He was wary of her needs though, he needed to remain unattached.

'I know what you are going to say and if you want to go through the *why not*, well then, be a spectator. Have a look around, Linda. Think what you really feel.' Victor knelt closer to her. She smelt of apples. He thought how apple branches bent easily as you pulled the fruit towards you; the shiny apple skin, such a thin film to protect tasty insides.

'You're looking at me weird.'

Well.' Victor smiled. 'Yes, I am.'

'Why?'

The cornea of her eyes glistened and reflected the studio.

The paintings were exciting her, and she was projecting that excitement onto him. 'You're beginning, starting to become.'

'What?'

'Linda, I like you, but I don't eat other men's fruit.' Victor laughed.

'You're such a weird man. I like you too.'

Her face was open and honest, like Emily's. That was his curse—everything he liked in a woman was what Emily had. Every time he found it, he shut down. Linda was ready to give, he wasn't. 'Look, you get it, obviously. Just let go, it's okay. Fulfil what you are capable of. I'll be around. I'll be here when you need me.'

'*When?*'

'Now, Victor.' Neon came over with the Kage Kids. 'Am I disturbing?'

'Always, Neon. My whole fucking life.'

'*Hey,*' said Neon, 'I got you a Soul Bug and you didn't even have to shoot it.'

Victor sighed. 'I like shooting them.' He looked at Tommy Bones next to Neon. If possible, he looked even more spaced than usual. Johnny Ease looked more relaxed. He was the man with the Bug Box. Ease was an unusual one. As Tommy Bones said *he ran a computer without a memory.* As much as Tommy was the peroxide firecracker, Johnny Ease was the mahogany thunder—dark hair hanging low on his forehead, deep set eyes with pupils floating in a murky pool of delirium. He spoke words long, pronouncing every nuance. He was a low rider. Stoned like Tommy, but clear as fucking sunlight when he said something.

46

'Now boys,' Victor started, 'we have here, a fucking Soul Bug.'

'Nice,' said Tommy. 'What you done there, Scram, cut em up?'

'Nope, it was Neon. Assault by painting.' Victor nodded over to the canvas.

'Flame fucking out, man. Can we?' Tommy Bones hopped over near the canvas.

'Sure.'

Victor moved over too. He hadn't seen Neon lacerate a Bug before. From where he had stood Neon had gone into a trance, slashing at the canvas like he was having a fit. Victor stood behind the Kage.

His vision melted—feathers floated slowly in a room, tears fell. Albert, his father, strode away from their house into the night. He saw a woman crying, his mother. He heard rushing air, felt himself being pulled away, watching his father get smaller and smaller. The meaning evaded him, different emotions fought in his heart— fear, anger and shock flipped sideways, becoming images on cards. The cards flicked out across a dark void to figures hiding in shadows. Large hands loomed forward holding the cards in their blunt, rounded fingers. At first they flicked through them, but a black mist formed around the bottom, squeezing the wrists, choking off life, slowly the hands stiffened and turned to stone. Each statue was left with a card facing up showing a warning sign. Everything exploded. Pieces of dust shot out of the void and dropped down over the city. The dust settled on skyscrapers, tenements and murky back streets. It landed on telephone wires stringing across streets. People walked underneath, oblivious to the warning dust and unaware of dark mist that slid around their ankles. When the mist touched, knives were drawn and guns cocked. Rage was infecting the city like a sickness and it was somehow connected to him.

The Kage talked excitedly as Linda scrutinised the painting. Victor felt a weight had been dropped on his forehead. He turned away, placing his hand there, but the slight release didn't change anything.

Neon moved off to the other studio room and Victor followed. It was dark and derelict, the peeling paint on the walls looking like laughing mouths.

'This feels like a parting of ways, Neon.'

'A parting of roles, Victor.'

'That painting is invasive. I think it sees into me rather than me into it. You know I'm not much of a one for questions.'

'I know.'

They walked over to the large window and looked over the city. Lights flickered here and there. In the distance a fire burned and sirens squalled as a helicopter beamed its light down like a hover fly. Cars jittered through the streets like segments of a centipede. The tone of the streets had changed from the old acoustics, now it was high pitched—screeching rubber, alarms, breaking glass and gun shots. This was a city running on adrenalin and running out of time.

'Something,' said Victor, 'is crawling through the city like an infection.'

'Yep.'

'Are you the cause or the cure?'

Neon's gaze stayed fixed, looking out the window. He wore silence like a suit of armour.

'I presume you got good reason, and I know, that you know, that I will go out there and burn those Bugfuckers out of every hellhole in town. But Neon,' Victor grimaced, 'what the fuck are you doing?'

Neon's eyes were gaping vacuums. Victor felt dizzy and sick looking into them. Neon was far over the threshold of what made them men. Who in their right fucking mind would do such a thing? The answer gaped back at him. This was a man who no longer had a mind, a man no longer constrained by individual limitations.

Victor felt Neon's hand on his shoulder.

'Hey, Victor,' Tommy Bones shouted, 'this Bug is coming up.' Tommy's voice came from another planet, from a small workshop at the edge of the universe.

'It is a plague, Victor, a plague from a dark land.'

'Why, Neon? Why? What are you doing?'

'I... puncture the role of mankind, I...' Neon looked out the window, mouth pursed, furious eyes glaring.

Victor looked down. The window ledge was raw wood, wood that had suffered a lot of water, which had left it parched and bleached. It creaked as the glass started to bulge out. Victor resisted the urge to limit his imagination, letting it flow forward into the space.

'Fucking Bug, man.' shouted Tommy Bones, amidst crashing noises.

The glass continued to extend out like a bubble. Victor saw bright silver lines tracing across it like a net. The lines blinded his eyes and soared inside his head imposing images, thoughts and fragments of words. His head drawers began rattling and old thoughts flew out. He watched one image—himself standing outside the Elgance Gallery on Carden Street. It was the night after he had first encountered Neon's painting in the gallery window and he had returned to look again. Shadows formed and retreated on his face as he struggled to comprehend the painting. What he saw, or felt, seemed capable of moving forward and entering his mind. Tumbling through *dimensional infinitesimal*, Neon had later told him. Victor remembered the fever in his senses. They were accelerated, powered by an imagination plugged into an unlimited resource.

I see you like my painting. Neon was standing behind him on the sidewalk.

As soon as Neon spoke, Victor felt ill; something wrong, some overriding force taking control. Visions of Dr's Frankenstein and Jekyll came to him. He thought of Jack the Ripper; lonely streets where the unknown waited with a scalpel.

'Scram, man. We're gonna fry this fucking Bug!' Tommy Bones shouted.

Victor stared where the window had been. There was a whirlpool of images, new windows opening and closing before him. He saw faces of the models he had brought here, Shelia G, Lucy, Frenchie and Liv, all now inhabitants of some new world. But only parts of them, parts stolen by this maniac, this possessed fool. Victor wanted to get his gun, shoot at the images, like at a funfair.

'Serious, man. Fuck sake, Scram!'

Then, once again, the glass before Victor was plain glass. He looked at Neon, but Neon just stared out. Victor wondered if he was sick. He rarely ate, living mainly off a diet of coffee.

Neon doubled over and grabbed at his head. 'Fuck! Turn it off, turn that fucking thing off!'

For the Distracted

Neon searched for paint materials, his spine arched like a cat. Linda imagined claws concealed deep within his fingers.

They were alone, Victor and the Kage having headed off into the night after the earlier frenzy. When the Soul Bug had gotten out of control, Victor and Neon had stormed in, Neon freaking out about Tommy's Bug Box, screaming at him to turn it off. Tommy froze and Victor roared at him, snapping the box out of his hands. For a moment Linda thought they were going to start fighting each other. But after turning off the box, Victor grabbed the Soul Bug like it was just a doll and dragged it outside, returning after a couple of minutes.

She felt sorry for Tommy Bones, who had looked heartbroken, but Neon had given him and Johnny some sculptures to take off, which left them happy enough.

She was going to have to tell Victor to be more careful with the Kage.

Neon muttered, making a noise with his lips like a drumbeat. Linda tapped a similar rhythm on the arm of her chair and then stood and turned away from him. The dull tug in her back informed her he was watching.

A red velvet curtain hung on the wall, the dusty folds

whispering of opulence, but screaming of secrecy. She turned back, pressing her stomach against the back of the red and white striped chair which looked like it belonged in a sports car.

What had come as a surprise to her were Neon's gentle ways. *'Just an eyebrow,'* he'd said as he stroked her face. The touch of his finger was soft; something unexpected. More telling, perhaps, was the lasting feeling on her skin afterwards. A warning? Yet, all he had asked her to do was to sit in a chair. No clothes off, no ingestion of drugs. She could be at the hairdressers.

He busied himself around an easel, brush in his hand.

She sat down. 'Where's my paintbrush?'

He didn't look at her.

She felt lost. Then she saw herself—that zooming feeling— she saw herself from above, in the bright room, the room deep in the damp, dark warehouse, the warehouse in a central position in the surrounding streets. She saw the streets like conductive pathways on a circuit board, and she, one tiny consequence in the vastness of a dream.

'What is your favourite period of history, Linda?'

Linda zoomed back, noticing that every time he turned away, he turned back and looked like a different person.

'Where's my paintbrush?'

'Because we can paint you in any era you like, any person, any style.'

'Where's my paintbrush? Don't you listen to people?'

His face was impassive and arrogant.

It should have been unsettling to be alone with a maniac she didn't know. But he seemed so set on what he was doing, that even if his intentions were impure, she didn't think he would get around to them.

Neon sat down on a tall wooden stool facing her, animated, restless, and seemingly ready to talk. 'You say, give me, but what do you give?' He held his paint brush up like a burning torch. His jaw jutted open, teeth hanging short like tree stumps.

Linda felt slightly repulsed.

'Let me tell you a story,' said Neon.

Linda saw a Doctor perched on his stool in a laboratory. She wanted to look down, but didn't. 'If you like.' She had the feeling there was no ceiling above her.

'Once,' Neon said softly, 'a woman went searching, like people do. She left the town where she had been born and the further she travelled, the easier she related to her surroundings. One day she arrived at a town, town like any other, streets and people, but something was amiss. Everywhere the woman looked, she saw curtains, curtains on windows, curtains on doors, it became apparent to her that there were curtains around the people's minds, men, women, children, even lovers. The woman, who had talent and charm, tried to open the curtains to see what was behind, but the curtains refused to open. She felt like she had gone to the theatre, waiting for a show that would not begin. The people were staunch and they ridiculed her ways, they accused her of being corrupt and chased her out of town.

'The woman felt alone, and walked for a long time. She walked until her feet became coarse and knotted like the olive tree. As night fell she entered a forest. She left the path, wandering amongst the trees and slowly, fear began to work in her imagination. Her vision started deteriorating. Images became surrounded by expanding borders of blackness. She stopped being concerned about the past and became truly lost. In the distance, she saw a light. Her heart lifted, reminding her of how it felt to want. As she neared the light, she saw a man wearing a long cloak. He had one hand stretched out holding a staff which had a lantern on the end. The closer she got, the drowsier she became and by the time she was within five feet, her eyelids were dropping and her legs felt like iron. She accepted a reached out hand and collapsed. When she came to, she was in a bed, without clothes. It was pitch dark and she couldn't even see her hand in front of her eyes.'

Linda noticed that Neon had started painting. She had a strange taste in her mouth, perhaps eucalyptus or pine.

Neon continued. 'The woman sensed that someone was sitting beside her on the bed, "Who's there?" she said. No one answered. She felt unsettled and exposed. She reached out, trying to find the edge of the bed, but it seemed immense. All around, she sensed someone, but could find no one. It started to incense her. She became desperate to touch someone, to feel the contact of a human. Eventually she stopped moving. She could still sense someone close, but they never touched her. Her body became ultra sensitive, as if it could even be bruised by someone's breath. Then she started to smell, she smelt her skin and the bed sheet, she smelt roses, small dainty flowers with layers of delicate intensity. She smelt all over like a small creature, exploring from a place of want. Her mind stretched out as if it was going to separate from her body. Suddenly a pair of eyes opened in front of her, she leapt visually towards them and in those eyes, another pair of eyes opened, and in those eyes another pair of eyes, she fell in, chasing the images.'

Neon stepped away from his painting. 'There we are.'

'There we are, *what*?'

'The finest song ever played.'

'What, I don't understand. Are you finished? What did the story mean?'

'Mean?' Neon stood before Linda but stared off into the distance. 'Meanings are for the distracted.'

'What? Of course there's meaning.'

Neon turned back, eyes glinting with menace. 'Not any longer. The rules are going, all is breaking down. Look around.'

'Here?'

'Always, but out there.' Neon gestured to the door.

'Outside?'

Neon's face was animated, one second a grimace, frown, mock smile, eyes wide, then squinting. It was like he was wrestling with himself 'Yes, the crack is wide, all hell pours in.'

'What are you talking about?'

'I'm talking about what I do.'

'And what do you do?'

Neon strode around like a tiger, but more, a menagerie, the whole fucking jungle. As he came close, Linda could see his eyes were singed red around the edges.

He swung his arms up. 'I don't do anything, nothing, nothing at all.'

'What? No painting? Exhibiting your paintings?'

'I know nothing of what you talk about.'

56

'But you're an artist.'

'An artist? An artist is obscure, unknown.'

He was fascinating. One minute she could see his face, then it was as if the handle of a slot machine was pulled and another person formed. She felt butterflies in her stomach, and the beginnings of panic. It was as if he was tugging at her, attempting to pull her into his world. Without taking her eyes off him, she concentrated on sitting in her chair. She felt the rough surface of the hard plastic armrests, the stubborn resistance of the seat under her arse. She became aware of her legs stretched out in front of her, feet snug in her favourite boots, ankles enjoying the cushion wrapped around them. She could feel the strong fabric of her jeans taut on her legs, snug fit, shapely, all perfectly held in place. Her best jeans, belt she liked, light brown leather, large buckle hanging low, slung. It was how she was in the chair, slung, presented; how she wanted to be seen. Neon's skittishness rattled her. Something inside said: *no, that is the path of danger*, but she thought of Victor, how much she admired how he committed to his actions. But *committed*?

She sat up. 'I think you're an artist. I think you're lucky.'

'Lucky? I don't want to be lucky, I want to be great.'

'But what you do is different, something new. I'd like to know how you do it.'

'Yes. So you say.' He was sitting on his wooden stool facing his easel sideways so that he could see her. She noticed that he was barefoot, paint dripping down to his toes.

'Would you like to paint with me?' asked Neon, his brush moving on his painting.

'Sure, then you might let me in on your secret.'

'Can you imagine where the dream begins and the day disappears?'

'You keep trying to misplace me, knock me off balance.'

'I'm trying to help you see.'

'What makes you capable?'

'It's not me.'

'Then what?'

'It. It is all around you.'

'Ow!' Linda felt a burn on her fingers.

'It is what is. It's what happens, when the other falls away. It's the dream, what falls in-between.' Neon was shaking his head, singing and painting rapidly. 'One more, one more to the Mantis.'

'Stop!'

Neon looked manic, his eyes were phosphorescent, like his brain had been scraped out and a huge light placed inside his head. His mouth hung loose and his voice seemed to be coming from somewhere else. His hands flung around the canvas like monkeys swinging through trees.

Linda felt the paint strokes riding over her. Swishing, touching her mind and body with some strange psychic connection.

'Stop!'

'Oh stop,' said Neon, grinning. 'Stop the life, stop the Bugs. Hah! You couldn't imagine the price, the cost of entry, little Linda Kalom.' He leered over his canvas, perched forward on his chair.

Linda focused hard on him. 'I know there's something

wrong with you.'

He stopped moving and swivelled his head around towards her. She noticed that he seemed to fit with the lurid colours smeared on the wall behind him, like they were his grotesque shadow.

'Yes. Wrong.' Neon got off his chair, staring off into the air. He pursed his mouth in mock seriousness. '*Wrong Karl*, oh they said that, you know. *Karl, you are wrong, that is wrong, is wrong, wrong, wrong!'*

Linda watched him transform into an angry child.

'And I was indeed wrong. Oh yes, but they were not so wise though. Just coincidence you see, that *I* happened to be wrong, at the same time... but it was a *different* wrong.'

'What was wrong?'

'I was one,' said Neon.

'One what?'

'One person. Just trying to be me, tied in my being, my effort to exist. I was important to myself, precious and tiny.'

'And now?'

'Now I am more, now I am the gang, the troupe, the spectacle.'

'You're mad, can't you see that?'

'No I don't see. I don't see. Can you get that, I, the I, no more. Lots of ones, and twos, and the three. Freed from expectation, yet damned to decipher.'

Linda felt a weight land on her shoulders. Her eyes felt heavy, weighed down by huge boulders. She thought of Neon's story of the girl in the forest, of her meeting the man and falling asleep. She did not want to fall asleep. Neon wanted her to roll over so he could take from her at will. She stood up. He watched her intently. Eyes on her like a Bug. She wanted to believe that he saw greatness in her. But another part just wanted to give it to him, to throw herself forward, and give it all away.

Linda became aware of sitting in the chair. She felt cold from not having moved, and sore from the frame against her back. There were three candles lit behind Neon. Shadows danced over his paintings, like the images had gone away into the night. She felt heavy and worn.

'It's the yo-yo.'

Linda felt her breath might stop if she didn't forcefully inhale and expel. 'What do you mean?'

'What you are doing.'

'How do you know what I am doing?'

'I don't care to tell you.'

'Bastard.'

It was time to leave, but she didn't know where she could go. Everywhere seemed so far away. 'What is the yo-yo?'

'The zooming feeling, being here and then zooming out to see the big picture, then back down again.'

'Why?'

'Shaking you free, Linda Kalom.'

'You haven't the right.'

'You wanted to be here.'

'Really, well where the fuck is *here*?'

'*Here*? Why don't you look at my painting...'

Lizard Shaped Melanoma

6

While Linda sat in the chair gathering her thoughts, Neon looked up at his paintings slumped against the wall. Looking at them was the only time he ever relaxed. They were pyramids preserving the tombs of unsaid thoughts. He often wondered what he had left behind in Palenque. Some nights as he hunted around for sleep, he would pace the studio, but really, it was the crumbling plazas of Palenque he wandered in. He could feel the humidity of the jungle, could hear the bodily vibrations of thousands of insects, the sirens of the city became howler monkeys, black pollution became ants, police helicopters were harpy eagles, circling, waiting—and that brought him swiftly back to Linda. He had decided she was a hawk, a kestrel, a buzzard swooping through his innards. No. She was the eagle who ate the liver of Prometheus.

And damn, he could not break into her codes. He looked over at her face, probing with his pupils. She had cheeks like question marks, lips like curling claws. He marvelled at her features.

But things were not as they seemed. For she—under the veil of beauty and promise—had undergarments of strong and wise, and this was causing serious delays. Neon pushed his awareness towards her, but again she escaped with ease into private plains.

He spun back into his own mind.

'*Neon 23, tell me of the situation we are faced with?*'

'*You painted her, the girl that sits before us.*'

'*Yes, you fool, this I know, but tell me of what happened in the inner world, my curiosity of madcap's mind?*'

'*We had to feed fourteen Neons to the Mantis.*'

'*Fourteen! What the hell? Why so?*'

'*You went further. She moves fast in the spectrum.*'

'*She does indeed. But more than this, what does she bring?*'

'*She brings the view of one, the individual.*'

'*Yes, one. But which one...*'

Linda approached the canvas and halted level with the easel, still out of view of the image. 'You didn't take very long,' she said.

'Long?' Neon felt a ripple pass over his mind, he imagined a stone being thrown into space with a piece of string tied to it. His brush-holding hand was trembling, which surprised him. He inhaled the paint smell, pulling the odour of Linda in with it. In his mind, the little Neons began stitching the two odours together.

Linda placed her hand on the top of the easel.

Neon dropped inside.

'*Neon 23?*'

'*Yes, sir.*'

'*What is the reading on her?*'

'*Well, we like this. She's all messages now. Her symbolic inference is streaking like a comet. See the lizard shaped melanoma on her wrist?*'

'Yep.'

'*Defensive, evasive, yet also quite threatening. See down there.*'

Neon looked down. '*Sweet.*'

'*Not there.*'

'*Where then?*'

Neon looked in at his own nervous and endocrine systems laid out like a rail map. Electrochemicals buzzed down the lines; reds, green and the blue. '*Take me into her.*'

'*Are you sure, sir?*'

'*All things come to those who dare.*'

A desert appeared before him. An inference landscape of bodily interaction. Linda's hormone releases became lizards on rocks; eyes watching, tongues flicking. His arrival triggered a response; hills changed, cacti moved and yellow and black signs appeared—*Danger, Attention*—blunt instructions from the genetic emblem.

Neon viewed the instructions with disdain. He didn't connect to, nor trust, what was fed automatically down through systems. He lived in the outside realm, orbiting his inner connections. *Don't cross, don't cross* read the genetic crime scene tape. Yeah, fuck you. He knew who placed them; the controllers, the crawling king snakers. He split from himself— leaving a dummy to distract the watchers—and flipped a little Neon to the rampaging Mantis. Freed from Overlord inspection, he scarpered off across the rutted desert-scape.

'*She following?*'

'*Following? Check the octagonal patterns in the cracked soil.*'

Neon saw glinting eyes in dark cracks. '*Nice. Deviant. Doesn't she know that I'm the hunter?*'

He came across a ridge and looked down into a small crater.

'Let it be here, 23.'

Sculptures appeared in the crater, his sculptures—animal skulls perched on metal, wood and fabric bodies. He walked amongst them, studying the infinitesimal changes of each sculpture since he had last seen them. *Long Horned Skull 3* had shifted slightly, the wood it was balanced on had curled in the scorching sun. The arrangement of twisted metal limbs on *Long Horn 4* glistened in mangled contortion, but there was one extra gleam.

'23?'

'Yes, sir.'

'Update?'

'*Long Horned Skull 3* has twisted from your reaction to Linda. She's cooking up your insides.'

'She's interfering with the outcome... soon to be joining though. Where is she?'

'See the tattered fabrics on *Long Skull Horn 4* flicking in the wind? That's her. She doesn't know how good she is.'

'You know how close to get?'

'Yes.'

'Say nothing.'

Neon walked down between the bone faces and metal bodies. Every piece was a stepping stone, gesture of Sheila G, desire of Liv, presumption of Albert, seclusion of Victor, illusion of the city, protrusion of the origin, how it all played out, and how it all could be played.

The scorching sun seared his skin. He offered no resistance, aware that reaction would give his position away. He was one step ahead, had to be, because playing with codes was viewed as stealing from *them*. He was familiar now with the warnings they triggered in his body. That was the first line of defence against anyone who ventured into these zones.

'Neon 23.'

'Yes, sir.'

'We're ready to take from her.'

'Well, yes. Well, you are.'

'And you are hesitating, 23?'

'Well she is one freaking fast mover, that one.'

'Move faster yourself.'

There were a number of bangs on the studio door.

'Someone knocking on the door,' said Linda. Her eyes were lidded, sleepy, but she was still standing by the easel.

Just one more step, thought Neon. 'Come on. Cast your eyes upon this.' Neon gestured to the painting.

Linda began to say something but froze on catching sight of Neon's painting.

Neon watched her eyes extend, the pupil translating the image into her mind. He followed the intertwining fibres, marvelling as he travelled down the connection between his painting and Linda's visual cortex—the uncrossable—and passed on into her body. All was revealed in the landscape of the glandular and nervous highway. The visual impressions created thoughts which triggered the hypothalamus to open chemical floodgates—magenta trickery swirled down to the ovaries, mauve waves crashed onto the thyroid, cobalt beams strobed the adrenals and vermillion hands ticked around the thymus. Neon felt a rush of pleasure as he watched—a feeling that swelled his own pituitary gland.

Linda's inner secrecy was breaking.

As he watched he became aware of something else, of something that was knocking him back, not only was she looking at his painting, but she was looking at his findings and transforming them, moving them forwards, backwards, changing the connections, designs and forms. This was new.

'*Neon 23!*'

In the studio, the door thumped with a sound to match Neon's heart.

Who the fuck could that be? The electromagnetic web was being severely interrupted by whoever it was—a large flash appearing where the noise was.

'Go open the door,' Linda said, shaking her head.

'You open it.'

'I'm not a fucking waitress.'

'No, you're worse, much worse.'

The door was thumped again.

Neon reluctantly pulled himself back into the clumsy visuals of the studio. Linda stood before him, her eyes trained on his painting. He could still feel her intense internal vibrations, but moved off and pulled opened the studio door.

'Fuck!' he exclaimed at a girl who waited outside.

'Must come,' she panted.

Before him stood a figure bursting with the sense of arrival. She was Japanese, late teens, in her hand a motorcycle helmet; black, thin shell, open face, with a white stripe up the middle. The helmet was very small, which might have explained why her cheeks were squashed, chubby and ruddy looking. Her nose was button, mouth puckered and pursed. She was stocky, forceful and bouncy, with pure river stone eyes.

'I have a message for you, Neon. Urgent, from Victor and Kage.'

'Fuck, are you the Pony Express?'

'They in serious fooking trouble, you gotta come.'

'I gotta come, gotta fucking come?' Neon noticed his body releasing adrenalin—he shouldn't react but this girl was an irresistible force. He liked the type, but it was the wrong time.

'Look, I'm fucking busy.'

'You gotta come, they in serious fooking trouble, real big problem.'

'Spodge?' Linda said groggily, from behind Neon.

'Linda? You okay? What the fook is wrong with Linda.' Spodge pushed past Neon into the studio.

'Don't be bloody pushing... fuck!'

Spodge walked over to Linda. As she did, she took in the room. 'Wow. This is your work,' she said, turning to Neon.

'You know my work?'

'I fooking love your work,' said Spodge, 'you paint colours in my heart.'

Neon saw her words freeze like water in the air. Common language, yet issued with hyper molecules that changed the air that they passed through.

Spodge stood protectively beside Linda, who was now sitting in the chair.

Linda looked at Neon, her brow knitted tightly together. 'You were following me.'

'What you done to Linda?' asked Spodge.

'Not enough.'

Spodge stepped in front of him, her determined, babyish face, forcefully present. 'You must go, Victor in big trouble.'

'Victor takes care of himself.'

'No. Too many Soul Bugs, like ten at the same time. Really serious trouble, something happened and the Soul Bugs rat-a-tat-tat, appear in rapid succession.'

Neon thought of the amount of inner Neons that had been fed to the Mantis. He looked at Linda, noticing that when she looked back at him, it was with a part of him. Fuck.

'Why were you doing that?' asked Linda.

Neon felt irritation swarm around him, a rising wind in the inner desert stinging his innards. He smelt Linda, sensing her furtive thoughts moving over the vast inner world. Her thoughts were clumsy like a new born antelope, but her strength would soon arrive. He caught himself marvelling at her in a way that he hadn't felt for ages. That was distracting.

'Neon!' said Spodge.

And *that*, was also distracting. Spodge had a face that wore its experience truthfully, and he could see anguish written all over it.

'Just wait.' He went into the other studio room. It was dark, partially lit by the glow of the city coming from the window at the far end. There was no furniture, just a cold, grubby radiator perched solidly on the left. The walls had a thousand tongues of peeling paint which picked up faint light reflections. In times of quiet Neon would sit on the floor and let the little Neons move out and use the licks of paint as beds. Each one curling up like a caterpillar.

From the window he watched the city below with its cardboard cut-out buildings. Following the line of vision he moved out and joined to what he saw, then stepped back into the dark, knelt down on one knee and bowed his head. He re-imagined the city, mimicked its layout, its force, its feed. On the dusty, brown and gray floorboards, images of the city coiled and congealed to form a solid black mass. As the image formed it became singular, separate. Within it was a piece of him — an *other*.

He passed his awareness to the other then took it back inside his body, experiencing an incredible lightness of person. His awareness was now a hundred times more powerful. With his hands, he gathered dust from the floor into a pile. At first he doodled, slowly tracing arcs, arrows and curves. His skin analysed the air around; draughts, eddies, temperature and moisture levels. With exact detail his hands began to mimic the movements of the surroundings, easing their way through and blending more with every movement. Around and around his hands went, creating a three dimensional spiral shape with the dust, first pointing downward and then rising, Toying with the dust, he was able to make the spiral move from side to side and then dance in the air before him like a snake in water. With gentle persuasion and minute manipulations he took dust up into the air, hands moving fast to keep it suspended with the least effort. The dust spread out to form a globe of shimmering haze. Slowly it began to clear and within it Neon could see a dark, small figure. It was Victor. With a cutting movement, the ball revealed what could be seen out of Victor's eyes.

The Soul Bug situation *was* bad—a large gang of Bugs were advancing down the street, their individual movements starting to merge together as one. Victor's gun jolted forward and before him lay a number of melting Bug messes. Victor shouted at the Kage Kids to stay focused. Neon tuned into Victor's heartbeat, his rhythm was getting closer to the heartbeat of the city. This was necessary. Cities were an ultimate force, they did not experience fear, could adapt to any situation—boom, bust, redevelopment, warfare, bombardment, starvation, inner crises, they took it all, broke down, reformed, ever changing and evolving. Victor was of the same type, but he was young in his development. At this point he could be overwhelmed and without Victor's force to serve as a blocker, Neon wouldn't be able to function in peace. He needed to be able to work.

Okay then, Victor Scram.

Neon opened his eyes and snapped his head back into place. He leapt up, letting the dust fall to the floor, and walked into the other room.

'Got transport?' he said to Spodge.

'Sure.'

Know thyself better

7

They had retreated back to Annapolis Street, down off Pelham and West. Not a bad move except for the fact that they heading towards the river and out of running space.

Soul Bugs were storming down the street. Fuck, Victor had never seen such numbers.

As he watched, he heard the hum that buzzed around him — the city hiss — and in it the phrase *know thyself better*. It was the mantra that Neon's last painting had set in progress.

'What the fuck?' Tommy Bones came up beside him. 'They keep coming man. Johnny's Bug Box is gonna blow.'

'Like your head.'

The Kage were as erratic as ever, Tommy Bones on the sidewalk practicing dance moves, Johnny Ease on the road staring up at the sky and Easter shouting at the bugs.

Easter was an inner city kid, so named for his similarity to the Easter Bunny, in reproduction anyway. He was handy, quick with a quip and a knife. It wasn't knives that were needed here though. The Bugs induced terror when up close, even from thirty yards they filled his head with the image of Emily face down on the sidewalk screaming — always screaming. He closed the drawer, the Bugs pulled it open. It just never ended.

'Damn.' He wished he had more ammo. The Bugs weren't in

full control of their movements, but they were moving pretty fast. 'Hey, Johnny?'

'Yeah, man?'

'You got any more Bug Boxes?'

'Not here man, been working on the new box, man. Like you be, man.'

'Like I be?'

'Yeah, man, it's the Scram Box, the Emergency Shutdown Box.'

'That's a big honour.'

Tommy Bones stood beside Johnny, nodding. 'Yeah, you the big machine, man. We like that.'

Victor figured they didn't get too affected by the Bug pheromones as they had so many chemicals cruising around their minds already. 'Where's your girl?'

'Spodge'll be back.'

'Yeah, yeah.' Victor felt a rush of dizziness and fell off balance, steadying himself against a car. His head felt too heavy. He looked at his reflection in the car window. For a minute he dropped into a blank zone, not knowing anything or anyone, especially not this gnarled face. It was like there was another person hiding in his reflection. Then he realised he was looking into his father's eyes. Shit, his father, the man who thought far into the night and then disappeared into it.

'You okay there, Scram?'

Victor pushed himself up, shaking his head clear. 'Not too bad, Tommy.'

'City poems, man. Surfing the neural down the reflective fibre.'

'Something like that.' He raised his gun, squeezed hard, once, twice, two Bugs twisted and fell to the ground. Their bodies disintegrated and the black polished shoes flopped forward—tick tock.

The front Bugs were wearing the standard Bug uniform, cream jackets, elasticised waist, cream chinos and black shoes. They were cat fleas, *Ctenocephalides felis*. But the two at the back—from here it was near impossible to tell what Bugs they were—were wearing different clothes. There was even a hint of style. *Square pants, with rounded edges* as Tommy had called it.

'Listen, Tommy,' said Victor, 'if the fucking Bugs are improving, we gotta raise it up.'

'We fucking getting on it, man.' Tommy threw his hands up, and frowned at Johnny.

'Hey,' said another Kage, Mark Baa. So called, due to a ridiculous lump of hair perched on his head that looked like sheep's wool. 'Lotta Bugs, you wan me boost a car?' He waved his hand around at the few cars around them.

Victor was tempted, but he had a hunch that something had to happen here. A saying of his father's sprung to mind, *Nothing comes to those that run away, other than more things to run from.* Pity he didn't take his own fucking advice.

He wondered where the fuck Neon was. Neon didn't have a phone, which wasn't too bad considering they rarely worked these days. But maybe, just once, he could be where he was needed.

'That's it, man,' said Johnny Ease, 'Bug Box finished. The night belongs to you now, Mister Scram.'

Johnny stood on the sidewalk, his face blank and calm. The

73

building behind loomed over him, its entrance doors watching like cold black eyes.

Tommy Bones grimaced and shrugged his shoulders.

They looked to Victor, not for approval, never that, but they definitely sought some legitimacy from him. Right now he didn't feel he had much to offer. His head was starting to feel over inflated. The gun in his hand—something he had always felt at home with—seemed pointless and clumsy. He felt if he fired it, he would have to run with the bullet in his hand, making noises like a child.

Black wires laced tightly between the buildings like a furious mesh of night. The zebra crossing thudded with its chunks of hard hitting black and white. A newspaper dispenser leaned over at an angle spilling out newspapers; lines of print, headlines, columns—inky placements... He remembered his father showing him one of his paintings when he was a kid. Those fucking designs, his dad was obsessed with them. Victor hadn't understood much of what they were, but one stuck out. The design was on a small square of light brown and gray cloth. On the cloth were maroon spots of varying size joined by lines. His father shook it at him, mouth alternately flashing smiles and grimaces, burning blue eyes flecked with gold and glinting with expectation and desperation. Victor had been eight years old, but he could still feel the old man's grip on his arm. He'd strained to understand, but just saw cloth. Next thing he remembered was his mother coming in screaming *leave the boy alone!* His father's eyes. One last look, long and strong. That night he left, never to return.

Supra-chemical Bug releases irritated Victor's nostrils yet

sharpened his vision and hearing. The Bugs were transmitting, he was receiving. *Calling to you, Victor Scram.*

Not a good voice.

A flare went up over the buildings, lighting the street in frantic magnesium. The set changed: barricade cars, trench-like sidewalks and a battlefield road.

Victor half expected to hear the crack of gunfire, but there was only the chainsaw sound of a motorcycle approaching. At last. Spodge and the Doctor. Spodge, head down, ball bearing eyes set forward; unstoppable and impressive. Neon hanging off the back waving a flare gun around.

The Bugs recoiled as the motorcycle veered through them. Victor could see their numbers were even greater than he'd imagined.

The white stripe on Spodge's black helmet tilted as she leaned side to side, more like an incision than a person. Neon looked manic; wild hair, eyes covered by flying goggles and flare gun conducting some inner tune.

At the end of the street, an Ambulance pulled over. The *Ambulance of Unforgiven Screams*? Just as quickly, it drove off.

The motorcycle skidded to a halt, heat billowing out from the white racing faring. On the faring was a green circle with the number twenty three on it.

Victor nodded, but felt detached.

Neon rolled off the bike. 'Like there isn't enough to do?'

Victor smiled for a moment, not sure how he felt.

Neon pulled off his flying goggles and flung them aside. Victor heard a large clang. He looked around. On a building to his right, Spodge was banging her helmet against a large steel shutter. The noise pulled Victor closer and closer to the edge of his eyeballs.

Neon stood watching Spodge, nodding. 'I like that one. I sure do.' He turned and tilted his head at Victor and walked around and around him.

Victor felt indecision and anger start to build.

'Now, Victor...'

'Don't start on me, Neon.' The noise from Spodge banging the steel shutter completely filled Victor's head and his drawers began rattling.

The Soul Bugs were hanging back, gathered about twenty yards away under a streetlight, pacing back and forward. The two differently dressed Bugs had moved to the front of the group and were exchanging high pitched squeals.

Tommy and Johnny Ease were leaning against a car, sharing a reefer and nodding their heads to Spodge's steady metallic beat.

'Victor, you getting the idea?' asked Neon.

'Get your shit outta my head.'

'You get out of the shit *in* your head, Victor. Feed the city.'

'What is this, Neon?' Victor waved around.

'One man's city, one city's man.'

'What the hell are you saying?'

'Connect, Victor. Cut the bullshit, all is before you, all the answers, but cut the aching heart bullshit.'

Victor went to raise his hand but his strength wasn't there.

Neon moved off towards Spodge, a rattling aerosol can in each hand.

Victor knelt down and gulped air. He was really fucking

76

annoyed but hearing the hiss of aerosol cans over by the steel shutters, gave him some head space. He placed his hand over his eyes and dove into the black. A light came on and Emily Merryweather was sitting in a chair.

'Sorrow,' she said, 'is the shadow of death.'

Victor bowed his head down, blackening further his eyes and heart.

'Will you not acknowledge me?' said Emily.

A coffin shaped lump formed in his throat.

He examined the brutal physicality of his body, every element tight; skin, flesh, veins, muscle, ligament, bones, cells, and the thumping heart. He remained still, head bowed and on one knee. He saw a horse drawn hearse, listened to the roll of the carriage wheels, smelt the horses; powerful beasts tempered by the solemnity of death. And then the hearse shrunk, dropping in size, tiny, hand sized and smaller still, until it slipped inward and the funeral procession resumed inside his veins.

The air felt thinner. Victor honed in on the acrid smell of the tyres of the car the Kage were leaning against. He smelt the debris on the tyres—driveways, highways, streets, gutters, grass, gravel, dirt, rotted food, pollution and dog shit—a smudged city mascara.

He smelt the street, the symphony of odour. The next street, the one beyond, he smelt quarters, whole sections including the underground, cables burnt out from frantic messages. He smelt into a new communication of the city and its people. How one odour could strike out over the city so one man could walk in the centre of the city at all times.

Neon was watching him. Victor nodded. Neon nodded and turned back to what he was painting. His arms moving like they were in fast forward. He was throwing colours like knives, streaks on the surface that looked like a code or magic sigil. Victor saw bright rays shooting over the carapace of his city. *His city.* He liked that.

'EASTER!' shouted Tommy.

Easter was walking towards the Bugs under the tree.

'EASTER! What the fuck?' said Tommy.

Tommy and Johnny ran down towards him. The air heavy with information the Bugs had laid out—a tea party for the glandular soul.

'Yeah, man,' said Easter, 'cherry pepper eyelids on a sweet Dakota soul.'

Tommy grabbed his arm.

'Le'go man.' Easter swung out at Tommy.

'Scrambling your fucking airwaves, man,' said Tommy. 'Pull the shit back.'

'Nah. Honey sweeter than narcs, man.'

The head Bug, a Bombardier beetle, *Carabidae*, was looking straight at Easter.

'Scram, man?' shouted Tommy.

'Sort it, Tommy.'

A dark shape crept into Victor's eye, he rubbed it and blinked but it was like there was a leak from his pupil.

'Victor?' Neon was grinning almost nervously.

The air between them was static, like it could explode.

Victor's ears began to hurt from built up pressure. 'What?' But as he spoke, air spiked his lungs with a sharp iciness and he became engulfed in a virulent paranoia.

Neon shook his head.

'What is it, Neon?'

'Listen and learn, Victor Scram. That's the call of the origins, the ones who are coming to shut down operations. You getting it?'

'I'm getting it.'

'Get it sooner. Make sure you keep the airwaves clean. I need to get going, don't wanna get caught in the open.'

Neon strapped on his goggles as Spodge kicked the bike into action. 'Got your army coming to help?' Neon gestured his head behind Victor's shoulder and shot another flare up into the air. Coming down the street behind the Bugs was a large gang of people armed with guns, bats, planks, pipes, and chains. There were street people, clubbers, men, women, young and old. They looked tough and they were closing fast on the Soul Bugs.

'Who are they?'

'They're your teeth, Victor and it's time to start eating.'

Soul Dance

8

The dark air tasted salty and Linda presumed seaweed, barnacles, discarded tridents and anchors strewn in the darkness. Tentacles stroked her face and hair as she climbed down the warehouse stairs, way further, it seemed, than she had climbed up.

Part of her screamed, ever so quietly.

She reached the entrance hallway. When she'd arrived it had seemed a key, but now, it was an embalming jar. Body parts floated around her; exquisite hands, beautiful clear eyes, calves, arms. She didn't raise her hands to touch, not wanting to break the spell.

The warehouse door clanged open and night air surged up her nostrils like darting sea creatures. She staggered and turned to face the building. There was a breezeblock base up to about ten feet, the large bricks appearing purple-grey in the night light. The higher floors were covered in a cladding of black metal sheets which were bleached-out and covered in white frosted water stains. Mariner Street was living up to its name.

Moving over to the sidewalk, she counted up five storeys to where Neon's studio was. Nothing gave it away.

The street was empty and immense. Victor had talked of the *Illumination of Thought*, Neon's grand scheme. Linda had imagined that it was a new way of looking at things, but this was different. It was as if *everything else* had changed—yesterday she'd looked at objects as solid mass, now they didn't seem so secure. *The power to transform. The ability of each...* Neon's words floated around her head.

Moving down the sidewalk, she experienced a child-like joy from having no reference point to how she felt. The street was immaculately lonely. Cars perched on the surface like toys. She marvelled at the chrome edging around their windows. The chrome screeched. When she moved her focus up and looked at the glass, the noise changed. It was a lesser screech, an easier sound. The tyres emitted a low thumping beat.

She inhaled cool air, but she also felt its colour. It had a sepia feel, but there were whites, silvers, greys, blacks and blues. All the colours of the city leaked out into the air; the black belch of roads, the grey thud of buildings, scorched blue squeals of metal, green shining glass and all the electric violins of the lights.

Following the air inside her body, she felt the oxygen absorb into her blood and feed into her system like bees returning to the hive. Everything occurred at once, and yet it seemed possible to be aware of it all. Her mind twisted in its feast of pleasure; a million flowers hitting bloom at the same time. Again and again, peaking and hitting more peaks. She saw herself standing on the street surrounded by the glow of million exploding thoughts.

She clasped her hands, exploring the pull of muscles in her body, her heart pounding in her chest, bones and skin placed like a cloak. She shrugged her shoulders and felt a rush of endorphins charge around her body. Jesus fucking Christ, she

81

felt like crying, like running and hiding to indulge this extreme ability. All the books of anatomy and body systems she had studied were playing in real-time in her head.

Then she hit on a noise; a rustling, sinister, scraping sound. She shook her head, focusing on the street around her. Adrenals triggered, pulling her heart down low and intensifying the feeling of her feet on the ground. She wriggled her toes in her shoes. *Feet in shoes?* It all seemed surreal. And then it hit her, how exposed she was, one girl standing on a dark street in the middle of the night.

The scraping sounded again, this time closer. Linda looked up and down the street, long, straight and black, as it should be, as it *should* be? The scraping sound was a primeval fingernail on an inner blackboard. An acrid taste filled her mouth; something was invading, some savage spell, cold like violence. Bug. The smell of it was unmistakable, an ancient, musty curse that cloaked, and soaked, into her mind.

She turned and ran.

In the instant she moved, she heard the complete symphony of the car she had been looking at, all its components singing of their place in potential movement.

Her feet rolled on the sidewalk, rubber soles gripping the cement. The sidewalk held the dirt of its ages and in turn, her boots dropped their message and picked up the exchange. She ran past other cars, each a genius of connecting metals that could move faster than her, yet nothing could match her body. Thigh muscles squeezing, releasing, pushing energy over the exquisite joint of her knees and transferring power down into the calves. She ran under streetlights and in the darkness, on the sidewalk and in the road. There was no one around, *there was no one around, just Bugs on the ground.* Her vision separated, the normal view, but also one from above, a grid of streets she was contained in.

Images rushed past. There were no people, just props. She was stuck in a rat's maze, yet blessed with feet; running, heart leaping, arms pumping. She ran faster, sucking cold air far into her lungs. Reaching an intersection, she stopped. It seemed like everything was spinning. Swaying traffic lights and pedestrian crossing lines boxing her in with their geometric patterns. All was a puzzle. She bounced on her feet, keeping her focus on her immediate environment. The scraping Bug sound was weaker. The street plaques said Shelley and West Lafayette, each one dumping their best buildings into the intersection. From West Lafayette came the preening and stocky Workington Place. It was all about the front; grand pillared entrance, three squat floors, bell tower at the top and iron railed walkways outside each floor. It boasted of history, yet it was fake, the windows too new, the angles of the corners dull like car bumpers.

She swung her arms out, twirling in the endless city twilight. She bounced, then felt silly and headed down Shelley Street, down any street. The importance was to run, to experience moving.

Indifferent street signs offered her nothing, stationary cars grunted, litter pestered and gossiped, puddles held stagnant city tears, shop shutters stared like tombstones, their outers broadcasting parties long finished.

The street was filled with malice, every object a hiding place for sinister sounds and fearful shouts. The wind squealed she was coming, that her legs could not move fast enough. She turned quickly to her right, moving into a side street. The element of surprise was hers. She leapt over a bench—kicking ghosts out of their sleeping state—and down a back street. She was dwarfed beneath the backs of buildings, but ran at full blast, avoiding piles of garbage and haphazardly placed bins. She was winning.

Above an approaching arch, drainpipes snaked all over the back of the building. It was a circuit pattern. She followed the lines, projecting her route and seeing how the Bugs would seek to trap her. Her mind starting layering drainpipe patterns of different buildings on top of each other—systematic transmogrifications. She saw a million connecting points within a million connecting points, fed the signals into her heart, laying plans where to release and hold energy. She was involved in a project of mass involvement with no margin for error. She exited the alley, twenty yards left, right, immediate left, forty yards, left, exit right. She arrived on a main street, and saw an ambulance pass at one end. *The Ambulance of Unforgiven Screams*?

'What you running from, girl?' a lilting, husky voice said.

She turned to see a man sat on the ground. At first glance he looked homeless, but Linda noticed his trainers were clean and his long and ragged robes were designed that way. He had long dark hair and beard; a person calm within his own appearance.

She eyed him, keeping her distance.

'Cat got thee tongue?'

'Just running.'

'Nice night for it.'

As he raised his hand up to his face, Linda noticed that there was blue digital writing on the back of his hand like the readout that a projection clock made. The writing said *Friend*.

'What's that on your hand?'

'What's that, girl?'

'I'm not a girl, I'm a woman. The writing on your hand?'

'Ain't nothing on my hand.'

The man rose up. He was over six feet tall, thin and somewhat dark, but his stance wasn't aggressive. In her mind's eye she could see his body set out in pathways of luminous lines. It was a complete network of his electric and hormonal movements, or she was totally fucking mad.

The man moved his hand but the writing stayed projected so that she could see it.

The scuttling, Bug scratching came again. It was further away than before but too close for comfort.

'What are you doing here?' Linda said.

'Just taking some air from the club down there, *The Headlong*. Come down, good people, good beats.'

'I don't know you.'

'Sure you don't, but I'm okay. I'm a weird man, I've always been a weird man, but in the world we live in, you gotta trust the ways of the weird. The name is Raucous.' He smiled and extended his hand, *Friend* still clearly visible.

Linda thought of Victor and felt a strong desire to see him. The wind blew hard around her, a tree to her left shook its dry leaves, a Styrofoam cup twisted and twirled and a car aerial shook like a wagging finger. *Get off the street, Linda*, everything seemed to say.

She shook Raucous's hand. The shake was firm, no ill intention. She could sense he was relaxed, at ease. He pointed up the street, and she moved with him, keeping a physical distance. The street was wide, cars meekly parked, trees enclosed in cages yet shop fronts unsecured. It was a street that said *Protected — if you want to fuck with something, don't do it here.* She hadn't been in this part of town before, but saw Germain Street written over a shop. When she got to the club, she would call Victor if her bloody phone worked.

'So, why you running so fast in this night?'

'*This night,* is full of strange things.'

'You know, I was jus' saying that. There is something amiss tonight, some bad Bugs got beat down...'

'What?' Linda said, but her voice drowned out by pumping music and Raucous directed her down some steps to where two bouncers stood. From the ordered street it was like slipping under a rug to an underworld. The bouncers exchanged multiple handshakes with Raucous. He introduced Linda as *a special woman-girl.*

She nodded, catching her breath as she saw both bouncers had writing on their hands; the same digital blue light. The one nearest her; short, bald, stocky man in a tight fitting blue coat had the word *Stubborn.* The other, a tall, thin man, with hooded eyes and wispy, plaited goatee, had the word *Tense.*

The door of the club was pushed open. Strobing lights, thumping music and hot recycled air puffed out. Linda moved into a narrow hall way. On her left was a ticket booth behind a steel grill. A man waved them on. The hallway was dark, people crowded in small groups; women in tight dresses, men with loose open shirts and tight, hard flesh. Everything had a dreamlike quality.

The main room was packed. It was dark, blue-lit and smoky. Music thumped against her body, hard bass pulling her into another world. Faces and bodies moved and vibrated around her. Some checked her out, eyes and expressionless faces floating in a vacuum of sound. It was nice to be engulfed, pulled into the womb of noise. She pushed on in behind Raucous, who was able to part the crowd with ease.

A girl grabbed Raucous's arm. Full moon cheekbones, eyes broad and wide, dark eye shadow contrasting brilliant white sclera. The girl looked at Raucous intently, head tilted, mouth open with scarlet, pouting lips. The blue light on the girl's hand said *unstable*. Raucous waved her aside. Her face dropped, and she glared angrily at Linda as she approached.

Linda stopped. The girl's eyes were trembling pools, vast information vats which rippled and Linda found herself somewhere else. She could feel her own body but had moved over the visual lines between her and the girl and was now inside *her* body. The club was louder, the music having a metallic twang. Her heart thumped fast as if afraid, but it was also filled with energy and desire. A throbbing between her legs pulsed rapidly all over her body—the desire to be touched, but edgy, dangerous and easily bored.

Linda moved deeper, experiencing the girl's feelings like she was watching a movie. She saw blood splattered on white tiled walls, red droplets slowly falling and sky-blue pills spilling across the floor. The image thudded down, as if the viewer had passed out. All was black for a moment. Then Linda realised she was in a dark, curtained room. She saw a bed with twisted sheets, hands tied to bedposts and bodies entwining and snaking. She saw hair being pulled and the girl's face arched in pain. Linda stared with amazement, but the girl in the image turned and looked sharply at her. Linda felt a shock of terror and images started snapping faster—bizarre, electro experiments with flesh, cables and crocodile clips; arms flailing, teeth gnashing and legs jerked askew. Then everything faded to black and she was outside in a bleak wind-lashed night. Lightening cracked. A tree was silhouetted against the sky and then a branch came smashing through the roof of a house. Inside the attic, the floorboards, walls and church-like ceiling were white, but it was a white that was shaded with menace, mould and cobwebs claiming the corners. A child, perhaps eight years old, sat on the floor wearing a cream dress with pretty burgundy flowers. The child had tired eyes, red with tears and was completely oblivious to the branch that had smashed through the roof. Her head bowed to what lay before her—razor blades, matches and photographs.

Linda leapt into another room which was completely black except for a table with a brown box on it. Wires, with big white labels on them, were plugged into the box. The holes where the wires plugged in also had labels above them. Linda saw an *Anger* wire plugged into *Security*, *Desire* pushed into *Fear* and *Pain* plugged into *Love*. The *Sex* wire—tugged, overstretched and coated in a sugary, sticky flesh, which had been rubbed raw—trailed off the table and plummeted down into darkness.

Linda zoomed out of her head and came to awareness in the

club. The girl was still glaring at her. Linda felt overwhelmed by knowledge and sadness. The girl pushed her away with beautiful, unmistakable hands—the ones Neon had multiple drawings of.

Linda moved off into the blue of music, people and smoke. For a moment she just danced. Enjoying moving her body to the music and feeling free from what was surrounding her. Her head loosened and past lovers came to mind; Eduardo, Philip, Lucian—especially Lucian. When she'd come to the city he had been helpful, attentive and considerate. She'd fallen for him beyond the limits of her inexperienced self, becoming dependent on his every emotion and mood. It had been a glorious, plunging journey into the feathered and velvet whims of a brilliant thinker. She remembered walks by the river, setting suns and laughter dancing across silver-gold ripples. She remembered the warmth of his hands, his *tap poetry*, forefinger tapping on her pulse as they sat facing each other, holding hands, *Morse Code for the Soul,* he called it.

Lucian showed her how to play with creativity, yielding to the powers surrounding it, like a flower plays with the wind. *Learn how to make moves of consideration,* he told her. She felt as if he thought inside her head, that he wandered in all parts of her.

One day he was the perfect lover, the next he was gone, all beauty recast by his sarcastic words: *I never actually liked your paintings. I was only trying to make you feel good.*

She'd been in her room putting the final touches on a self portrait when Lucian had arrived. He had this casual way of throwing himself over her sofa like a cloth, one of the simple steps to her heart that he knew how to take.

'Lucian?' she said.

'Yeah?'

'Do you have anything that you have never told anybody?'

'Sure, don't we all.'

'Wouldn't you like to just clean it all out, drop everything, let rip in the very fabric of your cells, the core of who you are?'

'Sure, but you must step with consideration,' he said.

'Yes, but from the inside, it's all true, you can just blast.'

'Read the books I've put you onto and you'll get there.' And he stood up, moving across her flat like a cloud rolling over the sky. 'I know you.'

But he didn't know her, not how she wanted to be known. She looked at her self portrait, saw lines etched into her face, layers laid with incision from her psyche, eyes staring with intention that didn't come out in her life. Lucian sat before her, held her hands, fingers on her pulse—how she liked it—warm and giving, and he started talking to her, soft words, words that felt true, gentle, giving words; the ease of water, the taste of the sea, shanties and poetry, songs and fantasy, she let her mind float with what he said. It felt true, yet something, some corner, seemed to be peeling. And then she felt a tickle on her hand, a tapping from another place. She opened her eyes. Lucian was before her, eyes closed, face passive, deeply communing with her, but on her hand she saw a bee. Her heart quickened and Lucian smiled, perhaps feeling her pulse increase. She watched the bee fearfully, yet she was unwilling to move her hand and break the moment. The body of the bee trembled and Linda marvelled at its tribal shield back pattern and its muscular body and tense legs. She saw the sting poised, such a precise instrument. She listened to Lucian's words, but found herself moving somewhere else. It surprised her, she thought that all she wanted was him, but at that moment she became intensely involved in herself—what made her, how far she went—and she began to find Lucian irritating. She took a breath, travelling over her inner world, *her world,* not the world of Lucian. And she started talking: *what I want to say, where I want to go* and he resisted, she noticed it, in his hands, a slight moistness, in his breath, a hesitance, a smell—what had before seemed like fresh fruit, now seemed slightly rotting. As she opened her mouth, the bee stung her. Pain shot up her arm, exploring and exploding in her mind and her words came out rapidly. She gripped Lucian's arms. *What talks in the night... what sings in dreams... where valleys meet mountains... the brutal contact of vision and sky... land that talks of the heart... systems that dream and live... insanity and the thoughts of ghosts and gods... tumbling flight... bees in the thorax... personal system of deformation.* Linda raced over an inner landscape, driven by the fire of poison that plunged into her body. The bee hung on but Lucian pulled back, ripping his hands free.

Linda let the music of the club pull her back, but she remembered Lucian's look of incomprehension and disgust. She'd broken his little china dream, smashed up his cellar and kicked his fucking windows in.

She danced on, letting herself be herself, watching other versions far away, distant memories of who she had been. Now she was alone, alone in the complete majesty of her inner self. She looked at the digital readouts that she could see: *Dominant, Aggressive, Enthusiastic, Prudent, Angry, Sensual* and

Introspective. Some people looked like their readout, but others seemed to go against what was displayed.

She watched *Introspective*, a man, early thirties, good looking, mousey blonde hair, slight tan, untucked orange shirt, tight leg jeans loose at the ankle, and clean white trainers. He looked outgoing, easy and loose, but his dance moves were a little stiff, the shirt was bright orange, clashing with his tan. Every so often, his eyes looked down to the left, sneaking in a little think, then he seemed to sigh and put the mask back on. Linda could have sworn that amidst all the noise she heard his heart beat and it was dull and thudding. The girl dancing with him had long, straight, blonde hair and candy floss eyes. Linda manoeuvred to see her readout: *Ambitious*. That seemed a disaster in the making. As Linda looked around she felt the heady mix of the club. It was a menagerie, a cauldron of human personalities bobbing around each other, their swaying bodies creating friction and triggering chemical releases. The air was awash with electrical stimulation, mass information feeding directly into the nervous systems of everyone.

A man was staring at her from the seats at the edge. He was good looking, wild hair, face ruffled, but eyes intent and alive. He waved her over with a hand that said *Absent-minded*. Linda smiled and shook her head. Her body released pleasure waves, curling tendrils that softened the ends of her thought and attempted to fog her mind. She realised how easy it was to get lost in someone.

She danced on, needing to get some sense into her world. She could drown here, washed over by the immensity of what everyone was. She closed her eyes, dancing, spiralling inward, vast landscapes lay before her, millions of receptors to the environment.

A hand snaked around her waist from behind. Linda lashed out, dug her elbow back, and twisted around. It was the guy who had waved her over, Mr *Absent Minded*. Linda snarled at him and he raised his eyebrows, now sneering rather than smiling. He brought his hands up in mock apology. Linda felt a blaze of revulsion flood into her.

'What the fuck do you think you are doing?' she shouted.

He just stood grinning and stupid looking. His readout was now *Resentful*.

Linda's head felt fogged, swarming with anger. She looked over at *Introspective* and *Ambitious* but they also looked changed. He was leering, she was looking tearful and irritated. His readout was *Bitter*, hers was *Delusion*.

Linda tried to clear her feelings, but they kept dredging up dark emotions. She read the nearest hand readouts: *Insecure, Liar, Cheat, Hater*. Jesus, it was like a plague. Then something brown, dry and musty filled her mouth.

Bug.

Linda quickly slipped off the dance floor and headed into the backroom where Raucous had gone. It was quieter there, the crowd spread out into three circular seating areas. The lights were dark blue, but clear enough to pick out objects and faces. There were low, fat curved sofas and round bulbous stools, perched on a black, rubber dimpled floor. Tables were piled with drinks and various drug paraphernalia. Calm faces looked up at Linda's entrance, eyes blinking, minds and mouths hazed and hushed. She turned and looked back at the dance floor which was thrashing and red. On the far side, the girl with the hands was talking to what looked like a Soul Bug.

Raucous came over. 'Come,' he said, leaning towards Linda's ear and brushing his bristles against her cheek. 'Meet some friends of mine.'

Linda looked over, seeing a tough looking bunch of men and women. Linda raised one finger and placed an imaginary phone to her ear. Raucous nodded and moved off. Linda walked over to the cloakroom area and pulled out her phone. Please work.

'Hi Victor... in a club... yeah, well, for now...some serious shit... *illumination*?! Insanity... he didn't do, well... yeah, but I mean, fucking hell, Victor... listen, there's a fucking Bug... underground club on Germain Street... smelt, tasted it... don't know, just fucking crawling, insidious musty... don't know which fucking insect... why would I?... what?... shit... really fucking close... basement... a fucking trap... oh shit... it's talking to a freaking psycho girl, amazing hands, Neon drew them... she, well, a long story... serious? Too fucking right... do, please... hurry.'

Linda stayed in the toilet hallway. A vicious odour crawled up her nose like needles of sulphur.

The Bug and girl came towards the backroom, glanced around before returning to the main room.

Linda followed, watching them as they crossed the dance floor. They left people shaking their heads; dance moves that had been lush and rounded became jagged and coarse. As they moved off the dance floor, Linda slid down, trying to hide within the crowd.

The two stood on a walkway above the dance floor, heads swivelling as if they were touching antennae.

Linda's stomach twisted and cramped. She danced on, looking around for some protection. But it was pointless. The dancers had loosened around her, as if instinctively moving away from danger.

The Bug looked straight at her.

'BITCH!'

Unforgiven Screams

9

'You eat?' Spodge asked Neon.

Neon shook his head, stirring his coffee absentmindedly and looking out the Diner window. It was getting dark and the last of the day people were scurrying home, nervous of the appetite of the advancing darkness. He had been disappointed to find that Linda was not at his studio.

'Got Victor's number, Spodge?'

'Sure.'

'Can I have your phone?'

'They rarely work.' Spodge slid her phone across the table and returned to watching the street.

Neon dialled.

'Victor... Where's Linda?... Why?... Bug attack?... *Alone*? We're all alone, THAT is the essence of it all!... Liv?... Ah, Liv... those hands, magnificent things... Sure, unhinged but capable. Not a team player... Really? That impresses me... Care? There is no care, only change... Dark harbours and their boats... Not so sure really... Exact? You want exact, go talk to a fucking scientist... Some linear simplicity? Yes, life is a text book, Victor... Yeah, and regressing back into a cunt makes you a moron... No, Victor, you piece-a-shit. Stop trying to apply old fucking templates to new fucking situations... Yes, people *are* in fucking danger. You want it to be my fault, but the fault line is

96

as much inside you, as me. You're not a thinker, Victor. You're *the doing*. Yes, Emily Merryweather is dead. She died... Sure and I don't care, I'm not doing anything for me. I do it because that is what has to be done. The streets of the city are corroding, they moved first... The outsiders, the deceivers, the fucking plague police, the Genetic Overlords, anything you wanna call them... You see, Victor. You don't see in straight lines, you don't see, you are, that is your strength... You, you're the colossus, you're the fucking blockage in the pipe... 'Cause I'm the fucking seer, Victor. I *know*, you *are*, that's why it works... Yes, Victor, but you shouldn't fucking listen, you never did until pain wrenched your soul. The Bugs killed Emily, but don't make it personal, your revenge will be more effective... Fall through the wires, drop into the concrete of the city, the mesh of human endeavour. Look around you, Victor. Where are you?... What do you see?... Bullshit, Victor. What do you see? Listen to the throbbing in the temples, pressure, brain suspended in liquid, eyes bulging, but not exploding. You got any sharp knives there?... Go get the sharpest one, cut your fucking brain out... Cut it out and place it on the fucking table. What the fuck is your brain?... Yeah... Nah, Victor, you're forgetting one thing, your brain is turned off... Sorry, Victor. Of course, you know better. Enjoying your life at the moment, are you?... Have you got your curtains closed?... Lights turned off?... It's perfect really. There you are, sitting there in the dark, in an apartment with the windows closed, no air circulating, no fresh food, the water in your pipes stagnating. You are suspended... Alright, Victor. It's okay to mourn, that we can do. But something happened, Victor, something happened to us.

97

You heard it, that day outside the gallery on Carden Street. Jesus, you heard it! The clarity of your hearing was so fucking loud, I felt it from miles away. You're the kingpin, Victor, you're the God of the City, don't you fucking forget that. Go get laid, take a break. I want that Linda. All these fucking things Victor, these pieces that fall from the sky, these people we meet, how the environment shapes our relationships, day, night, how we see each other, from mourning, from ecstasy, from the position we held in our family, from past experiences, from the programming of our social class, of our religious upbringing. A million configurations, mass importance and complete inconsequentiality. We live lives and we don't live life, and nothing is important and everything is important, and we care and what the fuck is caring... Nice, get Linda would you?... Did I? I don't mean a break, you know. You don't get holidays in this job... You want money?... Yeah, yeah.'

The Diner was covered in people pieces—flaked skin, grease and hair. It was filled with thoughts and conversations, intentions, desires and deceit. It was alive with hands rubbing, touching and scratching under the tables, legs rubbing together creating friction, repulsion and attraction. Mouths chewed, teeth pounded down on various lumps of food—bread, potato, sausage, bacon, burgers and sauces. Juices and saliva dribbled, dripped and dropped. Hands rubbed flesh, eyes and ears, people sneezed, coughed and then cloths dipped in dirty water containing germs and other remains, smeared it all across the tables.

Behind Spodge, a big man wearing a working man's jacket

was sitting in a four seat booth. Somewhere along the line he had been recruited by the capital machine, strapped into the system; a cog, a cell, one molecule in the vastness. His hair was impressive, shining and thickly greased back like it was an iron. His back was a mountain craned into place, preserved tomblike by the desires of others. His coat was likewise sealed, its breathability frustrated by the toil of living. The red vinyl of the bench held the man, but it had disdain; it had heard too much false laughter, accusation, gossip, plans and the pointless.

Neon stood up.

The Iron Head man had vast boulders for fingers; hard and stained. Ingrained in that dirt and filth was the history of the working man.

The Neons in his head were buzzing. Word was that she, Linda, was like molten lava. She was too much, unstoppable. She was out there in the city, growing in power. She could well be the one, the light that burned through the bullshit.

Iron Head rose from his bench. His face was stagnant, hard and heavy. He had eyes like stones, worn stones, and then, like a clam, they opened. Neon saw a flame, a turbine spinning at incredible speed. He was pulled into the whirl, ripped from his standing spot and whirled around at the speed of light. He fought back, removing his attention from his sight and inhaling the odours of this beast. He was blinded, but in smelling the tar, the ingrained filth of the man, he found a corner, an unsealed edge. Jesus! This was no working man. Underneath the odours, the clothes—the fucking mask—was another mask, and another fucking mask. On the tip of Neon's tongue was a burning sensation; the emittance of a caustic mind. Jesus, he hadn't encountered this since Albert.

'Neon?' the man's voice was heavy, laden with gravel; every intonation of the accent was masked by a twisting of the vowels.

Neon's eyes were spat out and returned to him.

'Who the fuck are you?'

'That is not so important. Who you are, now that is of interest. Come with me.'

Spodge looked at Neon, eyes shining.

'Not the girl.'

Neon flipped inward. *'Neon 23, what's the score here?'*

'Iron Head is a fluid occurrence of individual. Communication is mainly based in the preverbal. He is throwing moves all over the place.'

'Give me some details?'

'His right hand is hanging down, but it is tilted out with the palm of the hand showing. This is a gesture of openness, yet... the thumb is covering part of the palm, this is showing the desire to only share certain things.'

'Okay.'

'The left hand thumb is touching the tip of the forefinger. This shows self belief, but more, as it is moving left to right, it indicates that he has an accomplice, who he wants to return to.'

'Interesting...'

'The body stance is selling an image, it is dumped before you, but it is not all for your benefit. The head—left eye further back with squint, head slightly pointing down to left foot, and mouth open— tells us three things. He's got about sixty percent of his attention on you, he is using mental powers to keep his mind on a thought pattern,

100

and he could react extremely, if threatened.'

'Violent?'

'Not of the normal kind, this could be a mindfuck specialist. It's got Albert written all over it.'

'But Albert is dead.'

'Yes, he's dead, but there's similar beasts bouncing around this guy's box. This is a higher forming dude. We ain't been near one of these in a long time.'

Iron Head watched Neon with unwavering eyes. 'You coming?'

'Now, why would I do that?'

Iron Head's eyes flickered.

Neon tightened his nostrils and let the muscles of his fingers flex and retract. In his inner mind, he projected the man's features into wet oily paint; grey-white on the surface, but underneath, as Neon explored, were liquid yellow, ravenous red, poisonous pinks—loaded colours, drying and stretching Neon's concentration over the man's landscape. Each piece of the man's mask had been placed with precise intent.

Neon saw twenty images of the man, from the one in the cafe, through a myriad of spectrums; electromagnetic, frequency, power, energy, colour and mass.

Iron Head leaned down towards Neon. 'The city streets strain and bleed, the Bug Squealers are gaining more than even *you*, could imagine.'

'Can't remember asking.'

'Your creations aren't as well hidden as you think.'

'Really.'

'Maybe we can help.'

101

'Maybe...' said Neon, as he tried to get a fix on Iron Head's mind to see if he had been to the spectrum. The dude was more evasive than midnight. Neon changed tack and raced to the desert where he kept his equational sculptures. He looked for signs that someone had been there. Nothing had changed. The sculpture's dogged faces nodded at him in their way. The desert was silent, a silence that elongated time. And then Neon saw the anomaly—a glistening bead of sweat on a skull. Shit.

'Neon 23, you knowing what I'm knowing?'

'Just known it. That we did not expect. Neon 43 and 12 are on the case, we need to secure a fix on his origins, seems passive for now, but you better go and see where he leads.'

'Will do.'

'Let's go,' said Neon. 'Wait here Spodge. If I don't return, drink more coffee.'

Iron Head seemed relieved to be leaving. They exited the Diner like moths turning away from electric light.

They paused outside. Across the road, pimps and drug dealers clung to the sidewalk like grease. Shop fronts were boarded up with asymmetrical planks of wood. Cars cruised by, lowered windows revealing aggressive faces.

Iron Head was unmoved by the glares. His presence spoke volumes. No one would mess. Neon noticed his head turn right, and followed his gaze. There was an ambulance approaching, cumbersome and out of place amongst the slick, bass-pumping cars. The ambulance pulled up sharply in front of them, too quick for Neon to see who was in the front. The back doors burst open, banging against the sides. Iron Head stepped to the side, and Neon stared in at the bright interior.

102

There was a man standing inside, large, unshaven rounded face, worn sleeveless shirt hanging over a protruding belly, jeans and hiking boots. He had scarred cheeks like a boxer; not a man used to taking shit. There were two beds in the ambulance, in the bed to the left was a child with an oxygen mask over his face.

The big man in the ambulance looked down. 'The Man and the *other* man.' He looked at Neon. 'Quick, get in, won't be long before we get noticed here.'

Neon climbed in and moved to the back, sitting on a chair at the top of the empty bed. Iron Head sat on the empty bed and the big man pulled the doors. The ambulance sped off.

'Arthur Sven.' The big man held his hand out to Neon and shook hard. 'And you're the Doctor Neon man.'

'That's what they say.'

'Nah, you are, I've seen your stuff, you're a regular doctor alright, one dangerous muthafucker.'

Neon got the feeling of being kidnapped and realised that only by agreeing to come, had he removed the need for force. A sense of helplessness started to bring up feelings he had long buried. He ignored them. 'So, what's the visit for?'

Arthur Sven looked at Iron Head, then back at the kid he had on the bed beside him.

'You see this kid here?'

Neon nodded, observing the pink blanket rising and falling very slowly over the kid's slight frame. With the oxygen mask on, the kid looked like a shrunken fighter pilot.

'I go around, find sick kids like this...' Arthur Sven rubbed his cheek, pushing at the flesh like it was a hindrance. He stared at Neon.

Neon took a breath, as he breathed out, he stopped thinking, observing the silence that surrounded the sick child. 'Sick from what?'

'Oh *you* know.' Arthur choked a bit, and then took a sharp intake of breath.

Arthur and Iron Head were big. Neon was not. He had maniac strength, but he got the feeling that wouldn't get him too far. Worse still, he didn't seem to have access to his inner Neons so he couldn't get a feed on the motives of these two. He was being cloaked, forced into this moment and at the mercy of these and whoever was driving.

The quietness in his head made the inside of the ambulance seem bigger. It was like a holding cell. It didn't appear that these two were with the Overlords, they were coming from a different angle. If the shit got heavy though, he was going to have to use a weapon. On the floor beside Arthur Sven were two oxygen bottles, but they were safely secured with black straps. There were steel drawers just by his knee and no doubt they contained many scalpels, but he wouldn't have time to find them. The only weapon left was his mouth. 'Let's cut to it. You asked me here.'

Iron Head leant forward, placing his hand on Arthur Sven's arm. 'We worked with Albert Scram.'

'Okay, that makes sense. He was some man.'

'Yes he was, but maybe not so capable. You, on the other hand, *are* capable, question is, *of what*?'

Neon smirked. 'I don't see why that's an issue.'

Arthur's cheeks flushed magenta. 'I'll tell you why it's a

fucking issue.'

Neon clocked his clenched fists. 'No offence man. I do what I do, you worked with Albert. I worked with Albert. I don't see we're on different sides.' Neon noticed his voice echoing off the sides of the ambulance. The whole world had disappeared.

'You know why this child is sick?' asked Arthur.

'No I don't.' Neon looked at Iron Head and back to Arthur. 'What's with the questions? Just spit it out, if you've got trouble with me. Get on with it.' As Neon spoke he was trying to find some way of getting into his inner Neons. He needed to be able to work out these guys' motives. He felt like his head was wrapped in a heavy lead apron but there was a corner of his mind that wasn't fully fogged, there always was. If he couldn't get into his head, he would have to start anew. They blocked the past and present, he moved to the future.

Iron Head nodded at Neon, a small smile playing across his face. 'You're like a cop, Neon.'

'Yeah, how's that?'

'Well, how long we get?' Iron Head looked at Arthur.

The big man relaxed, 'Oh I dunno, I'd say about three minutes.'

'Three minutes till what?'

'Three minutes till you get a trace on us. Till you find some way of moving out of your head, taking an angle, *probing* our minds. Did you miss the bit where we said we worked with Albert?'

'No I didn't miss that, but I'm not Albert.'

'No... what *was* he up to?'

'You worked with him, but you don't know what he was

doing?'

'We knew he wanted freedom of choice. We transported some of his creations, things he didn't want seen.'

'Yeah,' Neon looked around, 'seems as good a place as any. Albert believed understanding to be mimicry. At the highest point of understanding he believed there was a point of crossing, a point where the mimic could steal the upper hand.'

'How'd he do it?'

'I'd like to know that myself, but it's starting. The problem with freedom though, there ain't no training for it.'

Arthur nodded. 'You know what happened to Albert?'

'I know he's dead.'

'How do you know?' said Iron Head.

'A light went out. Details—I'd like to know those.'

'He lay down on the railway tracks at Garelt. Laid his fucking head on the line and a train went right over it.'

Neon nodded. He had come to this world by freakish occurrence, but Albert had arrived through intense thought power. A building block of intense equations. A man who was too sane.

'If Albert was obsessed with freedom of choice, what's your obsession, Neon?' asked Arthur.

'You seem to know all about me, you tell me.'

Arthur stretched out his arms, seemed to be marvelling at them. 'It doesn't matter,' he said and looked up at the ceiling of the ambulance.

Neon followed his gaze, noticing that the ceiling was grubby. In fact most of the edges in the ambulance were worn like a tattered old suitcase. Save the modern equipment, the old

106

box could be centuries old.

The two men were talking quietly to each other. Neon's importance was secondary; he wasn't going to be taken seriously until he presented himself in the reality they wanted. This was coffin pressure.

'Tempted to flip out, Neon?'

Neon flashed a smile. 'I'm not the entertaining type, if you're looking for a reaction go find an extremist.'

'And you're not?'

'My reaction is excessive, but my aim moves with me. I am exact. This is boring, get to the point.'

'There will be no point.'

'Sounds more like my line. So don't let me know, but do let me out.'

'Miss the moon, do ya?' said Arthur. The two men laughed.

'Two comedians and a sick child for the sympathy vote, brilliant.'

'Shut yer fucking mouth,' said Arthur. The impact of his anger changed the grime on the walls into screaming faces, the oxygen tanks shook with rage, drawers rattled with screeches and stale air lay on Neon with the impact of a sledge hammer.

Neon's chest muscles tightened. He slowed his breath, placed his hand on the cold white surface in front of him and stretched his fingers. His head ached. 'Okay, I'm listening.'

Arthur gestured to Iron Head.

Iron Head turned around to face Neon directly. 'Right, this is important, very. Don't try to get a make on us, 'cause I'm gonna tell you everything with my voice, strange concept I know.'

'Stranger things have happened.'

'You're a dark man, Neon.'

'Depends where you're looking from.'

'Ain't that the truth.' Iron Head rubbed his hand over his face, like he was searching for the right face to speak through.

Neon couldn't tell if the ambulance was moving or not, everything was silent, except for the child's laboured breathing.

Iron Head continued. 'When a child is brutalised it creates poisonous images in their mind. They swirl like a tornado of razorblades. Even as time passes, the tornado repeatedly forces itself to the forefront of the mind plaguing and diseasing self-esteem and confidence. But humans are tough creatures and the quick-fire method of dealing with it is blackout, blanking the memory out for years, if not forever.'

Neon felt himself relax, dropping his suspicions.

'When the memories are blanked out, they leave a void, a cold, empty space.'

'So—'

'No.' Iron Head raised his hand, palm towards Neon. 'Listen. The memories spin out. But they don't disappear. The city is full of them. They like the city, hiding places are plentiful here.'

Neon thought of murky backstreets overhung by grim, shadow clad buildings.

'People know where these places are, there have always been places people don't like to go to. If these terror blots are left alone, they create rot in the world, small black holes of the human condition. But they are essential to each child and it's important to keep them close so that one day, little by little, pieces can be put back in. Maybe a moment of understanding, a forgiving, or just a shame-free day. Now Arthur here—'

Arthur looked away, staring at the back doors.

'Arthur does what few would do, what few could do. He finds the memories and he brings them in here and gives them a space to be at peace. You're probably wondering why your head is blocked, all fogged over and sealed. That's what this room does, this ambulance is a sealed thought chamber. And in here the thoughts become what they are: sick. This'—he pointed at the kid— 'this is not the kid. This is part of the kid. The piece that scarpered. When they come in here, they seal and remember that they are human and so they maintain an attachment to our world.'

'Okay.'

'When you work, we end up with those Bugs.'

'Soul Bugs, poisons of the splendid. I can't be responsible for what other people leave behind.'

'We ain't judging, Neon, but blanked out memories are gold dust to Soul Bugs. Food in the city. Soul Bugs thrive on the hate and anger of unlived thought, but they want more. Always more. They are drawn to the blanked out memories, and their aim is to reuse the horror on the child, or more to the point with the grown up. You can't act on hate if you don't know you have it.'

'What do you want me to do?'

'It's not what we want you to do. It's the people with blanked out memories.'

'Like who?'

'There are a lot, but in particular, Liv Adder and Victor

Scram.'

'Liv, okay, but Victor?'

'Yes.'

'Victor's hung up on Emily Merryweather.'

'He is, but you've got to take it back further. Although Albert scrutinised everything, I don't think even he knew of the dangerous effects of the void inside people.'

'Don't be too sure. So, what are you saying?'

'You're the hole maker, and now you're putting holes in holes. It's causing a catastrophe.'

'That's what you see, but you're buried under fifty tons of reinforced steel. You got fists, goodness and you got anger, but you're submarine men. Up top is raw, it hurts, it bleeds, that's what happens. Nothing changes with ease. What left a hole in Victor?'

'That's not your concern.'

'Fair enough.'

'You've started Victor on a road to rejoining with things he just can't imagine and with good reason.'

'Victor has potential beyond any of us.'

'You're more than right. But in taking Victor and Liv out into the open and infinitely expanding the blackness, the Soul Bugs will do everything to latch onto them.'

'They have returned to Liv.'

'Yeah well, she's got one hell of a void inside her. And now that the Soul Bugs are filling her with rage, both their powers will rapidly increase.'

'And Victor?'

'Well, don't you think it's a coincidence that Victor

encounters so many Bugs? The thing is, he's pretty fucking immense and we've been working hard with his lost memories.'

Neon looked at the child on the bed. The broad forehead and dark blue eyes. Washed out fighter pilot, who grew up to be a fighter pilot. 'Shit.' Neon's heart lurched in his chest, and a torrent of tears threatened to overwhelm him. Fuck that. But there was no doubt that this emaciated sliver was Victor Scram.

You wanna sleep with me?

10

The Diner had an ultra quiet period at midnight. At this time, the mirrors behind the counter lost interest in reflection. The glasses on the shelves shone mutely, cups and mugs were turned upside down and teaspoons and cutlery waited quietly in their containers. There were no outside hands to push, stir or spill, no sugar on the counter and no sauce, salt or food scraps on the tables.

Victor sat on one of the cherry drop stools. It was Linda's night to work, but she wasn't here yet. It had been three nights since the club incident and Victor hadn't bothered to get her for Neon.

Listern, the owner of the Diner, was pacing down the end of the counter where the hatch opened. Listern was never behind the counter, he liked to be on the outside so he could connect with whomever he felt might increase what he had—money, drugs, commodities. His was a life lived in pursuit. He was in his fifties, pot bellied, with a large moustache smeared over his lip and down the sides of his mouth repeating the pattern of his hair. There was no point asking *him* about Linda. Linda did as she pleased, she attracted people and Listern's greed easily overrode his desire to be respected.

Tracy, another waitress, was working the counters and doing the tables. She had already given Victor his constant companion, coffee. There was a faded aspect to Tracy. She did the job Linda did, probably a lot better, but in her plump face—skin slightly too gray for true health—she seemed to have random control. She would talk, but her top lip wouldn't move, or she would laugh and her cheeks would stay still. Her hair, dyed a matt chestnut brown, seemed like a wig, yet you could see the scrubbed cleanliness of the hair follicles in her scalp. It was like some essential piece was missing.

Maybe Neon could work with her, transform *her* experience. Victor mused on the way she wore her grey uniform; bunched at the arms, breasts and hips. Neon said that if people weren't in a state of bloom you couldn't connect to them. But her body was still firm, the bloom was in her even if it wasn't active now.

'Can I help you, Victor?' she said, noticing him staring at her. She looked at him with oval shaped, armadillo eyes.

'No, no, just wondering how you are?'

'I'm fine, well as good as can be with what's going on.'

'What's that?'

'Out there,' Tracy said, nodding her head towards the door.

Victor turned around and looked at the door. 'What do you mean, out there?'

'Haven't you noticed?' she said with a youthful raise of her eyebrows, although her motionless mouth let down the expression.

'If you lived in the world I live...'

Armadillo eyes stared and blinked.

Victor shrugged. 'Well I don't know. Is it different to how it was?'

Tracy looked down the counter to where Listern was busy

113

tucking heads with an undesirable.

'It's spreading over the city.' she said.

Victor could have sworn he saw a glint in Tracy's eye and imagined her tottering on armadillo feet and waving a small tail behind. 'What is?'

'We, myself and others, have been watching it, you see, because—' Tracy leaned forward, '—people rarely see what is in front of them. It's hard to unravel the puzzles that life presents.' Tracy puckered her mouth, her eyes soft like caramel. 'But when you get quiet, when quiet settles right into your bones.'

Victor thought that he was about as far from quietness in his bones as it was possible to get.

'If you just stay still long enough, you get to see things. Out there.' She pointed to the window. 'Where the people roam, where they gather at night.'

Victor noticed narrow nails, neatly clipped. 'The street?'

'No, not the street. The street is the trunk of a tree, but off that trunk grows branches, in the V between the trunk and the branch, people gather, some sliding down, some climbing up.'

'I see.' Victor wondered why he had never talked to this woman before.

'Well, now the tree is sick. It's oozing sticky tar-like nectar and people are getting stuck. It's one thing to settle, but another to be held down. People get cross, they get mad and their minds start turning in on themselves, snapping in anger, like an animal in a trap.'

'In this street, branch?'

'All branches of the city. If you infect the trunk, you infect the city.'

'TRACY.' Listern shouted from the end of the counter. 'Tables.' He shook his head and waved his hand around.

Tracy moved off. Victor smiled at her watchful eyes. He thought of her team of watchers scurrying around the branches of the city tree. There was no doubt the city was suffering, and maybe he needed a new way of looking at things. He was getting deeply tied into Neon, and Neon was tying him into his own head. Maybes this little Armadillo was giving him a new direction.

The door rattled behind him.

Shit. Victor swung around on the cherry drop. But it wasn't a Soul Bug, it was Linda.

Linda did not arrive dressed for work. She arrived dressed to kill. This was not a Linda Victor had seen before. Her face was taut, the skin polished. Her cheekbones were spiky; makeup heightening their features. Her eyes were sunflower heads, the iris surrounded by flaming sentinels. There was something frightening, not in the look, but in the intention; like noticing how sharp a knife was.

Her exposed cleavage was more shapely than ample and her body was lithe, like a panther. Tight top, short black skirt with a sash of grey netting and a leather strap. And her legs, long, clad in sheer tights, muscled, moving with a grace that Victor had not seen before. Black boots, combat style, rounded her off. They were tight to her ankle, offering easy movement rather than clumsiness. This was a body that had electric burning all over. What the hell had grown in the last three days?

'Linda.' Victor nodded.

She raised her eyebrows at him.

It was still Linda, somewhere amidst the dazzle. To say she didn't suit the Diner was an understatement, but she seemed to bring something in with her, like the space around her was interactive. Listern started up from his spot, but Victor glared and he retreated. It was one thing him looking.

Linda slid onto a cherry drop. 'Thought I would find you here.'

'Something keeps pulling me back.'

'But I wasn't here.'

At that moment, there was no Diner, there was no city, just this beacon.

Tracy scuttled past. 'Evening, Linda.'

'Hi ya, Trace.'

For once all of Tracy's face lit up. Victor wondered where she saw Linda on the tree. She was pretty high up in his mind and he couldn't imagine her getting stuck.

'You doing tables, Linda?' asked Tracy.

'Like that?' said Victor.

'Like what?' said Tracy

'Eh?' Victor shook his head.

'I,' Linda started, 'I want to thank you for the other night.'

'That's okay. You were in a tight spot.'

'You're a good man, Victor. I mean, you're a bad ass, and you're kinda fucked up, but there is something about you.' She threw her hands up and smiled.

Her eyes flaming over him. And her hand, when it moved, was like something was pulling, or coursing through, the fingers. He had seen that one in the good old doctor.

The door rattled again, jarring back on its hinges.

'Juice ball, Scram, man!' an excessively wired Tommy Bones roared. 'Linda, grrrrl. Going to a funeral?'

'No, Tommy.'

'Funeral? In those clothes?' said Victor.

'Huh?'

'Hey, Johnny,' said Linda.

Johnny Ease stumbled in behind Tommy. His eyes looked deeper than ever, like his thoughts had been drained and filled with black ink. Victor hadn't seen the two of them so wasted before. But losing Easter the other night wasn't going to pass unacknowledged.

'How you going, Tommy?' asked Victor.

'Fine, perfectly designed. Been working on some new things, y' know.' Tommy was standing out on the floor, his knees involuntarily bending and straightening. He kept putting his hand on his hip, where it kept slipping off. He wore a skinny, blue leather jacket, dirty, rock washed, skinny jeans, and pointed shoes with one big buckle. The door bust open again, Mark Baa buzzed in, his little wool hair-hat bouncing as he jiggered around. There was something of the vaudeville about Baa; waistcoat, tapered tweed trousers, a kind of inner tune playing in his head. Now he seemed to be spinning around in circles.

'Sorry to hear you lost Easter,' said Linda.

'No,' flashed Tommy, 'no, not lost, we're getting him back, see. Johnny building the fucking retrieval box, and I got new fucking moves.'

117

'You,' slurred Mark Baa, 'ain't got no new fucking moves, Tommy.'

'No? I got the fucking moves.'

'Nothing, Tommy. No fucking moves.'

Johnny Ease was watching the two of them; big old thunder eyes. Tommy stood with hands together, raised at chest height, elbows pointing out. Listern watched from the end of the counter. Listern had bad blood with Tommy, had tried to outdo him on a drug deal, but didn't have a fucking clue what wavelength Tommy was on.

Tommy leapt, or at least a scrawny leg shot out and hit the table in front of him—ketchup, mustard and sugar shot into the air and crashed onto the floor. 'Now, there's some fucking moves.'

'Fuck sake, Tommy,' said Victor. Listern's eyes widened.

'And now,' said Tommy. 'I will demonstrate the condiment bodysurf. He started taking his jacket off.

'Johnny,' said Victor. 'Fucking wrap him up, would you?'

Johnny bowed his head at Victor. 'Hey, Tommy, listen...' He laid his hand on Tommy's shoulder and spoke into his ear. Tommy's face broke into a serious frown and he started rubbing his chin. Johnny took him down the Diner and placed him at a table, where he collapsed, sighing and gesturing to himself like a scratching dog.

Listern advanced. Victor stood up and moved towards him, not letting him reach where he wanted to go.

'Leave it, Listern. It's sorted.'

'I can't have this kinda thing here, I have customers.'

Victor looked around, the studied night-heads were staring

down at what was in front of them. 'Customers are fine.'

'No problem, Mr L, all cleaned up,' said Tracy.

'Yeah, but it's that one. He tried to point at Tommy but Victor moved into his line of vision and he had to point sideways. Victor wanted to knock him out, but the Diner had importance to them and he didn't want to ruin that, not yet anyway.

Listern nodded, yet didn't meet Victor's eyes and headed back down to his cronies at the counter.

Victor sat back down.

'You gotta take care of your boys,' said Tracy.

'They're not my boys.'

'No?' Tracy asked, then moved off.

'My boys?' Victor said to Linda.

'Well, you fill in something for them. They're all covered in cracks. Shot through with them.'

Lind watched the Kage Kids with the same furious stare that Neon had. Linda's gaze seemed personal though, an edge of concern in the frantic intent. Neon was all for the greater purpose, the relentless progress. Linda seemed present, available. Of course, three days ago she was semi-normal and as much as he was enjoying it, she wasn't dressed up for him.

'You're going to see Neon?'

'I can't not.'

'I ain't judging you.'

'The potential is boundless.'

'Boundless sure, and the consequence?' Victor felt like a ghost walked through him and stayed poised in the middle. He could feel Linda's head inside his head. He didn't resist, it was like hitting g-force, you had to let it happen, resistance was futile.

'You're no innocent, Victor Scram.'

'Never claimed to be, but it's about how you get to where you want to go. Who gets hurt and whose head you set alight to achieve it.' Victor felt Linda retreat.

Linda smiled apologetically. 'It's not what I want. I mean, that's your head. But I think something and I am there and then I think something from there and I am somewhere else; *someone* else. It is about who I am. How many different ways I can see myself. Take it apart, dissemble, transform, mutate, relive the experience.'

'Cooking your fucking brain. You're like a Kage without the drugs.'

'No, it's exciting, it's creative. Without being full of shit, it's myself as my own creation.'

'Yeah, sounds like hell to me. Of course your world ain't my world.'

'That I know. But there's something that lurks...' She got up to go.

'Something, yeah, now you're talking about the *something*. There's a price, Linda. I don't stop things. I don't stop you. I don't stop Neon. I know something's right about what he does. It's undeniable. But there's a price, there's a price we all gotta pay.' Victor looked at her blazing eyes. The deep black circle in the middle didn't seem so perfectly rounded, like it was threatening to spill over, not tears, but some sticky oil of mind mechanisation.

'You gotta be careful with Neon.'

Linda looked back at him. 'Because?'

Victor opened his hands, pointing to Linda's clothes.

'You see what *you* want to see, Victor. It's not what others see.'

And Victor realised she was wearing jeans and a leather jacket. 'What?'

She flashed a smile, looked at him with hardening eyes, and slipped out.

When he'd arrived at the club the other night, Linda's eyes had been a lot more frightened. It hadn't take him long to suss the situation. The Soul Bug pheromones were spreading over the dance floor creating wickedness in people. It was like giving people a rash that they couldn't itch. Or maybe, as Tracy had pointed out, it was making people feel stuck. But when he saw Liv, even he got shivers. Communicating with the Bug. Straight up, side by side; dark and darker.

Victor had chosen Liv as a model for Neon about three weeks ago. Had stumbled into her at Sparkies Bar over on Lincoln. She'd hooked into Victor and he'd hooked into her. There was no doubt she was present, or as Neon said, *full bloom*. She was leaning against the bar counter, her body brazen — one leg cocked open, wide mouth, head rolling back with laughter, her open eyes inviting people in. It wasn't simple sexuality, it was raw heart, willingness and daring. Something Victor understood. She'd been eager to get to Neon and he shameless in taking her. Neon's agenda didn't judge what came its way.

When he had seen Liv the next time with Linda in the club. It was the same willingness, but this time with a Soul Bug. She and the Bug staring at Linda with riveting hate. *Bitch!* The high pitched wail of the Soul Bug had screamed. A black wasp, *Sphex pensylvanicus*, ferocious. Victor took pride in the fear it exhibited when it saw him. Maybe it was because he didn't have the Kage with him. With no Bug box to repel them, it was gonna end in annihilation. The dance floor whipped into a frenzy. The Bug laying pheromones heavy on people and making it difficult for Linda to get over to him. He couldn't start shooting, well he could have. But that dude had appeared—Raucous, Linda had said his name was—and cracked the Soul Bug with a pool cue. Liv had melted away fast, but not before taking one deep look at Victor. The look had troubled him. It was a look that said, *game on.*

Looking around the Diner he saw some new heads—many from the gang that had given the Soul Bugs a pasting on Annapolis Street after Easter had gone down. After they'd done the Bugs, they'd raised their weapons, looking to Victor like he was some fucking leader or something. And, the dude, Raucous, at the night club, giving him the nod, as if to say, *I'm with you, man.* Really?

The Kage was one thing. He looked down the Diner to where they were sitting. Spodge had joined them so they were quieter. She was no angel, but she only seemed to cause trouble in the right places.

Victor swung off the stool and headed for the door.

'You take care out there, Victor,' said Tracy.

Her eyes reminded him of a comfort he no longer had in his life. 'Yeah, I got that covered. See you soon.'

Victor walked without looking at people. He concentrated on the buildings, the lights, the street signs. Each street had its swagger. Crow Street secretive, filled with shadows and dark eyes alert and watching. Mariner Street tough with worn buildings and bleached mind people.

The weave of city fabric helped him unload his head. He thought of his mother, Clarice, hadn't seen her in years. When his dad had left, something had gone out of her. Hadn't spoken to his sister, Lucile, for years. He stepped onto the sidewalk, looked at the dirt between the paving stones. He could smell it. Was he turning into an animal? He thought of Armadillo Tracy, out on the streets, sniffing and watching. He stopped and looked at himself in a shop front window. Jacket sitting square on his shoulders, high collar sticking up, framing his neck and face. Head tilting forward. *Here stands Victor Scram; one man.* Like the message was being relayed across the city. Come take your piece, he gives to all, just not himself.

There was another reflection beside him and no mistaking the stance. Liv. Hands on her waist, hips thrust forward like she had an aggressive cooch, right shoulder pulled back, head tilted to the left and mouth puckered and snarly. And fuck it, if there wasn't something so goddamned sexy about her. He didn't turn around, feeling a warmth on his back. Where was the sense in that? Liv hated life, befriended Soul Bugs, the creatures that killed the only woman he'd ever loved. He turned around and the warmth moved to his chest, his eyes, his face, over his flesh and inside his body.

'Liv.'

'Victor.' Her lips moved like two snakes sliding off in

different directions. She was dressed achingly similar to how Linda appeared to him.

'Surprised to see you,' he said.

'Are you?'

'How'd you find me?'

'You come up on my radar, you beep like a red light. I think I could find you anywhere.'

'Always had that ability?'

'For a man like you.'

'And what is a man like me?'

'Something real.' She moved closer.

Her mouth was open, teeth lined out like white gravestones next to the blood river of her lips. Her tongue was wicked, pointy and lashing. Long, prominent nose with a slight bump in the middle. She had a lot of makeup on. Hair short, black, bob-like but high on her forehead and off her neck. Her eyes tunnels to dark parts.

'Shall we go for a drink?' she said.

Victor couldn't place her accent. It was changeable, maybe English, perhaps Russian, probably fake—the villainess of the movie. Part of him said, this is mixing with the enemy, but there were no rules. *No rules.* He liked that. 'Sure.'

As they walked he had a nagging feeling some part of him got left behind in the window reflection.

They settled into a booth at Laceys, a bar on East Fifth. It wasn't a place Victor usually went, a bit up market for him. The seats were velvet and still had bounce in them. The tables were clean. Victor sat on one side of a booth, Liv on the other. Behind each of them was a wood frame and set into that was a navy, leather cushion, punctured with gold studs. The wooden backing went up about six feet and at the top of each was a dimpled piece of coloured glass. The table was dark, polished wood. Liv had a Daiquiri and Victor had tequila with ice; twenty five years old and as smooth as glass.

Liv toyed with her stirring stick.

Those hands, *the Cadillac's* as Neon called them. They moved slow and elegant and he could only imagine the touch of them, so sure and poised, long fingers pushing and retreating like dancers. How did *she* get blessed with such specimens?

'You keeping some bad company the other night, Liv?'

'Don't know what you mean.'

'No? Notice anything strange about your friend in the club the other night? You remember. The one who got pulverised with a pool cue?'

'Oh him, don't know him really.'

'Nice conversation?'

'Dunno, just a man.'

'I see, and you're just a girl.'

'I guess that's about right.' Liv looked at him, swizzle stick in her mouth, bottom jaw veering to the left. 'You wanna sleep with me?'

'That doesn't matter.'

'It does to me.'

'What matters is, *if* I sleep with you.' Victor watched cool brown eyes that had cried a thousand tears. He saw broken dolls, lip sticks slamming into counters, mirrors smashed—eyes that screamed, yet dazzled with jewels, eyes that lied, yet held so many promises.

'When I was a girl, behind our house was a forest. The Stolk Forest. There were stories about it, scary stories, stories of depraved horsemen, of crazed killers ripping people's heads off. Veterans hiding out and resorting to cannibalism.'

Victor saw trees in the lines shooting out of her pupils.

'As a child, I was never afraid of the woods. What happened in my house was far worse than ghost stories. I found it strange that people watched horror films. That they would search for things to be afraid of. I never had to look far. In fact, going into those woods seemed to set me free. I left *me* behind in the house, cowering in my room. I remember loving those trees with the soft flesh hidden under rough bark.'

What the fuck was it about trees, thought Victor. Twice today, people are telling me about trees.

'Are you listening?' asked Liv.

'Yeah, of course.'

'I'm telling you something personal here.'

'Nah, you're trying to seduce me.'

'Don't flatter yourself.' Eyes flashing, chairs being thrown around, glasses being smashed by the dozen.

Victor smiled, he toyed, but he wasn't joking. 'Liv, you're all woman, you're so much woman, I don't know where to put myself. But there is more than that, the past—yeah, I see it, I know what you're talking of. I know horror. I know it more than I can fathom, it is my every breathing moment. Did you know my girl was killed by your fucking friends?'

Liv's head pulled back a bit.

'Yeah, stomach that. But you know what, it didn't start

there. It wasn't then that I realised horror, how it cuts through the folds of the brain so deep that it seems to have sliced it in half. And it wasn't when jets I used to fly malfunctioned. When the ground is rushing up so fast it's like the universe is about to clap your head into oblivion. Nope, not getting beat up as a kid, taking the punches, taking the kicks. Not my dad leaving, no it's something else, it's the horror that makes all these things un-horrific. And that's you. You're the same. These things don't bother you, you couldn't give a fuck, cos something has always been worse.'

Her mouth didn't pout. She placed her arms on the table, folding them, hands on elbows.

He didn't know why he'd said it, why it'd bubbled out of him, apart from that she angered him. That her disregard for herself, was the same disregard that he had for himself.

Liv ran her finger over her bottom lip. She eyed Victor as she took a sip of her drink.

He could smell the thoughts in her head. She poured from deep. Above her in the frosted glass, images began forming. The navy leather cushion behind her seemed to be rippling. She was breathing life into the environment.

'Don't ya want to hear about my forest?' Her lips moved with her eyes and her body coiled beneath.

'I don't know. How far you gonna take me in?'

'Oh I think with you, there wouldn't be any limits.'

Victor pushed the key into his apartment lock, imagining Liv's legs. He'd gone and slept with the enemy. What the fuck had he been thinking?

He turned on the apartment lights, stepped over pizza boxes and discarded beer cans and ripped open the curtains. Dust choked him. How long had it been since he'd last opened them? The window sills were covered in a black grey fluff. His home was like a museum, there was no life here. There *had* been. The sofa where he used to lie with Emily, the kitchen, now stinking, unused, but once, the smells of hot chilli, conversation, tequila and Emily's hot body.

These things were always going to occur, it was inevitable. Emily was going to die. He was always going to sleep with Liv. His resistance was a tug on the inevitable. He never had a choice. But Neon—and this was the key, the god in the man—Neon was an interruption. It was in something that Liv had said. She'd gotten angry when he asked her about Neon, said she was annoyed about the fact that she succumbed, that it didn't feel like *her* destiny, that Neon had changed what was inevitable for her.

And now Victor had explored his inevitability, the *know thyself better* mantra. It was inevitable that he would sleep with Liv, but in letting the inevitable build to a scream, he had felt the tug, the connection from here to there —who he was to who he would become. Yes he had done it, but the reflection in the window when Liv had met him on East High Road, the other that didn't, had activated a beacon in his head—choice.

The Bee

11

'Do you think I should pose for *you*?' Neon said, adjusting one of his sculptures.

'Not tempting,' said Linda, 'You don't understand.' She was sitting on his sofa, stretching her leg out and exploring how the jeans disappeared into her boot. She enjoyed her legs, liked the shape of her calves, the curve slipping into her boots. But what really excited her was the leg formation; the accumulation of millions of years of running, jumping, thrusting, kicking, bending and exposing; the growth of the cellular implants, formed in caves and around protective fires.

Linda saw the forces of the past everywhere. In fact what she saw, and how she saw, was staggering. It had grown over the last three days. She'd ruled out everything—drugs, brain tumours, mental illness, none added up, nothing but the desire that engulfed her. It was an urge deeper than the base of her thoughts, bigger than the furthest reaches of her imagination, it was something that had travelled through time and space from the umpteenth galaxy before somersaulting through twenty five parallel universes. It was the fire to unravel and create, to enact change where there was none. Descriptions spilled around her head but none of them fitted. When she found a word, she immediately changed it, improved on it, added images, odours and tastes. She revelled in her mind and she

129

revelled in Neon's work. His creations crawled with synergy. It was staggering, and yet the secrets of how it was done were hidden inside this stubborn bastard.

'*You* are saying *I* don't understand?' Neon sneered.

'You don't understand that I only desire to paint myself.'

'It's self indulgent. Desire is futile, it will shred you to pieces and leave you looking for more.' Neon stood on the other side of the long dining table, head tilted, hands flat on the table.

When she'd arrived Neon was pensive. She saw information bristling all over him but didn't dare enter his head, figuring that would be suicidal. Yet he emitted information, everyone did. She had seen it on the street on the way here. People vibrated, each one leaking personal details without knowing it. Neon though, there was colour and in the colour was an odour, and in the odour taste, and in the taste, memories, and in each of those memories there was colour and it went on; a majesty of information.

'I see,' said Linda. 'I'm self-indulgent and you, some great dictator?'

'*I*, I don't do the *I*, there is no I for me. The work is all.'

'I could help you.'

'You couldn't. You don't know what I do.'

'I know what you tried to do to me.'

Neon pulled out a chair from the table and sat down. 'Why were you so elusive?'

'You can talk. You think you are the only one who is creative?'

'Creation is dullness following inevitable progression.'

'*Your* creations are extraordinary.'

'I know.'

'And that's arrogant.'

'It's not. I don't take credit for my creations. Just continuing where others left off.'

'Oh, so humble.'

Neon looked thoughtful, and then disinterested. Little clouds floated around his head like his brain chemicals were emitting moisture. The clouds were white and puffy, then turned dark grey and filled with mathematical equations. It was a tease, a display. Neon did this to her, made her angry with him, displayed arrogance, then humility, then did something interesting. It was playing hell with her self esteem. He was such a difficult man, but then looking around at his looming paintings, what could she expect? 'Whose work are you continuing?'

'You come here with your questions.'

'Yes, I'm here to torture you. But really, where else could I go?'

'I wouldn't want you to go anywhere else.' Neon walked over and sat on the sofa beside her. He lifted her leg and placed it on his lap. His hands were gentle, gliding over her jeans.

She felt vulnerable lying on her back. 'You know, you're very backwards coming forward.'

'I'm limited in the choices I can make, maybe your elusive patterns could help me.'

'You mean, I have something you want.'

'Oh, you have a lot of things I want.'

'I'm not going to sleep with you.'

'I don't want to sleep with you.'

'You don't want to sleep with me?'

'I'm not going to sleep with you.'

Linda floated in a white wonderland. Snow covered everything, no footprints, no landscape, just the infinite loss of all identity.

'You ready?' said Neon

Linda zoomed out of the canvas in front of her. She wriggled and pushed her boots against the floor, tilting forward onto her sitting bones. The canvas' emptiness seemed mocking. *Okay, listen up, Linda, you sold your soul to get here, so make it count.*

'Right then, Linda Kalom.' Neon stood behind her, smelling of sweat, damp clothes, saliva and coffee with hints of night-scented stock. 'You have to keep your eyes focused on the canvas, and drop down inside yourself.'

His voice was serious. He could be playful, definitely elusive, but never without intensity. Last night, before he had given her his bed to sleep in—such a gentleman—he had let slip some pieces of his puzzle. Something had happened in Mexico, before then he referred to himself as Karl Long. He was deathly sure of what he was doing and he definitely had a lot of voices in his head.

Linda thought of how different his studio seemed from everywhere, yet she felt at home. She was welcomed, not by Neon, but by the furniture. The tattered sofa seemed familiar, the Parisian lamp beside it shone a light that reminded her of herself. The books, the pine table, the paint splattered floor. It was like she was always going to end up here, no matter *what* choices she made. But the best of it was that Neon's art was welcoming. When she looked at his paintings, all thought of self

132

disappeared.

In Saks, where she was from, the artist was the freak, the Satan of the town. There had been a man, Jean Le Martin, a little French painter. As a child, she used to sneak and watch him paint by the river at the north of the town. It fascinated her, how he would wave his brush around, getting angles and dimension right. He would mutter to himself in French. His hair neat, and moustache precisely shaped and moulded. She had always been a little afraid of him.

Neon handed her a paintbrush like it was a baton. 'Hold the brush light, close your eyes and drop back into your head, like you're diving.'

Linda closed her eyes and relaxed her shoulders. The studio was quiet, temperature cold enough to make her skin prickle. She sensed Neon behind her; not imposing, but very close. In her mind she saw laces being tied, luminous green strings zipping around and around. Ahead was a black tunnel with faint lines on its walls. The lines fluffed out like spikes, at first black and then yellow and black, like the fur of a bee. There was a burning coil like the one inside a light bulb and the piercing buzz of a bee. Blue and purple flowers spun before her, fine petals beckoning like a kaleidoscope of jewelled fingers. A bee came into view and began moving around the flowers. The droning buzz lulled her softly inward; so quick and seductive. The bee landed on a flower and she felt invaded. She was being pulled out of her head, tugged forward while her body remained behind. The tug was strong, but there was a link restricting her, holding her back. *Something has to die.* She fell forward, her breath cut off and voice strangled. The vision exploded, eyes ripped a million miles wide—ripped apart by the sting of buzzing drone and the feverish pitch of freedom. Death.

'FUCK!' She couldn't breathe. Opening her eyes, she swung around on the stool and struck out. But there was nothing there. It was inside.

'It's okay, it's all right,' said Neon, taking her blows and placing his hands on her shoulders. 'Easy.'

'What the fuck?' Linda's eyes stung. Her image of Neon jarred into a spasm of luminous lines and then back to a person. She heard his life like a bang. *Malfunction,* her brain screamed. Giant wings flapped above her. The bee. The air pricked her skin with the sensation of a million needles. Her eyes became laser beams and her heart ached. She wasn't coming back from this one.

'I didn't know it would be the same for you. You're one wild flower, Linda Kalom.'

'The bee...'

'Yes, the bee.'

'It...'

'It's your death.'

'What? No! I can't believe... no, it's hallucination. It's fabrication. You're just playing, you're fucking around. You—' but Linda saw Neon as fractured shards, entrails and brain waves, sounds and smells dripping on luminous lines. It was overwhelming but it wasn't frightening. The frightening bit was the trembling that surrounded it, the knowledge of how this was done. The pin point accuracy of the one thing that gave her

134

definition more than anything in existence. Her death.

'You see,' said Neon, 'you give a lot, you get a lot.'

'Say it. Just say it fucking clearly. And don't miss a fucking word.'

For a moment anger flashed across Neon's face, but then he became calm. 'If you want to see clearly, well then die, die a little. Come.'

He took Linda's arm and brought her into the other dark studio room and over to the window. The city was laid out before them. 'You see all this?'

Linda looked at the lights, at the buildings, the images were sharp and stage-like; shiny glass, coloured lights, cars highlighting the roads, pinks, reds, blues, set against a rusty, torn and jagged skyline. A cloak.

'This, this is illusion, the representation of function and force. You're coming home Linda, no longer crawling obediently into the jaws of death.'

'I don't understand.'

'Understanding will come from doing not from words. You get to create with open eyes. Eyes opened by befriending death. They—' he waved his hand at the window, '—they all have it hidden inside them.'

Linda looked out. She heard the drone of the bee, imagined a bomber moving over the city, bombs dropping, exploding structures and extinguishing life. The skyscrapers as massive tombstones.

'It passes in importance, eventually. But your death will take you, one piece at a time.'

'So if mine is a bee... what is—'

'You wanna know mine?' Neon raised his eyebrows and smiled, 'Praying Mantis. One badass. You see, I think you got something beautiful there. You got a bee, one sting. Only one chance for that. But the pollen taking, that's nice. You get the exchange, the spectrum that the bee lives in. You die a little, you live a lot. Praying Mantis, well, it's not so gentle.' Neon acted out something getting its head bitten off.

'But, if I don't create, then nothing happens.'

'Can you not create? You think that's possible? You got the riches, girl. You got the world lying down before thee. Would you not want to dance?' Neon was animated, moving his arms erratically. 'Now I may be obsessional.' He grinned at her, raising his eyebrows. 'It has been said, and it is true, but only sometimes. Sometimes I'm quiet. Not often, because it takes some getting used to, this knowing, this depth.'

Linda felt anger like a giant match moving along the strip, sparking, then igniting. 'You did this to me.'

'Did I? Were you planning to be immortal?'

'No! But I wasn't planning on being at my own funeral, every fucking day for the rest of my life.'

Neon snorted. Took Linda by the arm again and brought her into the main studio and placed her in front of his paintings.

Flowers, trees, pillars, dancers, lavish colours, dirty city nights and ecstatic nature. And underneath; people, places, thoughts, feelings, and underneath them; the challenge of force, the parasite of manifestation and the enthralling shakes of the carnival of life. The pictures were vast movements, lives strung on implication.

In a flash Linda felt cheap, and then in a flash she fell in love. She fell in love deeper than she ever imagined possible, into her heart and beyond. She travelled through Neon's paintings, walked in exotic gardens, smelt wisteria, drank rich wine, laughed, felt thoughts lifting her into landscapes, journeying over the mind, over thought patterns, the reason why anything was, or had been. A sunset arrived and as quickly it was dawn again. Everything changed—*that* was the key to these pictures. And she was about to turn to Neon, to smile at him, to let him know that she knew. But then it wasn't that everything changed. It was that nothing changed, that everything was, and it could not be anything else. It was a flux of change and a flux of being. How everything outside her would change and everything inside her would change, which made everything outside her change, and everything inside her would change and...

So now she was mad too. But she got it. With riches like these, could she ever be a poor girl again?

Three days. Three days she stayed in the studio and painted endless parts of her life. She gave to the bee and the bee gave to her. She explored how to make colour and how to destroy it— how to see with eyes and ears and touch, how to touch taste and taste hearing. She learnt that the stars were not as far away as she thought and that she didn't mind getting her fingers burnt, nor wet. Light exploded into vibrations, visible and not, she cruised over the gamma rays, x-rays, burnt high on the ultraviolet, scored deep with the infrareds and screamed out into micro and radio waves. She learnt that Neon liked to paint her, but that she only wanted to do self portraits. She learnt that

137

everything had life. That the studio was a magic box, a conjuror's bag of tricks. She learnt that coffee was a god, the bang in the firework. She learnt that madness was an ocean, that within that ocean were islands, lands occupied with people, and each little person had a pearl of wisdom to tell. Each little person could change everything. She liked these people, she liked all the people inside her. As the sun set, she would find an island, and there would be great parties, carnivals, where her body organs slid happily against each other.

Neon was the can that held the worms, the factory that made thought, the devil that designed devils, multiply that by a thousand, paint it, sculpt it, sand it, weld it, burn that further and you would be at the starting point. Neon had little Neons and those Neons had Neons, and they all talked, and they all worked together passing parcels to each other like some galactic game of pass the black hole.

At the end of the third day she decided she couldn't stay in the studio forever and set off back to the diner. At the junction of Shelley and West Lafayette, there was two, three hundred people; street gangs, call girls, regular folk, ghetto boys and swivel sisters, all jostling and cheering. In the centre was a mass brawl, people being laid out left, right and centre. The police were there, walking in the crowd, their black and white bug-like cars lined up, but they weren't doing anything. It was like they were there to ensure that the event happened.

Linda moved on quickly, weaving through the twisted shop shutters and broken glass of West Lafayette. Strewn amongst the debris she saw vests, sweat shirts, pants, trainers, hairbrushes, makeup, photographs and phones. It was like people were throwing their lives away.

When leaving Neon's studio, Linda always came off Mariner, down Bleeker, into West Fale, down Shelley, across to West Lafayette. In each street there was the right place to cross, the right number of steps. As she reached her crossing point on West Lafayette, a shop, or ex-shop, caught her eye. At first glance, the building was a standard city merchant's shop and house. There were three storeys above the shop, brick work cream-grime, with a reddish mortar. Each floor had two sash windows with distorted glass. The overhang above the windows gave them the appearance of sad eyes. The top of the building ended in a cross gable with a large spike on top, like a wizard's hat. There was a hint of magic, but the creepy shades, tones and the gaping shop entrance implied the magic had long gone bad.

Inside, the glow of the streetlights revealed a floor covered with broken cameras; hundreds of them smashed into pieces, their lens covers looking up like distorted eyes. It was frenzy, even the plastic that had held the cameras had been broken, the shelves had been broken, counter splintered into dust. Misshapen pieces of metal showed the brute force of the violence.

Why didn't people just steal stuff?

Linda knelt down and picked up splinters in her hand, moving them over her fingers with her thumb. Odours of bromide and iodide kick-started a merry-go-round of photos in her head—gormless baby pictures, stiff faces in starched

139

dresses, her dog Adam, garden days with her wild brother, pointless portraits with her critical mother, goofing in photo booths with friends, party drunks, old friends and boyfriends. She shook her head clear and moved deeper inside the shop, her nose building a model of the layout.

Something moved in the back corner of the shop.

'Who's there?'

The words sunk into the darkness. Nothing moved but the smell of stale, woody breath and sweat. Her sense of smell told her there was a person: male, afraid and excited but with anticipation not aggression. The intricate knowledge made her feel powerful, she had nothing to fear, not yet anyway, and the smell, bergamot and tobacco was so, so familiar. 'Lucian?'

And there he was, standing in the corner. It was hard to see but there was no doubt about the outline. 'I found a way, Linda.'

'Found a way to what?'

'I tapped, Linda. I tapped right in.'

'I don't think you should have done that.'

'But it makes so much sense.'

Linda smelt a real stink; a feral nightmare. 'Lucian, what are you doing hiding in here?'

'Don't come any closer.'

In that instant Linda hated him, she hated everything he stood for. She smelt right into his veins, into his poisonous brain, she smelt over the carcasses that lay inside him. His smell crawled all over her, it invaded her being and threatened it with destruction. This was wrong, a mutated helix of disastrous decision making.

A passing car light illuminated Lucian's face, but Linda already knew. She had smelt right into his Bug shell before she saw the bug plates of his face.

'It's the right order, Linda. The progression.'

'What have you done, Lucian?'

'Absolution of self and integration with the creator. Isn't that the way?'

'No. Why would you want that?' A coldness passed through Linda's chest, a chill of error.

'What else is there?'

Ghoulish faces swarmed her head. She saw herself afraid and small, threatened by the immense city, her mother, lovers and haters. It was a kaleidoscope of fear and failing, the spike in her heart—thirty years worth of the internal doubt.

'Fuck off, Lucian.'

She ran, afraid of what was in the shop and inside her. She sprinted down West Lafayette, cut across to Hamfell and down Tamworth.

Soul Bugs were one thing, but this was worse, it was personal. As she ran, her straining body eased the pressure in her mind. She had to work out what she wanted. What had seemed clear an hour ago—the sharing of Neon's world—was now clouded. *Sharing*? Was she letting herself down?

Up ahead, some kids were systematically kicking a bus stop to pieces.

She ran past.

'Hey, girl.'

'Whoa, slow down.'

'Hey sister, wan' a little fuckie?'

141

Shit. She ran on, hearing them pounding behind and encouraging each other. Faster. Down Roundhill, cut across to Tattle Street. She didn't need to look behind as the excited yelps let her know they were gaining. The fucking Diner was the opposite direction. Her body only had so much fuel. It was laid out like a video game; nitric acid levels, lung capacity, fear triggering adrenals converting dead waste into energy. She rounded the corner into Sidfield Plaza. In the centre was a dry fountain; big, stone fish mouths gasping for air. On top of these, a statue of some dead God with a trident in his hand—no saviour there.

A chainsaw buzz sounded to her right. Jesus, not in person, but Jesus on a motorcycle: Spodge. There was no mistaking her as she sped past Linda's pursuers, weaving expertly between them and skidded up beside Linda.

'Get fook on!'

The Diner was empty and after glaring at a moon-eyed Listern, Linda slumped down on a table with Spodge.

'What the fook you doing, Linda? Streets aren't safe anymore.'

'I was okay. I usually am. Just got thrown off my concentration.'

Spodge stared. 'You different, Linda.'

'Yeah, I different. I just don't know if it's all good.'

'Oh, you good, you got stars in your eyes.'

'Thanks, Spodge.'

Spodge's eyes shone like polished metal, perfectly formed, the pure flow of will. 'I seen Neon's picture of you.'

'Huh?'

'I try and take him some fooking food. He never fooking eat. And he painting this picture. It big, yellow and fooking crazy, and I see you and a Bug man. But there was red and black-pink, demons and little devils eating away at you, all spite and hesitation. And this, black congeal, drippy fooking inner swarm of thought. Like you troubled, eating yourself? So I went looking, cause it seem happening, you know, true.'

'I didn't see it.'

'Crazy fooking picture.'

'Crazy alright.'

'You pokey with him.'

'No. Somehow, just not at all.'

'That good, you strong Linda, more than any people. '

A sense of relief washed over Linda. She didn't know whether she wanted to laugh or cry. This was the beginning of her life, she knew it. What she did now was going to matter. She felt Neon stalking, or perhaps manipulating her. She wasn't going to let him have it so easily.

'You like Neon, Spodge?'

'Yeah, he crazy, but, he true. He paint the colours of my heart.'

'They must be beautiful colours.'

'Yeah, you nice, but we wanna see what you do.'

Linda wasn't sure if she wanted anyone to see what she did. And even *if* she could do anything, did she really want to?

'Linda.' Victor arrived at the table. 'How's things? Looking a little sweaty there?'

Victor seemed looser than before.

143

'She got chased by some crazy fooks on the street. I save her ass.'

'Good work, Spodge.' Victor sat opposite Linda, his face lined with stains and secrets.

'Neon's creating entities on the street,' said Linda.

Victor smiled. 'Hey, boys?' he shouted down to the Kage kids, 'Neon's creating entities on the street.'

'Get the fuck outta here,' said Tommy Bones. He came over, clicking his fingers; all bends and zeal. 'You mean *again*.'

The bunch at the counter laughed.

'Sorry,' said Linda. 'Am I fucking missing something?'

'Linda, you been away a few days, things are moving fast. This isn't the city that it used to be. Now, we knew the Soul Bugs were something to do with Neon. But fuck, now the place is in uproar. Whatever you and Neon have been rubbing,' Victor winked at Tommy, 'must be some hot shit, cause the city is burning hot.'

'Fuck you, Victor.'

Look at the Eyes

12

Neon stared at the studio door, eyes wandering over the white painted wood and into the dirt. The door opened out to the right, so people always placed their hands on the left as they exited and there was a large concentration of grime there. He walked over to it and sniffed it; onions and chocolate.

He walked back to his sofa. Looked at the bookcase. Back to the centre of the room. Looked up at the light. There was dust inside the glass which covered the bottom of the metal shade. How did that get there? He walked over to Linda's easel and her self portrait. Pah! He turned away, three steps forward, one to the left, and then he turned around, walked back to Linda's easel. His hands scratched each other, back muscles starting to cramp.

'Nothing!' He threw his head up. The light was so fucking bright, a downward thuggery in its gravitational push, and it was so willing, so interested in *her* painting.

Ochre mixed with mauve, interesting to some. He extended and smelt into the contours she'd painted of her cheek, up a little bit, the eyelash, beige tinged black, but more, the sweep of her brush, it took him to the beach, to the curve of the water on the shore, not bad, like her pelvis, the shape, a tugging down, and rising up. The white of the eye, not purely white, nothing ever was, except desire at its hottest. The eyes, saucers, badly drawn. Neon walked away, he tried to walk away. He came back.

'Neon 23?'

'Yes, sir.'

'What is happening here?'

'It's exquisite?

'What?'

'The painting, it's exquisite.'

'No.'

'Yes. You have to go into it.'

Neon looked again. He moved back. A face. Just a face, what was that going to achieve? The cheeks were like dancers' bodies, impressive, the tilt of the mouth, almost crude, suggestive, perhaps a smile, maybe a sneer. The chin, like a boulder, so unladylike. Neon smelt the burnt grass of the skin, he smelt the flavour of hormonal releases in his body. He lay on the floor.

Dropping into the vacuum of his head, he saw another Neon sitting on a black floor, naked.

'Another fucking Neon.'

The other Neon looked at him. 'Just the one, the one she sees in you.'

'I don't need to see another fucking Neon. Why are you naked? Can't you see I have enough to be getting on with?'

Neon opened his eyes, shook his head clear and got off the floor. Did he need to be bothered with this? But he couldn't stop looking at the painting of Linda's face. The contours of the brush strokes. He had seen that face in real life, but not this face, not the inner face. There, her mother, nestling beside her ambition; colouring and crushing it. Over there, her youth; bruised knees, tears, public and private. Curves swept through his head and over his shoulder, like a train journey; tracks laid down, plans for the future. All this with the brush stroke. He envied the self knowledge, he couldn't deny that. But with self came baggage, it was everywhere. Like that Arthur in the Ambulance, those scars on his face, wearing the emotional disturbance of what he saw.

Neon lit a match under the eyes and dropped inside them. Who was this girl, where did she come from?

He found himself standing in the Diner, but it was not the Diner, because there was only a number of props. It was a Diner for dramatic purposes, and there was Linda in her uniform with her back to him. So what? He cared not.

Linda turned around, coffee pot in hand, and walked past him as if he wasn't there.

He smelt her rustling, how every crease had purpose. Nice body. Nice body movement. He followed her. The coffee pot did not have coffee in it—interesting. There was a swirling liquid, like oil paints that didn't run into each other. Linda took it to a table. There was a man sitting there, with his back to them. Fuck sake, it was him.

Linda poured liquid into a tall, sundae-type glass.

'*Another Neon?*' he said to the man at the table.

'*Oh yeah, she's good.*'

'*Well, what the fuck are you doing?*'

'*This.*' The Neon at the table held up the glass of swirling colours.

'*Well, what the fuck is that?*'

147

'Emotion.'

'Emotion? We don't do fucking emotions!'

'You gotta taste this stuff.'

'I don't fucking have to taste stuff.' Shit. Neon walked over to the Linda who was completely oblivious to his existence. That face, that goddamned face. The way the mouth pouted forward a little, like she was thinking, yet arrogant, and the nose, what gave it the right to take the air in like that, take it and analyse it, separating single smells, like some artisan.

He avoided the eyes.

Neon went back over to the table, where the seated Neon was wiping his mouth after taking a gulp of liquid. 'Listen, Neon, I'm not so fucking sure that I like what you're doing.'

'What's your problem?'

'Time. Fucking time. We have work to do, we don't have time.' Neon walked back over to Linda. She had hair, hair like fibre optic cables, like a coconut. No, she had hair that swept, that lifted him like wind racing over tumbling valleys, like a train easing around a bend, clowns juggling, dogs leaping through hoops, flames in a fire, and why? Why? Because it all swept down to her eyes. NO.

He stormed over to the table. 'Neon, put that fucking glass down.'

'Okay.' The Neon placed an empty glass on the table.

And the table dissolved, dissolved like the colours in the glass, and Neon fell into it.

He smelt his studio and found himself in front of Linda's painting. *Just look at the eyes*, the mouth said, but it did not move. *Just look at the eyes*, the cheeks said but they did not move. *Just look at the eyes*, the sofa chanted, and the light chanted and his own paintings chanted, and the floor chanted and the walls and the world chanted.

Silence passed under Neon's heart like a knife. The last threads of his resistance became one note in the trembling heart string of a one string choir.

He walked through the desert to his sculpture valley and took some metal plates off a sculpture. Sitting down on the cracked, red earth he began to bend the soft metal. He created a small Linda and placed it on the ground. She began to dance and when the dance was fast enough he fell into the spin that she created.

Emerging from a mental whirlwind, he walked in a courtyard under a large leafed tree. He looked at the great vine roots of the tree, smelt vanilla, rose and geranium oils, and saw a goddess, a shimmering green and golden goddess, every inch of her like polished tear drops. The eyes rose up, curled around his face and held his body in the dark. The back of his head was stroked, his arms were ripped off, his legs thrown overboard — naughty girl — simple was the pleasure and long was the leisure, of happiness.

'Shit. Shit, shit, shit!'

'Right, Neon 23, get that Mantis cranked up.'

'Is that wise? We're all a bit thrown in here.'

'Bit thrown out here too, but that woman, jeez, that woman, what on earth is she creating?'

'It's self, Sir, a mastery of self, there is a beautiful place there.'

'That be as it be, 23, but there ain't much fucking beauty out here.'

'But she is something, I mean, can't we —'

'No we can't, we don't, so just leave it.'

There was a knock at the door

'Who?' Neon spun around.

'Spodge.'

Neon ripped the door open. 'Spodge, my angel, your beauty swings from the heavens and lands in my heart.'

'You crazy.' Spodge said, smiling. 'I bring Linda back.'

'The Linda, the Linda...'

Linda scowled.

Neon stepped around Linda. 'Anything new, Spodge?'

Spodge bowled off into the night after giving Neon the low down. Neon turned to Linda who was scowling at him.

'You fucking sonofabitch!' she said.

'I see. Any particular reason?'

'That fucking painting you did of me?'

'A tricky one, *The Manifestation of Fear*. You're one moveable feast.'

'Do you fucking know what is out there? Do you realise what you are creating?'

'Realise what *I'm* creating? Go closer to home.'

'What do you mean?' Linda paced around, pulling out paintings.

'Do you think I am playing a game?' Neon asked. He felt his blood warming, and rather than sidestep it, he let himself go.

'I don't care if you play games. What I want to know, is do you know what is out there? Do you know there is a man out there, being turned into a fucking Bug?'

'Interesting.'

'It's interesting? It's *interesting* to have someone mutilated?'

'What did you see, and what did you believe you saw?'

'Don't start playing with my fucking head.'

'Do you think I fucking play?'

Linda stood in front of him, her face twisted. 'No. But what are you doing, why are you doing this?' She raised her hand as if to hit him.

Explosions of blue light shot out of darkness, the lights were a web, a tangling mesh that spread over every part of Neon. And in this, Linda moved. That was the beauty of her. Even though she was angry, she was still busy renewing and reforming.

'Go to your easel,' Neon said. 'Here.' He took her self portrait off it. 'This, by the way, is amazing. An incredible majesty of self-creation.'

'Is it?'

Neon placed a new canvas on her easel. Then he went and got one for himself, put it on his easel. He sat down by his easel and Linda sat by hers. Then he got up, went over to some paintings that were behind her under the pine table. He pulled out one from behind a cloth. 'This, by the way, is *'Manifestation of Fear, and Other Oedipal Thoughts.'*

Linda stared at it for a moment, shaking her head, smiling and grimacing. *'Oedipal Thoughts?* Lucian? That's almost funny. You should take some fucking responsibility for what you put out there.'

'You should pay more attention to what *you* put out there.'

'What? Why do you never say what you mean?'

'You're so pragmatic. Bloody humans.'

'So you're not human?'

'Not like you'd think. If you want to know the present, why bother having one?'

'What bloody world do you live in?'

'What world do you live in?'

'I just asked you that question.'

'And I just answered you.'

'I'm not surprised Victor wants to shoot you.'

'Victor wants to shoot me?'

'Well, I don't know, I can only presume he does. So, wanting to understand is wrong?'

'Oh, you go to the top of the science class, now we shall discuss the Narrative of the Obscene.'

'The *Narrative of the Obscene* doesn't get taught in science class.'

'But it should. Before people act, they assess other choices—I might do *this*, I might do *that*, I want to do *this* or *that*, quick run past convention, expectation, laziness, doubt... whatever. Eventually action takes place, but the narrative leaves a backwash of indecision and wasted neural mass. Most definitely obscene.'

'*Obscene*?'

'Of course, it is an imposition?'

'But you said it was assessing choices?'

'Choice, of course, choice, yes. We believe action to be a consequence of internal narrative. Nonsense. Narrative has a hive agenda, *way* more insidious.'

'Hive agenda?'

Neon leapt up, pointing at Linda. 'Ah ha, questions again!

The hive is not a home, but a control mechanism. The control mechanism that controls what isn't controlling. Simple, wouldn't you think? But stay with me. We start by exploring choices, but the Epi, around and within, makes us take the same pathways through possible choices. Right there, forms calcification, intricate hives of ponderisation, and down these little sinkholes, future considerations rat-shoot away. No input, no choice.'

'We're creatures of habit, so what?'

'That's what *they* would like you to think. The capture of enrapture, the seal on the inner genie. Think of it, Linda. *Here I am in this beautiful vista, but what is that line around the edges, that hexagonal vice?* It pervades Linda, the hives are built from the well of materials, from the materials of the materialiser, the input facilitator.'

'You're insane.'

'I am, yes, of course I am insane, but *I* am not.'

'You speak in riddles.'

'You lie, I see all over you and you lie, you hide and you manipulate. You ain't got no hives, bee girl. So pull off the fucking covers and let me know why.'

'I'm no girl, and expose myself to you, really?'

'Yeah, go on, transfer the swarm over here and I shall dissect, then perfect, your wings.'

'You don't get me.'

'Get you? I get them all, that's what I do.'

'So you get Victor?'

'No one gets Victor. You can't contemplate the man, he's an illness, a pervasive dichotomy of independence and repulsiveness.'

'A good friend of yours?'

'He is the very best man. The key to them all.'

'And me?'

'You are uniquely the most infuriating and beautiful woman I have ever met.'

'Well, aren't you the charming one.'

'Neon 23?'

'That's a bit of a spill you had there, Sir. It isn't going to go unnoticed. The assessment of Linda is off the scale.'

'I can't get a grip on her.'

'Nor can we, every time we get in her head, she moves. She constantly changes, it's unreal, but we all like it. We're ready to give it to her, you know, if you just wanna fuck her, we'd be delighted.'

'Neon 23, that is crude and rude.'

'Look at her, sir.'

'I have eyes.'

'Then look at her eyes, sir. There lives the goddess, the ticking clock of humanity, the smile, the charm, the snake, the lover's alarm that wakes you in the middle of the night, the insurrection of the soul, hands that know not what they do, that leap over bodies like wild goats, finding pleasure in touch, connections that sensulate the fevers of the soul, human and gods entwining.'

'Ah, 23, you're good. All of you in there are good, but I trust you the most. You have been spokesman for the insiders for a long time now. But I have a job to do, like Albert before me, think of what Albert gave up for chrissake! Now, I like your sentiment, but if you get after that again, you're next for the Mantis, understood?'

'Of course.'

Linda jutted out her chin, eyes trained on distant nothings.

That troubled him, he went out, she went in.

Her head was infectious, it tilted and he was pulled towards her, the sail on his imagination filled with her features. The way her spine shot down, like a horse in mid air leap. With her there was no city, no songs to be sung except hers and that was dangerous. Yet the way her lip curved up at the top like a drying leaf... *blow those leaves away!* He should put her easel out. This Linda with her shoulder, how the bone dropped down, and the muscle rose like an arched cat.

Out there somewhere—Neon looked through into the darkness of the other room—Mr Black Hole, Victor, was hooking up with Mrs Black Hole, Liv. Spodge was annoyed and Neon understood that, he was a bit fucking annoyed himself, but Victor was transforming and Liv was everything Emily wasn't.

'23?'

'Yes, sir.'

'*Because Albert opened up the spectrum, the Bugs got through and killed Emily, ripping Victor in half. Do you think that was what put Albert on the railway?*'

'*Would it put you there?*'

'*Let's skip that one.*'

Neon painted the first stroke of Linda. She looked over, eyes sharp. Brush in hand like a sword as she slashed a stroke on her canvas. Across the floor of the studio, a line shot up, as if bullets were raking up the ground. They stung right into his body like nails, through his legs, up his spine, throat and brain. It tightened his resolve. One more stroke. Linda smiled, her lips pulling back like a theatre curtain, lush velvet fabric, her eye lids were perfectly level, nice shaped teeth, front bottom left slightly turned in. She smiled, left side bias, three C's forming on her cheek, and her nostrils played tunes with the air. The studio was quiet, an occasional passing car. To Neon's right was the coffee pot, he wanted to reach it but his stomach felt tight and he thought his bowels might explode. It was like being in the jungle again, right at the beginning when it had all happened for the first time.

He couldn't actually believe Linda was challenging him. Reaching back for the coffee pot, his fingers closed on the scorching glass. Shivers shot through his body, but he kept his eyes on Linda, slowly bringing the pot around and delightfully ignoring the neurotic screams of a body wanting to move away from pain.

Strung between them was the specta-rope, the wavelength he would travel across into her body. A little figure of hers began walking on it like a movie star sashaying down the red carpet.

His eyes began to water, sweat dripping into them.

'Neons to the Mantis.'

He edged back into his seat, spilling coffee carelessly into a cup, hand tightly gripping his paintbrush. One slash, paint oozing across the divide between man and mind—Linda's figure stopped walking across the rope—but something sharp was behind his neck, claw-like, cold and wet. Closer, closer, Linda's eyes were bloodshot, the red on the left sclera more pronounced. Neon slipped under the veil of his consciousness into the spectrum. Linda was a fairground; creativity like he'd never seen. It seemed her thoughts had thoughts, everything helixed out into a voracity of forms. But it was all personal—the claw on his neck was from a lobster. When she was eight years old, she'd stolen it from the local restaurant to save it and then kept it as a pet. Everything affected her.

Rounded vowels gathered in his mouth. How vile, it was his caring. The caring of a person. A person he was not.

'Neon.'

Linda's hand was on his arm.

'What?'

'I don't want to do this. I don't want to challenge you, to fight against you, seeing who can go further.'

'That is slightly disappointing.' But her hand and her arm, and her breasts, and teeth, hair. It took him back, way back, to when he cared. Shit. Next he'd be wondering where mommy dearest had ended up. 'You're right. The city weeps and we must help it. I need you to do something, something very important.' In her eyes, he could see the both of them curled into infinity like a fractal, so tempting. 'I need you to paint Victor.'

'Victor? No. Victor has turned into a shit. I can't believe it. I like Victor. I mean, you can rely on Victor. But at the Diner, Victor, the steady and strong, is arrogant and full of shit, like he knows it all.'

'Yeah... we all have our moments, growth can make assholes out of any of us, but that's not the point. Victor is a lynch pin, these little details are of no importance. I need you to do it, your style, your way. I don't know if it's because you're a woman, or because of who you are as an individual, you're too changeable.

But we need Victor, not the Victor you know—the other Victor. I can't say any more, you need to do these things yourself. But you can learn, you can grow through this, feel free to be an asshole even.'

'Well, I've got a good teacher.'

'Indeed.' Her face was intravenous coffee. It woke him up and he was already more awake than any man. It was time to hit the streets. 'I will get Victor to come here, once he gets me a model.'

'A model?' Linda raised her eyebrows.

She was so tight in the genetic bloom of her life, it staggered Neon. If he was to judge, he would have to say this very second was her peak; peak concern, confidence, playfulness and strength.

'Are you a model?'

'The use of the word is derogatory.'

'I don't use words.'

'You do.'

'I, don't *use* words.'

'Keep talking.'

'I don't have time.'

'You're such a shit.'

'Neon 23?'

'Yes, sir, feeling a bit left out in here, sir.'

'Shut the fuck up.'

'Yes, sir.'

'What's the Little Neon situation?'

'It's a bit serious sir. Your interaction with Linda seems to take

158

place on so many levels. We're down to 170 Little Neons.'
  'That'll do it. I don't care what it takes. We're hitting the streets.'
  'Isn't that gonna bring the Overlords down on us?'
  'Yes. It's the endgame.'

Neon held tight onto Spodge as she bumped her bike onto Levern Bridge. She weaved expertly around abandoned cars, some overturned, some burning and others just emptily idling. On the walkways, under the suspension cables, people cowered. Many of them looked shell shocked, others looked angry. Neon and Spodge sped past towards the mighty central bridge towers with their gothic arches. Rain stung Neon's face and he tasted smoky particles of grime as it trickled into his mouth. Spodge skidded to a halt before the towers as if she knew he wanted to marvel at the solidness and power of those great granite slabs. Did they manhandle the steel to hold up the bridge, or were they impaled in the mesh, forced to be useful, to go nowhere but here, stoically watching the city with eyes of torrent grey. He could identify with that.

Neon nodded at the large gang in the Diner. Victor was doing well. At some things anyway.
  'Neon, monument to the aeon,' said Tommy Bones standing at the counter.
  Neon eyed him. The kid was frazzled, a new breed, with him there was hope. But he was all short fused, drug addled and scarred by ridiculous emotional upheavals.
  'I was,' Tommy started, 'wanting to juice with you, man.'
  'You was.'

'You see, we been crystallising you on the massive, man, urging the curly rays.'

'If you don't speak in a language I understand, I won't fucking listen.'

'Eh... Johnny?'

The dark eyed one shuffled over. 'Hi, so, I been making boxes.'

'I don't like those boxes.'

'No, and that is something. But you work somewhere and we work somewhere else. And you work with tools and we work with different tools. But when we see what you do, we see the instant persuasion of all form, and we roll your work down the curling wave of electronic transfer, we pull it under, transforming the intention into presentation. Leaving the essential pieces in the black, the unknown. We, *not know*.'

'Nice, like the asshole is feeding rather than expelling?'

'Yeah, you could say that, although we regard you guys as the asshole.'

'And well you should, I like that.'

'So within this spectral visual. Being nothing, we become.'

'You guys are crookeder than a cross-dressing cockerel.'

'Well, thanks,' said Johnny.

'You have the luxury of knowing nothing about yourself through your drugs and the derangement of your—no past, present *or* future.'

'Knowing everything by knowing nothing, studiously,' said Johnny.

'You're serious people, I see that.'

'You see, we got you as God.'

'Don't do that.'

'There is God in what you do.'

'For better use of the word, yes. But that would never be the answer.'

'Well yeah... we're a bit fucking lost.'

The heads of Johnny Ease and Tommy Bones hung in unison.

'Well you should be, kids. That is essential, be lost, get fucking lost, the bitter taste of the pill should be a timely reminder. *Revolution*, it's in the word. Revolve, take the spiral staircase into the velvet interior. You guys are the spatial architects, you got Victor Scram, the man with the plan, the lay low, the ground work, but the particles, that is you guys, your thoughts are spatial, no consequence, as it should be, you have to grow with no roots, be instable, learn nothing, terrorise all climates, this is the dream, the correlated essence of reason.'

Johnny Ease stood stark. From his hand dropped a cup, which spun on the floor. Tommy Bones stood beside him, for once still; the maniacal mannequins.

Neon was impressed and moved down the counter. 'Raucous, you okay?'

The flowing, hairy man turned around. 'Neon, peace.'

'You guys know each other?' Victor came over.

'Sure,' said Raucous. 'The dude painted the mural in the back of my club. Been cooking the headlong for some time now. Yet we chill while the heat turns up.'

'That makes sense.'

'Victor, a word,' said Neon.

'Sure, come into my office.'

They sat on a table down the back left of the Diner. Neon liked the layout, always left of the door.

'How's things, Victor?'

'Can't complain. The city is falling to shit. I mean it really is falling apart.'

'You got a plan to fix that?'

'Me? No.'

'Listen, I need you to do me a favour. I need you to let Linda paint you.'

'I don't need a portrait.'

'And you won't get one, but I will.'

Black Holes

13

Victor sat alone in the four booth. He picked up the ketchup bottle. The thin red plastic left a spiky, clock-like mark on the table. He rubbed at it with his finger, *she paints me, she paints me not.*

The Diner was relatively peaceful after the evening rush. All over the tables were plates, cups, crumbs, brown, and bizarrely, blue food pieces. Listern hung at the end of the counter like a drop of grease. He was too cheap to hire anyone else with Linda gone, so it was fair enough Tracy was letting her standards slip. Tracy's information was proving useful. The Soul Bugs hadn't been around lately and that seemed wrong. Tracy told him what was happening in city tree and the nesting caught his attention. He figured it would be the next step of Bug evolution. He had started looking at the naturalism of it all, infestation, nesting and finally—reproduction. Not rocket science, but big shit was definitely heading from the fan.

'Victor, check it!' shouted Tommy.

Shit.

Liv had just walked in the door.

She was looking hot. But beside her, two Bugs, smart dressed Bugs. They filed over to the right.

Victor moved up to a cherry drop stool beside Tommy at the counter.

Liv wore a spray on, short black dress, shoulders exposed, skin powder-like and hair shiny. The Bugs wore tight black trousers, combat boots, green, short, army style jackets, with large pull over belts, turning them into a double breast. Behind the Bugs, came another, and another. Victor put his hand in his pocket, wrapping his fingers around the comfortable grip of his gun.

'You got the box, Tommy?'

'Yep, loading up.'

Victor felt a hand on his shoulder. 'No,' said Neon.

'What?'

'No. Tommy, put the box down.'

The Bugs were filling up the tables on the right. Liv standing before them like a wicked Queen. She stared at Victor and Neon, a smile on her face, teeth glistening, red lips, and a body like boiling treacle.

Tommy looked to Victor.

'Neon, seriously?' Victor said. 'What the fuck? This is not what should be.'

Neon's face was impassive, but studied. Victor felt if he put his hand in front of his eyes, it would get burnt.

'Victor. Just hold steady. You're not seeing what this is. You're not listening. Start listening.'

The Diner became a swirling cauldron of noise. It was so vast, Victor felt he could drown. There were voices, thousands of voices. And there was the fat frying in the kitchen, the hissing coffee machine, sweat crackling down Tommy Bone's face. Neon's breath, so fucking calm. Victor heard his own heart beating, blood pulsing around his body. He heard the sea of feelings, he heard taste, he heard Liv talking to Listern, not what she said, but the *ooh* and *ahh* of her words, the intention. He heard her hearing him, heard the crease of the skin on her neck, and he heard the Soul Bugs clattering in their uncomfortable skins like drawers of utensils. 'Neon, what the fuck?'

'It's the impasse, like clasped talons. It's beautiful, don't you think.'

'I think we should set upon them, sort this out.'

'No. That wouldn't sort it out, it would only prolong it. Relax. See.'

Pots of coffee were being shipped over to the Bugs who were sitting at tables now. A waitress Victor had never seen her before was serving them. 'Where's Tracy?'

'Don't worry about Tracy, she's doing her thing,' said Neon

'So that one?'

'Bug friendly, there's a few out there. Take Liv for example. Oh, I forgot, you already have.'

'Don't look so pleased with yourself, Neon.'

Neon was rubbing his hands together and walking towards the Bugs. He stopped halfway across the Diner.

Victor figured there was a line not to be crossed.

'Neon,' said Liv, approaching but not crossing the line either.

'Liv, my darling.'

'Fuck you.'

'Nice. You're looking well. How's the darkness working out for you? Filled any gaps in yet?'

'You stole from me, Neon.'

'Ha! Your life is theft, I took nothing, well... maybe a little. But you're raising the stakes there yourself.'

'Believe it, Neon. Only one place you're going. They know all about you.'

'Yes they do, and I know all about them. See you out there.' Neon nodded out at the street. 'When you're ready of course. I guess your guys got a bit of growing to do yet.'

Victor, the Kage, and Raucous all stood watching. It was like a veil had been torn down. No more hiding. No more waiting.

'Victor,' Neon called over, 'I need a model.' And he walked outside.

'A model, where the fuck?'

'Hey, man,' said Tommy. 'I know a girl.'

'That's good, but is she what we need?'

'Man, she the Lady Fox. She's Easter's sister, man. The best dynamite sneeze.'

'Dynamite sneeze?'

'Like that old shit, you know, cocaine, but black powder, way more infinite.'

'Where is she?'

'Spodge's, be here in minutes.'

'Okay, do it.' Victor started heading outside and Liv walked beside him. 'Liv.'

'Victor.'

'Seems like our sides are well and truly chosen now.'

'Yeah, I guess that's just the way. Always a piece for you though, Victor.'

'A piece of that?'

'Fuck off,' she snapped.

Victor smelt rotten flesh. He smiled, the Bugs around her were hissing, not too loud, but they were getting a sneer working.

Neon leaned back against the Diner window, staring at the building opposite. It was a chunky, six storey office block made of giant, pebbledash cubes. The cubes were placed in a haphazard fashion and the windows, with security wire glass, were set into concrete tunnels. The entrance was squat, sunken and unwelcoming.

'Now. What is that?' Neon asked, waving a hand at it.

'A building?'

'Something more dangerous.'

'One of your paintings.'

'Exactly.'

A big boom made Victor instinctively bend down. It was what they had heard on the Street last week, but sounded closer. 'Shit, hadn't you better get going?'

'No more going, Victor. I'm on the outside now, part of what turns. Linda is on the in. Go see her.'

'I don't know if that's a good idea.'

'It's the only idea.'

'I'm needed here.'

'We got people here. Raucous is good for the job.'

'Yeah, but—'

'Ah Victor, you'll always be my number one.'

'Don't give me that shit.'

'Nah, you are, you're special. Way back, Victor, way, way back. You have to go to your role. You take your place. I have

167

my place, even they,' he jutted his thumb at the Soul Bugs, 'they have their place. We all fit nicely together.'

The buzz of Spodge's bike sounded as she rounded the top of the street. There was a tall girl on the back. Spodge skidded up, and the girl dismounted.

Tommy hadn't been telling any lies. The girl was blooming all over the place. She looked like she had been plucked out of a nightclub, scrazzy hair, wild on the curls, compelling in its suggestion, attitude spewing eyes, bright and murderous, luxurious lips folded over glistening teeth, neck tight, shoulders angular, chest perfect, loose silver top draped like a casual glance. Gold mini skirt, long shiny legs, dazzling and muscular—a pop up character from sexual fantasy class.

'You Neon?'

'Seem to be.'

'I'm the Lady Fox.'

'Ain't no mistaking that.'

'Is this gonna help get the muthafuckers that took out my brother?'

'More than you could imagine.'

'Take the best shot with your cannon then, doctor.'

Neon smiled, bit down on his lip and spun a spray paint in his hand. Tommy, Johnny and the others piled out of the Diner and they all started moving across the street.

'Come on, Victor, if you can drag your eyes away,' said Spodge, kicking up the stand of her bike.

Neon stopped and turned back. 'Victor, you watch out for that Linda one.'

'Why's that?'

168

'Well I tell ya, if I'm the doctor, she's the fucking neurosurgeon.'

'Escorting me to the door, Spodge?' Victor said as they arrived at Neon's studio.

'Who know what could happen. I say bye now. Good luck, Mr Scram.'

'It's nothing to do with luck.' But Victor felt nervous and wondered what Neon wanted.

He knocked.

'Victor.' Linda was dressed in an old shirt and jeans with a large belt. She looked like a pirate.

'Linda.'

'Come in.'

Victor looked around the studio. There were a lot of canvases strewn around. The air smelt of burnt coffee. 'How's things been going?'

'Not bad,' said Linda.

'Sorry about the other night. I was tired. Didn't mean to be off. A lot of stuff has happened, is happening.'

'It's okay, we all have expectations of other people, maybe unrealistic ones.'

Victor noticed a strain on Linda's face. It couldn't be easy being Neon's concubine, but that wasn't fair. Who was he to judge?

The big Neon paintings still lurked along the inner wall, but a painting on the easel in front of him didn't look like a Neon. 'Is this yours?'

'Oh, yeah. It's not a Neon, we work in different ways.'

The painting was Neon-esque in the instability of the image. It was Linda's face, kinda brutal, done in rough brush strokes. But that was just the beginning. The image seemed to slip over his eyeballs and back into his head. There was a sudden jarring. The painting was a television screen and there was Linda, or a Linda type person, but as Victor looked around he found himself in a Diner of sorts; a few props in a black room. Seated at a table was himself.

'*What the fuck?*'

The Victor sitting there, turned and looked up at him. '*Just the very person I was looking for, Victor Scram.*'

'*I could say the same. You know me?*'

'*Oh, I don't know you yet. We're about to be introduced.*'

Linda approached, she ignored him, smiled at the seated Victor and poured colourful liquid from a coffee pot. She was wearing her waitress outfit, her tied up hair exposing the soft skin at the back of her neck. Victor inhaled the lemon-rose of her skin and felt lifted. Her uniform transformed into a feather dress and push up basque. She looked down at herself, laughed loudly and shook her head. '*Expectations of others*'.

Victor's head felt like a balloon.

Linda turned and looked him straight in the eye. '*Don't worry. I'm not Neon. Neon takes. He manipulates, delves and twists. But that is not what I do. I am the knowing. I am the doorway to who we are, a little touch of me, and a whole lot of you.*'

'*I know who I am. I am Victor Scram.*'

'*Of that there is no doubt. And there you are, projected along your memories like a movie.*'

Victor saw snapshots of his life—joys, pains and the in-betweens. He saw things he remembered and things he did not. His father, his mother, his sister, a small red car he had as a child, where his knees always hit on the metal when he tried to pedal. His friend Brett, down at the swim hole chatting up girls.

This was not hard. He could do this. In a blink he was back in the studio sitting on a red and white striped chair, opposite Linda. She was still wearing the loose shirt.

'I remember when I sat there. Seems such a long time ago,' she said.

'Do you regret being brought here? It's often crossed my mind.'

'No, I don't. As you said, there is no point in being a spectator.' She put her brush down and crossed her arms. 'I was cross with you.'

'I said sorry.'

'No, it's not that. I was cross that you slept with Liv.'

'But you're with Neon.'

'Not like you think. We're working together, higher up not lower down. But you've thought about me, and I've thought about you, and those are strong things, things that bind people. I knew in a way, when I met Liv, that you would. But I didn't want that to be true. A hangover from fairy tales. I guess I just wanted you to stay my big bear protector and not get distracted.'

'Well don't worry about that, that is one thing I *can* do well.'

Linda smiled.

It reminded Victor of when he had first met her. So, what do we do now?'

'Now we go in.'

'But we already went in.'

'No, that was *you* looking in. Now I'm going to see what you're not seeing. Because there is some part of the puzzle that hangs around you like a ghost.'

'If it's to do with Neon, there is probably a lot of the puzzle I'm not seeing.'

'No, this is personal, something in the hardwire of who you are.'

From blackness came the drone of a bee. The vibration caused Victor to shift sharply through emotions, like someone was pushing on his eyes, ears and throat. He moved away from the pressure and the blackness lifted. The sun was shining and he was sitting on the ground in a country garden. There was a long strip of lawn between flower beds with dark evergreen trees at the ends. He got up, wandered around for a moment, looked at flowers, looked at the sun. The air was clean, distilled, the stink of the city far away. It would be nice to just sit, relax and shut his eyes, but the landscape seemed unstable and he felt if he closed his eyes, he would sink through the ground into oblivion.

He started walking. The garden pathways led into others, like a maze. Leaves rustled, water and children's voices slipping in-between, but they were ancient voices, ghostlike gatherings of memories.

In the blink of an eye the landscape changed. Gardens were replaced by streets—cobbled roads, lined with tightly packed, rounded stone houses. There was the smell of freshly cut herbs. And then he was walking next to an immense wall, sand stone arching up into the clouds, like a Spanish castle. This transformed into a suburban house. Shit. *His childhood house.* In the background the familiar trundle of the overnight goods train.

'Victor?'

Linda's voice came from the house. Victor walked past the shabby picket fence, over the cracked mosaic porch, past cobwebs and rotting logs. There was no need to open doors, he just appeared in the entrance hall. The floorboards creaked. They were laid across the hall rather than up it. A large staircase led away to his right and the green tulip lightshade above cast dreary shadows as it swayed in the draughts.

'Victor.'

It was his father's tense, emotion-filled voice.

Moving down the hall. He saw Linda standing outside his father's study.

'Do you remember?' Linda asked, as she looked into the room.

Victor took a deep breath. It was as if he was breathing twice. Once now and once in the past. He looked in. 'That's me as a kid and that's Albert, my father.'

'What's he doing?'

Victor saw his father gesturing to something on a cluttered table.

'I don't know. I think he's showing me one of his little art pieces he used to make. He was obsessed with them. They were just dots, pretty much, but why here, what's the point?'

An acrid burning smell stung Victor's nostrils, tearing through the images of the polished streets he had walked on,

173

past the garden where he started, under the ground, under layers and emotions and body organs until it reached the middle of his head. He felt something nuzzle against his mind drawers, something comforting, like the folds of his brain were being warmed up.

'Go in,' said Linda.

'They know we're here?'

'This is memory, we're not here.'

He took a deep breath and entered. All around were small art pieces on scraps of paper. They moved and jerked like distorted television channels. The one in his father's trembling hand seemed different.

'It's all worked out,' his father insisted, showing the child Victor a piece of fabric.

'I don't get it. Why here, who cares? The guy's a nut.'

'Come here.' Linda brought Victor behind his father.

Young Victor's face was screwed up in frustration and fear.

'What the fuck do I want to see this for?'

'Go.'

Out of darkness came a shabby old theatre. All the seats curled around the stage were occupied by him as a child. Him pulling faces; grotesque, funny, angry, sad and scared. Each one reminded him of how he felt when he was a kid.

The auditorium squeezed in on him, chairs and kids pressing into his head.

He stared up at his father's mad, burning eyes. He felt what he must have felt as a kid— needing a wee, wanting to please his father, not knowing what to do, smelling the acrid burning again. The smell made sense to him now, the Golden Silk Orbweaver spider, *genus Nephila*. It was coming from his father.

A spider perched on a web between their eyes. Cold black eyes stared down at him. It was enormous and it started to crawl towards him, he felt warm piss streaming down his leg and he screamed, but he did not shut his eyes, he opened them wider. The spider reached him, those cold black eyes, and his head started to fill with inky liquid, those cold black eyes.

'No.'

He saw his father sitting in the Diner fastidiously folding a coat. Face tight and intense; folding, refolding, folding, refolding, getting upset and doing it again. It wasn't the coat that was important, he was mapping the layers of Victor's brain. He was stalking, seeking and stealing the thoughts that Victor would have when Emily died. Mimicking the action and reactions. Fold: *I can't live without Emily.* Fold: *I'll throw myself under the D train.*

What the fuck? Stolen his thoughts, stolen his future... last fold of the coat, scrawling on a piece of paper and then setting it on fire, confusion, money thrown on the table and out into the cold city streets. It was *his* path line he was taking, walking where *he* should have walked, all the way to the train station. Fuck, what was wrong with the man? This was a horror film. Pixelated information display announcing impending train arrival. The smell of tar and electrical burning. Dad lying on the oily stones of the tracks, jacket placed so his head was angled towards where the train would come. A cushion to watch the stolen death.

'My fucking death!'

Victor steeled himself, neck muscles tight and fists clenched.

175

'MOVE. MOVE!'

But his father did not move. He didn't move until the train wheel reached his face. Until the blood and bone and brain and neck were smashed. Muscles, sinews, childhood innocence slaughtered again and again as the wheel went around and around.

Linda caught him, lifted him with strong arms, pulled and shoved him out of the room, his childhood scream curled towards him with black tendrils, the mind trying once again to shut the images out.

Victor smelt paint, turps, coffee and stale clothes. He heart the hum of the fridge, could feel sensations in his head but not in his body. He did not care. In fact, the only thing he cared about was that he wanted to die. That he *deserved to die*. He would wait till Linda was gone and then he would shoot himself. No one would care and no one would feel anything, least of all him.

'Victor?'

If only Linda would go away.

'Victor. Drink this.'

Fresh coffee. The odour slithered up his nose, down his spinal cord and out into his extremities like a caress. There was a cushion under his head and the rest of his body. He must be on the sofa. It felt like someone had punctured a hole in his head and broken into a secret room. His legs were useless. He was scared of opening his eyes, of being shamed. Shamed to be so childlike and in need of care. Failure was the overriding feeling. Why had his father done it? What was he thinking, trying to show a child something like that? For fuck sake, what type of man was he?

'Victor, come on.'

'No.'

'Open your eyes.'

Victor could see one pinprick of light through his eyelid, and that was enough. Because one more and his brain would shatter.

'Victor?'

'Why are you here?'

'I met your father in the Diner.'

'I know.' Victor sat up. The light was frightful, like someone was pouring a pot of white acid in his eyes. He rubbed at them, pushing at them until he couldn't bear it and then he looked at Linda.

'Remember. I told you the story, the first day you came in,' she said.

'I know. It should have been me.'

'You asked me if he was drunk?'

'Listen, I fucking know, okay. This is a fucking horror show. I mean, why would a father do that to a child?'

'I think he must have had a reason...'

'A reason? Yeah, *hey, I'll commit my son's suicide,* but let's not stop there, let's fucking show him a preview when he's seven. One smooth fucking operator there. You know what, I don't even fucking care.' Victor thought of his father's face. His hands reaching out, as the spider crawled forward. 'And another thing, a fucking Bug in him?'

'Well...'

Linda described what went on inside her, Neon, and presumably in his father.

'What's the difference between you and a Soul Bug?'

'Different direction, we're going, they're returning.'

'Returning, why? And don't give me the Neon line, the fucking Negative Karmic Backbites.'

'Why? If that's what they are, then—'

'But why, Linda? You know?' Victor looked around. He saw Neon's paintings hanging like curses on the wall. The air was peppery, stinging his nose and eyes.

Linda looked pale, slightly sweaty and seemed concerned. God, he wanted to sleep with her.

'You don't. You're trying to avoid thinking.'

Victor clenched his teeth, his jaw muscles, his temples. 'Why is everyone taking fucking licence with my head?'

Linda laughed.

'Is any of this fucking funny?'

'Nothing, everything. There's just no way back. No way for me, no way for you. You started me on this journey. You're tough enough to take this and a hell of a lot more. There is one thing...'

'Just the one?'

'I think when you saw your father's death, you were obviously distracted. But his whole life, up to his death, was played out.'

'Yeah?'

'Well.' Linda frowned, looking down for a moment. 'He worked with Neon before he died.'

First Love

14

Victor stormed down Crow Street towards the Diner.

Linda had wanted him to rest up for a while, but he was adamant about going straight to Neon. She wished she hadn't told him about his father working with Neon. It had just popped out, mainly because she'd been shocked too. She didn't know how Neon would react. It felt like her loyalties were being torn in two different directions.

Around them, buildings were smouldering and charred, cars too. Gangs were roaming everywhere, but no one crossed Victor, especially as his face was so deeply ingrained with anger. He saw Neon's silence as a betrayal. Linda wasn't sure. Neon left stuff out all the time. But it wasn't usually personal, there must be another reason.

She hardly recognised Crow Street—smashed windows and sidewalks strewn with tables, phones, broken guitars, ironing boards, car seats, baseball bats and then there was the graffiti. It was Neon to the extreme, twisted mutations of bodies crawled over the buildings. He had spray painted everything—walls, windows, doors, cars, trees, streetlamps, the sidewalk and the road. Linda trailed her finger on a distorted face on a car, marveling at the colour blasted mangle of person and automobile. The picture's radiation tripped a thousand pistons in her optical chemistry. She drove across a thought line, out across a hydraulic system of compulsion and down the automorphic mesh of person and motor city frenzy.

She guessed Neon was around, waiting and watching the watcher, calculating distance and hormonic outlay.

She dropped and flipped, finding herself in a desert, hills speckled with tufts of hard grass and irregular cacti. The air smelt of frankincense and sandalwood mingled with sweat and scorched metal. Odours moved and danced around her like inquisitive creatures, leading her up to a mound overlooking a crater.

Below, in a basin of scorched earth, strange limbed sculptures were stumbling around like bizarre robots. Metal limbs, fabric, cow skulls, long bones, and twisted wood pieces were strung together by rope, wire and a very profane influence. Tilted cow skulls gaped up at her with bleached death masks. She moved down the hill, pulled closer by the bigger fear of not being able to see them. The closer she got, the more she felt them push inside her head. They surged like a visual inhalation, swarming every part of her head. She took a breath, the air hot, warming her lungs. Lungs deep inside, the deep inside of her, deep inside the deep inside... it was infinite. Up the other side of the crater stood Neon. He waved in the air, talking to himself, and then ran down, changing something on a creature and running back. Was he some evil Bug lord? Was it all a con and Neon was destroying humanity?

He saw her and smiled manically.

'Welcome to the factory,' he shouted.

'What on earth are you doing, Neon?'

'Not on earth. This is the workshop.'

'For?'

'One moment.' He ran down the hill, bent a piece of metal, pulled a cord tighter, and a creature did not lumber so crudely. In the air there was a large thwack like the thump of a helicopter gunship. Neon ran up towards her. 'Time is short.'

'For what?' Linda saw a look of fear pass over his face, very briefly.

'Well, these little darlings have no creative permission.'

'What is the whacking sound?'

'That... that is the very threat to the city, the people, but especially to us. There is a great tendency towards conformity. Material conformity is especially embedded within us. It is of us, you see. The mask we wear and who makes the mask, the fear, the tear, the angles of your face, how your hair is formed, dropping down millimetre by millimetre. Well, never mind that, but we will be annihilated. Most definitely, one, possibly both of us...'

'So stop.'

'No. This is the great work, this is what we do. We carry on the legacy.'

'Yeah, the legacy... I painted Victor.'

'And something was missing. What was it?'

Linda ran through the details with Neon.

'Damn, tough breaks.'

'I also told him that you had worked with his father.'

Neon smiled. 'My Linda, how did I ever stay alive without you? Never mind. All pieces need to be fitted anyway.'

'Which pieces?'

'Return to the street and see.'

Like coming up out of water, Linda re-emerged on the street. She walked into the Diner, shocked to see what was sitting on the right hand side.

'Well if it isn't the nightclub bitch,' Liv said, walking up to the divide.

'And you would be Liv, or should I say, species traitor.'

'Aww, you're kinda sweet, little girl.'

Linda watched Liv's mouth twist when she spoke. She remembered exploring her in the nightclub, her first fumbling in the spectrum. There was something cleaner about her now. All her features were outlined sharply, around the eyes, the nose holes, the shape of the mouth, her tight bob haircut on her neck, and her cleavage; all sharp, teasing and dangerous.

'Like what you see?'

'More interested in what I don't see. Troubled childhood, Liv?'

'Fuck you.'

Linda turned away and saw Neon down at an end table. He waved. She nodded and acknowledged Raucous and the Kage at the counter. Then headed down past the busy tables.

'Where's Victor?' she asked.

'NEON!'

'That's the one.'

Linda stepped out and let Victor sit opposite Neon. Victor sat, elbows leaning hard on the table, fists clenched.

Listern looked over, his little piggy face looking concerned for his precious Diner. Linda wasn't too surprised to see him ensconced on the Bug side.

'Neon,' said Victor. 'Why shouldn't I just grab your neck and squeeze all life outta it. One fucking reason?'

'Albert made his own decisions.'

'Did you know me when you knew my father?'

'Yes.'

'Did you know he was my father?'

'Yes.'

'Didn't you think you should fucking tell me?'

'If I thought I should have, I would have.'

'Fuck you. Did you know he was going to kill himself?'

'That's difficult. He was a complicated man.'

'He was complicated? Why the fuck did you pick me, why would you involve me in this shit, don't you think I had enough on my plate?'

Linda could see Neon wanted to smile, that he wanted to reach out to Victor, but couldn't. There was a real possibility that Victor would kill him.

'I didn't pick you Victor, you were the only one capable. *You* were the only one who could see.'

'No. Fuck capable, Neon. What are you capable of? Where is it going to stop?'

'Some things I don't have the answer for.'

'Doesn't stop you, does it.'

'Didn't stop Albert, either.'

Victor slammed his fist down on the table. 'Don't mention his name. Why did he work with you?'

'Cause he knew I could do it, I would finish what he started. Maybe he couldn't face that you were part of it.'

'Well I'm fucking not.' Victor pushed up from the table,

rocking the bench back. 'That's it. Finished. This is complete shit!' Victor shook his head at Linda as he passed.

'Hey,' Tommy started, 'Scram, man?'

'Forget it, Tommy, it's finished. Go plug your fucking heads back in. This show is over.'

Victor ripped the door open and walked out.

Linda started moving after him.

'Leave him, Linda, leave him,' said Neon. 'He's gotta go on his own.'

Linda's heart sank. This was her fault. She went to the window and watched Victor stumble down the street kicking debris. 'Shit.'

'It'll be alright,' said Neon.

'Really, you think so?'

Neon looked away, staring out the window for a while, before picking up a couple of spray cans. 'Better be.' And he walked out of the diner.

The door of the Diner burst open. Everyone turned around to see a large frame block out the street.

'Tony!' Linda ran over to the door.

'Lil' sis.' Smiled a beaming face.

'Fucking hell, how on earth?'

'Well I knew you had worked here. I sent messages?'

'Yeah, sorry, been working.'

'Nice. Strange clientele.' Tony looked around, taking in the Bug side, the Kage, Raucous and friends. 'I hope you're not responsible for this.' He jutted his thumb out at the street.

'Well, there are a few things I might need to fill you in on.'

They found a free table and Tony listened to Linda's story.

Linda talked—using generalisations and avoiding Bugs—but Tony's face didn't look too convinced.

'I've come to take you home, sis.'

'I am home.'

'This?' Tony looked around. 'You call this home?'

'Yeah, I do. These are my friends.'

'Linda, come on, you've had your fun and now it's time to go.' Tony put his hand on her arm.

'I ain't your little sis any more, Tony. You left long ago, and sorry, but I grew up.'

'Look at the fucking streets, Linda. The city is going into meltdown.'

'As I said, we're working on it.'

'What, you're working on it, with who? You and this fucking guy?' Tony jutted his thumb at Tommy Bones.

'Welcome to Planet Hex, dude,' Tommy said.

'Shut the fuck up.'

The Diner door clanged open and Neon wandered over. 'How you doing? I'm Neon.' He extended his hand.

'*Neon*? What is this, a fucking joke?'

'A joke, a joke? What are you, a fucking caveman?'

'Don't fuck with me, man.' Tony said rising up. He towered over Neon.

'Fuck with you? You're fucked, man, real fucked. Take a look out there.' Neon flung his arm towards the street. 'Anything out there you recognise? Anything you can see on that fucking street that bears any fucking resemblance to anything you have known before?'

'Neon, this is my brother. I don't know if—'

'No,' said Neon. 'You do know, Linda. You know. You know it all, we... knew it all. This is the end. The end of yesterday and the end of all the tomorrows you ever imagined.'

'What? Who is this fucking guy?'

'This fucking guy?' Neon slammed his fist on the table. 'I'm the fucking guy who is gonna tear the soul out of this fucking city, and when I stuff it back in, not one muthafucker is gonna recognise it.'

'That's the words, Neon,' said Tommy Bones. 'Pipe his fucking brain in.'

Liv arrived at the divide. 'Hey, big boy.' She wrinkled up her nose, and winked at Tony. 'Wanna come over to my side?'

'Yeah,' said Tommy Bones, 'that where you gonna be, man.'

'I told you to shut the fuck up.'

'SHUT UP!' screamed Linda.

Everyone stopped.

'Now, this is my brother, okay. And these are my friends. Well, not her.'

'Bitch.'

'Don't call my sister a bitch.'

Linda smiled. 'Sit down Tony.'

The others moved off to the counter

'This is my world. This is where I fit.'

'But what about Mom? She's worried.'

'Really? Worried about what? When has she ever worried about anything except herself?'

'That's not fair.'

'Is it not? What did she ever put into our lives? Eh? No, I'll take that back, remember her boyfriend, Dean?'

'Dean?'

'Cowboy Dean?'

'Oh yeah, Cowboy Dean, he weren't no cowboy.'

'No he was a string of piss, but that didn't stop him coming into my room one night, drunk, looking for a good time.'

'Ah shit.'

'It's alright, I hit him with that bat you left me.'

'Good girl.'

'But Mom didn't believe me, said I was making it up to cause trouble for her, that I was jealous. Jealous of Cowboy fuckin' Dean.'

'I wasn't there.'

'You weren't, that's okay. But no more, I'm never going back. Never.'

'And these guys, you trust these guys?'

'These are my people. We're all part of this. Life isn't as it used to be.'

'Look, come outside?' Tony took Linda's arm.

For a moment Linda saw her big brother, the strong arm, the concern. But his eyes were wrinkled and hard, an inanimate brown, and his jaw jutted forward like an aged salmon.

They stepped outside. Tony looking up and down the street.

'Look, Linda, I know certain things. You know I'm working for Aswi now.'

'Really? Jeez, Tony, why would you do that? Corporate pharmaceuticals... didn't they pollute the Flam and kill all the trees?'

'Nah, that was that artist freak.'

187

'Jean Le Martin? Oh come on, for fuck sake.'

'No, this is serious shit, Linda. Things are going down, you don't even fucking know. And the city is getting hot. You gotta get out of here. I shouldn't even fucking tell you.'

'You don't know what is going down.'

'I fucking know, I know freaks, like the little French freak, and other freaks are fucking with things. Science belongs in the laboratory. And this shit ain't gonna be allowed. The city is being shut down.'

'Who's shutting the city? Which freaks?'

Tony's eyes darted around, drops of sweat rolling down the side of his face. Linda could see Neon through the Diner window, watching. Calm, but with eyes of malice trained on Tony.

'I don't know this shit. I heard the big fucking heads at Aswi saying something big is coming. I ain't there for the talking, you know, I just do what I'm good at. So, just come now and don't fucking say anything.'

Linda saw Tony as something she had never seen him as before: a thug, a big man who was small in terms of making his own decisions.

'Tony, there are people here. Lots of people, people I care about.'

'They won't be fucking here for long, sis. I gotta get going, and if you have sense...'

Linda, with Neon by her side, watched Tony weaving off down the street.

'There goes the last exit,' said Neon. 'No one else leaves.'

'What do you know about him?'

'Nothing.'

'What about Aswi? And the city being shut down.'

'Nothing. Everybody wants to be important, feel like they are playing a part. We're all nothing.'

'You believe that?'

'It doesn't matter what I believe.'

Neon's graffiti was so layered up that it gave the illusion of movement. But there was more—there always was. The repeated application, the mimicry, the placing of lines on lines; removing those lines, placing them in-between, teasing out the magic, placing it elsewhere, causing an effect and effecting cause.

'How many little Neons have you got left?'

'A number.'

'What number?' Linda watched a pulse beating on his temple. Temple seemed the right word.

Neon turned around, his eyes glowing, perhaps a tone more than before. 'Forty two. And you?'

'I'm not a maniac. I haven't classified my brain and split it off into numbered people. And when you get to the last one?'

'Full tilt.'

'And then you die.'

'Creations take a lot of effort, you know. What do you want?'

'I want you not to die.'

Neon smiled. 'You're a dangerous woman, Linda Kalom. But the work demands it.'

'Who demands it?'

'This.' Neon gestured to the street. 'The edge of life, the lines that define. The whip, the cat, the scorpion tail, the ooze, Linda, the incredible and the desperate. Yes, baby. This is the time.'

'And me?'

'You? You gotta take care of your boyfriend.'

'Boyfriend?'

'You got a Bug Boy out there, ain't ya?'

The buildings on West Lafayette seemed to have lost their desire for cohesion. In front of each were piles of brick and plaster that had fallen from their facades. In their peeling state the buildings' personalities were exposed. To the left was a sulky, brown office building, twenty, thirty storeys high. It wanted to impose itself, to lay down *its* law, but it was too squat and lazy. Squeezed beside was a tall art deco type, a one emotion screamer, unsure of its function but propelled by architectural zeal. Over the street was an ultramodern, glass skyscraper, there was little decay there, more dismay, it was the one that would give loyalty to the highest bidder. To its left was the onion, a stumpy twelve storey, corroded and built in the wrong place—a corrupter of residents.

The Camera Shop where Lucian was, appeared more anonymous than before. Everything else vibrated and emitted electromagnetics, but the Camera Shop had no emission. Linda switched to sound waves, hearing a dull thumping compression. She turned away and walked to the glass skyscraper. It emitted a friendly, confident whistle—a lie.

Spodge had given her a set of spray cans, but she wasn't

Neon, didn't have the urge to be so... rude, confident, so... casual and graceful, so... loose and cheap. He flogged his images on people—did they really want to see them? Well, they did. People couldn't resist them and that challenged her. Weakened her somehow.

The rattle of her spray can seemed deafening amongst the empty buildings.

Behind her came a grunt and an almost unrecognisable face peered from the Camera Shop doorway. She turned away, her fingers tapping the spray can nozzle lightly. She dropped, savouring the drone of the bee on its ticklish journey inward. The wings tilted as it began its descent to the garden of her precious flowers. Her hand swung in the same curving arc and paint leapt and wobbled towards its destination.

The thought of Neon and the ease which he created pushed her further, made her vision tighter to the mirror glass of the office building and its impenetrable ice rink surface. She stepped out of herself, moving across to her reflection and staring back, face to face. The mirror was perfect, painting from within and without. Her arms moved, chasing the spray can in her hand. All her senses merged; images emitting smells, body movements having flavour. She flung arm over arm, swimming into an ocean of multi-macular awareness.

Lucian whimpered and Linda turned. His face was horrific, the skin swollen, hardened and calcified. Rectangular blocks had formed across his forehead and down the sides of his face. The nose, mouth and eyes had dropped back, and his hair was swollen out in clumps. It was clumsy though, as if the process was being rushed. He reached a claw-like hand towards her and she smelt Scale Bug, the parasite. Was that Lucian? Had he lived off her all those years ago? He'd always seemed at ease and knowledgeable when she'd met him, but maybe she'd been too immature to see a hidden agenda.

Before her, on the glass, was a picture of herself, just that, nothing else, but each time she painted she saw someone more familiar.

Grunt. Lucian shuffled like a nervous dog, making an effort to speak but his jaw was restricted and his tongue just flicked out. Linda walked over to him

'Naaaiiiiiiight, thay coooooome.'

'Who comes?'

Lucian struggled. It was as if his mouth was being sealed as they stood there. He raised a claw to her. Linda recoiled. But he shook his head and tapped his claws together. Linda smiled at the memory, felt a bit repulsed and held her arm out. He tapped Morse on her wrist.

'The Bug people come and make these patterns?'

Lucian nodded.

'Why?'

Lucian beckoned with his claw, towards his lair.

The blackness in the shop was ten times that of the dusk outside and the damp earthy odour smelt terminal, but Lucian's eyes were still bright and had a soft innocence.

His little Bug face wobbled as she stepped forward.

Linda gestured him to go in front and followed him in. The mess crunched under her feet.

Lucian gestured at the staircase, waving his claws up and down and rubbing his knees together.

'Don't you fucking touch me.' And she meant it, she hadn't come this far to end up with a Bug boy.

Lucian shook his head again. He was excited, eager to please, maybe that was his problem.

Linda creaked up after him. The stairs were greasy, as if something had slithered over them. On the first floor was more carnage. There were three rooms to the front and a toilet at the back. Everything was smashed to small pieces.

'Why is everything destroyed?'

Lucian turned to her.

Linda tried to avoid looking revolted. She slipped into the spectrum, the valley of black ignited by luminous lines. It was easier as there was very little of Lucian. Most humans would have a full representation but Lucian was only a small dot. It wasn't just that he was forming into Bug, he was relinquishing having ever existed.

Lucian tapped on her arm. *The city will conform to instruction.*

Linda figured it was the wrong time to argue.

Lucian went up the next flight of stairs. The third floor was not as destroyed as the others but the furniture was broken and ripped like a cat with steel claws had set about it. In the front left corner of the large room, there was just a mass of book fragments. The walls around them were battered as if the books had been set on with furious violence.

Lucian and his books. He had worshipped them. Looking at his Bug face, she felt sad and responsible. She had never thought that it might be masking a deadly inadequacy.

They went up a small back stairs and climbed out the landing window onto a flat roof. Leaning over a parapet they could see the street below. Rubble was strewn everywhere, but there were cleared paths moving out from the centre like a candelabra.

Linda knew the pattern. It was the pattern that the Bark Beetle left when it bored it into trees and created Dutch Elm disease. She remembered how Dutch Elm disease had killed the trees in her hometown square. Most blamed the artist Jean Le Martin, because he'd been painting the trees before they started dying. Others said it was the Aswi Corp, not many though. Aswi had so much control in the town. Now after Tony scarpered, the city was being infected. As trees attempted to clear the infection they effectively strangled themselves. The debris in the streets was having the same effect on the city. Victor needed to know this.

Linda felt a tapping at her arm.

'Fuck off, Lucian.'

Lucian bowed his head.

'Sorry, just...'

How many times had he put a hand on her arm? And now it was a greasy, blond haired, serrated claw. Lucian's face still had human eyes, and in those eyes was a love for her.

Lucian signalled to go back in the window. She gestured for him to go first. Lucian's movement was clumsy, but within the clumsiness there lurked Bug exactness.

He went into the room with the shredded books and started furtively hunting around. The room was bright, but on the floor in the corner was a dark jellified mess. It was about three feet across, two wide and about one foot deep. It reeked of menace. Lucian was bent double, straining, as if he was being pulled

194

towards the jelly. He looked like he was desperately trying to find something.

The black jelly was an absence. Mass that had reversed its form, vomited out the plasma of belief and filled it with emptiness and despair. She too had arrived in the city filled with belief but those beliefs had slowly dipped and time had peppered her with holes.

The black jelly pulled at black thoughts in her head. An image of her face zoomed out of the darkness of her minds eye, it turned inside out, happy face, sad face, newspaper headlines spun towards her, a day in the life, life in a day; pictures of her as a young girl, playing, laughing; colder images, her face hardened from cruel taunts and motherly scorn. Growing up, running away, falling in love and stumbling in hate. She saw herself climbing a vast tree, twisting to reach paintings hung on thorny branches, paintings of her as successful, strong, and independent. But the tree was so slippery and she slid down, spiked by thorns, down, slice, slip between, in the darkness hexagonal cells were being sealed with a black inky sludge. Zooming out, she could see they were tiny cells within her pupils. Warning sirens wailed about core failure. Looking into her eyes she saw her eyes seeing her eyes, seeing her eyes... the black jelly wanted her to forget that she was, it wanted her as part of its mass congeal. She smelt pure fear—hers.

Lucian grunted, shaking a page in a claw, his face desperate.

'Fuck off, Lucian.'

He was a plague of doubt and indecision, unwilling and unable to act. All existence shrinking into a globulating darkness.

She plunged into the dark. On a table sat her calcified heart and beside it bounced a bee. She looked into the vast bee eyes. Eyes that knew another way. The ocular bee head poured possibility into her. *Be everything else, yes, but be goddess as well.* Part of her vibrated with an intense personal fear of death, that singular drop of loneliness and extinction. But other parts expanded, growing with an accelerated vastness.

A pinch on her neck.

'Fuck sake, Lucian.'

In his claw was the page, which he pushed at her.

Linda laughed.

'Don't get stuck in your own narrative, Lucian.'

There was a sucking noise. Lucian's eyes flashed black. He raised a claw. Linda dodged as it thundered down, splintering a chair beside her.

'Bastard.'

She moved back, her bee buzzing like a chainsaw. She leapt into the spectrum, noticing Lucian's light fading. She chased her thoughts through the moving network of neural understanding and dropped down from the main spectra field.

'Don't stray from the path, little girl.'

'You die.'

Alarm sounds, harsh electrical, ear splitting music.

It was annoyance, junk waves in the head. She pushed into the black lines of the spectrum, squeezed into the cracks between mental floorboards, her stomach turned as she plugged dirt up the nostrils and into the eyes of the laborious parody of herself. She surged forward, black laser wire lacerated all space. Forces of life and death twisted without

196

division, image or errant biography.

Linda came out of the spectra and saw Lucian writhing on the floor. Fabric, splinters, dust, hair and fragments of skin, were being pulled into the black jelly and manifested into a voodoo subterfuge of the soul. Pushing her hair out of her face, Linda went to the wall and smelt her way down the maroon striped wallpaper, over the borders of gold and into the navy background. Her senses rode on the paint surging out of her spray can. In the mist she saw another person; the unknown Linda grinning at her.

Bee drone filled her head. She felt the plucking of the pollen from her flowers. She did not mind. Her hands performed dances and pirouettes before her; wall and paint, lying down like lovers. She remembered Lucian's eyes tracing over her face; the way he wanted her. How she wanted to be seen and which part did the wanting. She laid the images down, let them fall into the spectrum, snaking between the cracks, seeking out the last pieces of her strangled selfhood. *Her Lucian.* She took enchantment from the shelf of meaning and purpose, hope from the shelf of fear and doubt. And when Lucian stuck his head out of the tomb of first love, she killed him.

The Starting Point

15

Neon drummed on the table in the Diner. 'Coffee, Tracy.'

She looked at him with watery eyes. 'Does everybody have to get hurt?'

It was these ones that got to Neon. He used to have fun with them, but not anymore. The days of getting away with what people didn't see were behind him. Albert taught him that every step on the equational path had to be perfectly balanced.

He pictured Albert's face; round eyes, boyish cherry cheekbones, but worn, like they had been exposed to extreme hot and cold conditions. And those epic wrinkles, wide, sweeping, granite steps, leading to the supreme court of his eyes. The brilliance of those eyes made Neon's seem pale, especially when Albert proclaimed, *all is not predestined*. What he *didn't* say was that destiny was one hard sonofabitch to take on. Which led Neon to question why he had to listen to anyone. People had inevitable questions and to the answers—inevitable reactions.

He turned to Tracy. 'When you set a building on fire, furniture gets burnt.'

She frowned. 'Do you really have the right to make decisions like that?'

Neon stood up from the table, waving his hand down in front of him. 'Take a look. Tell me what you see?'

Tracy pursed her lips tight together and shook her head.

'Nothing. I see nothing.'

'That's right ,Tracy, nothing. Nothing at all. I know that you can see well. I watch you seeing, your eyes like film recorders. You see what happens out there,' Neon jerked his thumb towards the street, 'in a way others can't. Your lack of pretension lets you see with clarity. That's good, you get to help the ones who can't see in your way, like Victor.'

'What have you done to Victor?'

'I've done nothing to Victor.'

'You can tell me.' Tracy sat opposite Neon.

Neon sniffed at her. What a curious creature she was—the way her hair was neatly bunched at the back, hair pins evenly spread out. She was an old fashioned believer in right and wrong. Albert had talked about the good, how they might be a bigger hindrance than the others.

'Neon 23?'

'Yes, sir.'

'What are we faced with here?'

'A curious specimen, the Armadillo specialist. Good intentions, but limitations on what they are willing to experience.'

'Why is she bothering me?'

'Well, it appears she wants to mother you.'

'Well, holy shit.'

Neon thought of his actual mother, Margaret Strech, a long nosed, dark eyed beauty. He could still smell her smoky, violet perfume and feel the touch of her strong, leather gloved hands. No father, no questions; fine by both. She had expected a lot of him. *'Khhharl'*, she uttered his name like an accusation.

Then she disappeared.

199

Bang! Seven years old, a lawless mind and a senile grandmother who didn't pay much attention to him.

'Tracy, there is nothing to say.'

'Not even to those ambulance men?'

'And what do you know about the ambulance men?' asked Neon, tilting forward.

Tracy fidgeted.

Neon had a begrudging admiration for her perseverance. Her face was easy on the eye, once pretty, but now without sexual connotation.

'I know,' Tracy started, 'that the ambulance men keep the cells of the tree healthy.'

'The tree?'

'The city is a tree,' she blurted. 'The streets are the trunks, side streets the branches, buildings are leaves and people are the nutrients that travel between, keeping everything healthy.'

'Are people that important?'

'Life is important, people *are* important.'

'Yeah, yeah, you don't know what I do. Don't judge.'

'I see the effect you have on others. Victor, Linda, the Kage, they all look to you.'

'No, no, they look, but not at me, perhaps because of me, but I am nothing. What happens, happens without me.'

Tommy Bones bashed into the table. 'Neon, spark your sockets, man. Serious shit on the outside.'

Tracy nodded at Neon. 'You will heed my words?'

He laughed. 'You're annoying me.'

'That is because I am touching your heart.'

Neon threw his head back and roared. 'Oh, you're good.

200

Make sure you hang around and we can pick this up at another time.'

'*Neon 23, bookmark that woman, she is completely insane. I like that.*'

'Will do. There is serious Bug activity happening outside.'

'Endgame?'

'*No, but one mean streak of viciousness. And it is coming from a low level of the spectrum, way lower than before.*'

Neon stood up, eyeing the manic Tommy Bones with his staircase grin. 'Vicious Bug activity in the infrareds, Tommy?'

'That's right.' Tommy pulled at his jaw, muscled by amphetamine chewing. 'Do you know it all, man?'

'Yeah, all of it. Every last fucking detail.' Neon knelt on the bench by the window, his leg quivering slightly.

'*Neon 23, what the fuck is the leg shake?*'

'*A slight adrenal release. The absence of Victor is leaving us exposed.*'

'23.'

'Yes.'

'*Find out the Neon that gives a fuck and eliminate it.*'

'Yes, sir.'

Neon pulled the metal blind apart, the metallic crack disturbing the dust of exfoliating people. The street, with its exquisite graffiti designs by himself, was in uproar. Over on the corner where the junkies and dealers hung, a team of Soul Bugs were kicking one living shit out of the street people. These were not the Bugs of old with their juddering movements, they were moving fast and fluid, shattering bone and life with swiping blows.

Neon turned to Tommy Bones, noticing his razorblade pupils. 'What you gonna do, Tommy?'

Tommy's shoulders shuddered, tongue flickering out over dry lips. 'Well, man, we got a problem see. Bug box ain't working.'

'Come, Tommy. Put your Bug box away. The new tunes,' he said, tapping Tommy's head, 'are in here.' Neon slid off the window seat and walked towards the door, falling into step with Liv.

'Neon,' she spat. 'Coming to see our new forces?'

The way she tilted her head back and spoke down her nose reminded him of his mother. Something epic.

'*Our* forces? Found a new father figure, Liv?'

Her anger licked around her like blue flame, yet she remained untouched. She had developed an asbestos centre, brilliant idea, but essentially flawed. Her brow lowered, eyes flashing murderous looks, somehow erotic. 'Your time is coming fast, Neon.'

'And yours faster still, murderous childe.' Neon loved the crude polarities. In the repulsion of people and place was an incredible attraction. Victor had chosen well, this shithouse Diner was gonna cook them all eventually.

Out on the street Neon headed over to Johnny Ease, Lady Fox and Tommy Bones who stood next to a car graffittied with turquoise, yellow and sky blue.

'What's doing, Neon?' asked Johnny.

'Right there, you have the Milkweed Assassin Bug.' Neon stretched his arms up, turning them in their sockets'. 'They are reprogramming the city. Destroying the genetic failings of the

202

test-tube.'

'Right in front of us?'

'Sure. They are Bug, the obedient.'

'Are we gonna stop them?'

'If we stop them, they'll improve. We can take this as a lesson in understanding.' Neon faced the Kage, enjoying their shapes as they stood framed by his graffiti. They became an extension of his creations, so perfectly did they blend with the back drop. Johnny Ease slipped into the black lines in-between, the defining aspect. Tommy Bones was the sky blue, rocket fuel magician, and Lady Fox was the ooze, the groove and potential of form.

'Now, you guys work with wavelengths, eh? You create virtuals on your mainframe, codes of molecular electricity that take form with visual and aural transmissions. Am I right?'

'Sure,' Johnny said.

'And you use machines, tools, chemicals and the electrical, merging and blurring the lines between person and virtual person, between thoughts and sayings. Then you leave memories hung on the new wave, postcards of conclusions?'

'You got that right,' said Tommy.

'That's pretty fucking impressive.'

'Yeah, we got the fucking moves, man. We're the new heartbeat, flooding the mind with magnetic tentacles.'

'And that's good, Tommy. But bring it here. Take a snifter of this air, let your mind travel out to what you see here. Take in the Bug scene, the violent movements of uniformity. Smell the air, feel the pressure on your face of being here, that slight push from the outside, tap, tap, tap, goes the outside starting to come in and—'

There was a ferocious high pitched scream.

The four looked in amazement as the Assassin Soul Bugs began falling and writhing upon the floor. One by one they fell to invisible lacerations.

'What the fuck?' Dropping into the spectrum, Neon located the source of the attack. Across the street from where the Bugs were, stood Linda, her arms a flurry of movement as she graffitied a boarded up shop.

They all moved down towards the scene, stumbling over the rubble of crumbling buildings. Liv moved to their left, her mouth agape, arms tight against her body.

Neon raised his eyebrows at her.

'Thought we were leaving the Bugs alone?' said Tommy.

'*We* were...' said Neon, holding an elbow in each hand, his arm muscles clenched. The intensity of Linda's painting made him shudder. How dare she be so audacious?

'*Neon 23, what the fuck?*'

'*Oh boy, this is the outrageous. She's splicing the very fucking molecules of air and imprinting them with images.*'

'*What changed?*'

'*There is nothing left of her on the outside. Concerns are a thing of the past. She ain't gonna be asking many more questions. She's painting full tilt now.*'

The spray of the aerosol came out like an utterance and a Linda self portrait began to take shape. Flame-like hair flicked over the boards and eyes stared from deep within the grain. The splintered boards seemed to lay their fibres down in obedience. Neon heard drums beating but realised it was the pulse in his ears. The painting of Linda's face was stark in its expression and although it was self obsessional, although he should just walk away and find it self-indulgent, it pulled him into its details: the tragedy in the cheekbones, so harsh against the city night, like a moon freshly shaped with a razor blade — had beauty, had a wild torture that called his name.

'Struggling to find meaning, Neon?' Linda turned.

It was difficult to separate the person from the picture.

She stood tall, head tilted, wild hair pulled back into a pony tail with long wisps hanging over her face. Her bottom lip hung low, top sneering. Hips were tilted sideways, one leg slightly bent, the other straight. A cheetah after the kill.

'What you doing, Linda?'

On the paving stones around her there were blue digital readouts. Street names — West Lafayette, Shelley, Over Street, Black and West. They were not laid out as they would be in a regular map order. And they flashed on and off, moving into different places. There was some form of order, but it wasn't obvious.

'Interesting. Neon 23, what are we receiving here?'

'Well, this is some holy shit, we got Neons 56 and 43 investigating. This is a spontaneous projection of mind juice.'

'That's not one hell of a scientific answer, 23?'

'Well, sir, this ain't any old science, this shit has never happened before, this is live, there's nothing to compare it to. If we could join together?'

'I told you about that shit, did I not? We have the work to do and no other. This is nice, I know, we'll use it, we'll take it and use it, and no more shit about joining.'

205

'Of course. It appears to be a parallax.'

'Details?

'She is too slippery, but it seems her mind moves through patterns of development, repeated access points to the underside of her thought. She doesn't stay still long enough for us to get any closer.'

The Linda on the building was slightly bulging, inflated by the night air. The painted eyes were large and cartoon like, but that was the cheap sell, for they were symbols that cart-wheeled over the threshold of the normal. The hooks of the image sneaked out like 3-D projections disconnecting from their source. They sought to invade the mind of the viewer. Curling visions that caressed the iris, sclera, pupil, retina and snaked down the optic nerves.

Just like he would do it.

This was unhinged. The creative electricity threatened existence, but its brilliance was such that it excited every part of it.

Neon poured in, voyeuristic to the extreme. He crawled around Linda's face—the real one, not the picture. Her tight jaw and tense neck, sinews and tendons stretched beyond the elastic of gravity—taking too much, giving too much. Down over her shoulders and breasts, the spill of shape, mounds, curves and shadows; symbolic transmissions to his over-nervous system.

The heat of the city rose like there was a steam-spitting boiler beneath the street, a satanic squall cooking cocks and sexual glands.

'Shit, 23, this is scorching.'

'We gotta get all over her, sir.'

Linda's heart thundered, gunshots staggering the air, the liver stripped down her blood like a practised street gang stripping a luxury saloon, the lung space was a measureless cavern. Neon's wonder poured into the painting, and he let it, fascinated that he was helping lift the still-life off the boards. *Caress me*, it sang, like the dawn chorus had slipped off its branch and taken to seducing sanity.

It was talking to him.

'23, *what you getting? This is not seduction.*'

'*You're right, it's more. She is dangerous, isolated in her modernism, she seeks to destroy all that has gone before.*'

'*Us?*'

'*No. She can't... she won't, it's creature-like. It feeds, we're food. For now anyway.*'

Linda stood stock still, lynched by her own compulsions.

Neon wanted to drink her, to swirl his paintbrush right through the spectrum of her existence, dipping into the keynotes of her derangement.

Behind him, Liv edged closer.

Neon turned. 'Don't fuck, Liv.'

'Why ever not? Do you think I am afraid of you, Neon? You, your girl, and your fancy spray cans? Don't you think life has dealt me enough to be able to deal with you?'

'Go cut yourself. Fuck off.'

'I believe you're nervous, Mr I-have-no-fucking-emotions. You know what your little girlfriend has done, don'tcha now? You fucking soul stealer.'

'For what it's worth. I didn't know.'

'Didn't know?'

Liv's head was slanted like a Mantis. Her hips leaning the same direction as her head. And while Linda stood out from the street, Liv fitted in, which meant the city was slipping to the Bugs and Victor was still out of the picture.

Liv was spilling pheromones—iron sculptures and rusty figurines, born of her poisoned blood, ghosting around her.

Despite himself, Neon started salivating. It was like she was something bad to eat, too much sugar, too much grease, a bitter chocolate with drool inspiring sourness. Maybe she had more to offer—as if on cue, she raised her hands. How the fuck she had ended up with hands like that was beyond him. They were long when stretched, deftly curved backs with slightly see through skin, just enough to expose a bluish swirl of veins below. There were slight dips where the knuckles lay, beautiful joint bends in the fingers with perfect rolling skin hills and valleys sweeping down to sad moons rising over a sea of nails. The nails were talon-like, yet warm and individual, each a family crest for its finger, entire histories with poignant individuality and intelligence.

Neon shook his head. 'Outrageous! You carry on, Liv. Who the hell is gonna stop you.'

Liv scowled. 'Listen to the whacking skies, Neon. The dismantlers are coming to stop you.'

Linda sat opposite Neon in the Diner. A semblance of normality had resumed. The Bugs were on their side and the opposing team on theirs. Linda was still vacant after her street painting rage.

'Neon 23, what proof do we have that Albert was right?'

'There is no right or wrong in mimicry, only recognition.'

'Yes, but I put it to you, 23, that Albert was playing more than we've ever imagined...'

'Indeed. Think of this one, sir.'

'Lay it on me, 23.'

'Albert induced trauma into Victor.'

'By showing him his suicide, yes.'

'But it was the trauma of a death, that was itself caused by the trauma.'

'Why so?'

'Victor wouldn't have gone through the events leading to suicidal thoughts if he hadn't seen the suicide previous.'

'A past caused by its future, not the other way around. A goddamn reality breaking, knot tying... So why did Albert kill himself?'

'The inevitable had to be lived out, it's too strong to be rejected — fucked with, yes.'

'Death seems too simple for that man, too final. We need to find out more.'

'The only way to find out would be to look at Albert's paintings, everything was detailed. But does it matter?'

'Everything matters, every little piece is fitting tighter and tighter together.'

'What did you say?' mumbled Linda.

'I didn't.'

Linda's grogginess evaporated and her eyes shone with the lights of the Aurora Borealis.

'Nice eyes.'

'You think so?' she said with a barely concealed smirk on her face. 'I designed them myself.'

209

The Diner bent around her shoulders. Half an hour ago, she'd pushed against the air, been stark against it. But now, the air was pulled around her, as if desperate to get inside. Neon thought black hole. He thought danger, because his mind felt the same pull as the air. It was one of the reasons he avoided the mind, it was weak, a petty actor. Yet Linda's face, so settled and peaking to the fullness of the skin. Her mouth stark and alone, lips like the petals of a dark red rose flowing over the flower edge, hair thrown like a shawl, eyes of peril, exact in their watching.

'You're fucking delightful, you know that?'

'Well... *something* happened.'

'That doesn't matter.'

'Nice.'

'That was getting here, the vertical. *This* is the horizontal. But, I'll tell you what does matter.'

Neon laid out what he knew of Albert.

'What type of man was Albert?' asked Linda.

'It's too easy to judge. What did it take for him to go where he went? I have no idea. When I say I worked with him, that's not to be taken in the traditional way. By the time I met him, he was far beyond normal communication.'

'I met him, briefly.'

'Yes.'

'He gave me a painting.'

'What?'

'Well, he left it behind, small, intriguing. I still have it.'

'Shit, how fucking convoluted was that man.'

The clock over the coffee machine ticked aggressively. Everything in the Diner glistened—the grease, the sweat, the eyes, all were drying, infinitesimally moving towards a new state and a new point of departure. Tommy Bones and Johnny Ease were locked in discussion with the Lady Fox at the counter, *but about what?* The Lady Fox laughed, her head rolling easily on her neck, the whites of her eyes a startling void, unwritten pages, but why? She had arrived here, changed the scene, her words, her luxurious lips, the shoulders, hips, the silver sequin top, out of place, out of time, yet confident of her role. He had painted her, had stormed over her balustrade. Information had poured out, the fever pitch, broken hearted revenge that she desired. He had cooked the street on the soul of a white hot, black goddess. And of course that was the right thing to do. But there was something in the way she watched him watching her, like she knew something. They all watched him, every one of them waiting for him to make the next move. It was too geometric, mechanical, equational even. Had Albert set *him* up? Did Albert know that he would meet Victor, who would meet Linda, who would meet him, then she would rise and eventually sit here before him, telling him about Albert's last picture... all of these little pieces like a stream of dominos.

Albert had admired what he called the *Living Action*, of Neon's work. He had been excited at the pace Neon was moving at and had helped him shift into internal constructions, the place where the endgame was to be finalised.

'Neon 23, could Albert have completely outsmarted us?'

'We don't believe so. The Mantis sees all.'

'Yep, but does it tell all?'

Neon felt a grinding inside his head; the oil of confidence ebbing away.

'What was Albert's painting of?' he asked.

'Nothing, blotches really and title.'

'What was the title?'

'The Starting Point.'

'Where the fuck is it?' Neon said, rising out of his seat.

'Don't get shitty. It's in my apartment. Wait, I want to talk with you.'

'No time.'

'We need to talk.'

'I need that picture. Spodge, we have a mission.'

The Kage zipped over.

'Wait,' said Linda. 'There is something we need to consider.'

'What?'

'It's the layout of the City. There is something I found out earlier.'

'Which is?'

'Bark Bugs, Dutch Elm disease. It's being replicated in the city.'

'More fucking trees. Tell Tracy about it, tell Victor.'

'But Victor isn't around.'

'Then he needs to fucking return!' Anger tore around Neon's body like a virus and he rode on it into the inner desert.

Unbelievable. Linda's street painting hung on a desert hillside. Her style was so fucking haunting and individualistic. Out of place, wrong, selfish. It slowed him down, it was so fucking distracting. He needed to work, to unravel this fucking mess. She was pulling him as an 'I' and that did not work. The

'I' had too many repercussions. He needed to get a handle on Linda. He knelt down, letting the sun bake his back as he stared at her painting. One thing about her though, there was a delicious humour in the stark contrast of her urban portrait against the bleached, cacti-scattered hill. The painting threw down a challenge. The shape of the painted mouth, poised to speak. The sweep above the lips, epic, cliff-like. Concentrating on this made the rest of the face strange and un-personal, a mythology rather than a reflection. It was as if the self was another self, something distant, a dummy, a quick sell while truth worked underground, projecting out... and true enough, on the desert floor were street names in blue lights. They changed to words: *erotic intentions, illusion, tragedy, helplessness, love, expected, expected, expected.*

'Neon 23! This is invasive.'

'Sure is, she's into you, you're into her.'

'It won't work, too human, happy and sad, I won't go there. Look at the words, dripping with ineffectiveness.'

Neon returned to the Diner. 'Your street name projections, the blue lights on the street. What of them?'

'Yeah,' said Johnny Ease. 'Like a parallax, the trigonometric pattern of thought.'

'Go on.'

Everyone looked to Johnny. He placed a map on the table. 'Well, what I noticed, what you laid out, Linda was that you kept West Lafayette, East and Black and Mariner Street in place. The three streets beyond them moved, like they were doing an orbit. Yet they had their own individual orbits, ever changing. Also, the centre three streets did not stay in a fixed place, they moved across the City. Then the orbits started to re-occur but at different angles. A place in space of ever-increasing, psycho-geographical intensity.'

Neon shook his head. 'You remember all of this from seeing it once?'

Johnny wobbled his dark mass of hair. 'It's not memory, it's always there.'

'Of course it is.'

Johnny resumed, 'It's like strongholds are formed and new points charted from them. New thoughts, producing spontaneous creation of thoughts unlinked. Trigonometric manifestation of placement. Walking through the city, your body on one street, your mind on another, your hearing somewhere else, taste, smell, it's fragmented, derangement as a labyrinth equation in order to pinpoint where you actually are. I am impressed, really, beyond the saying. This is new, but to the point that the word new just disintegrates in its presence, falls to the dust, like a new electrical current travelling inside the old and shattering it just by the fact that it exists. It all leads to the ultimate conclusion.'

'Which is?' said Neon.

'Her starting point is a self replicating advancement, it consumes the past.'

'What is her starting point?'

'You.'

'Consume me?'

'I wouldn't.'

'It's him,' said Neon.

'Who?'

'Albert, the fucking puppet master!'

A thousand dominos fell.

Neon felt cold, frozen, stuck at one point as a boiling fever starting pouring down from the top of his head and spotlights burned holes through his skin. Sweat rolled down his face, picked up debris, stacking up excretions from his hormonal system and feeding them back into himself, triggering further secretion. The faces around him elongated into sharp arrowed points, all pointing at him. He tried to escape inside his head, but there too, everything expected him, mocked him. All his thoughts were formed of thousands of needles.

'Fucking hell.'

Liv and her cronies stared over at them.

'And the fuck you are staring at?' He whipped out a couple of spray cans and started spraying on the table, sending everyone diving out of the way. Cups and plates flew off, shattering on the floor, the remaining ones transformed by passes of blue and green paint.

'Hey!' shouted Listern. 'My table.' He ran over.

'Stand the fuck down.' Tommy Bones jumped and stood in his way. 'Don't be mixing it, man.'

Spodge stood behind Tommy, her eyes boring into Listern's head. Listern had little desire for a fight, especially with Raucous looming in the doorway.

A Bug next to Liv started squirming and squealing in pain.

'Fuck you, Neon,' shouted Liv, 'your time is coming.'

'No, my time is here.' Neon ripped over his inner landscape. His hands whirred under him like a running chimp, knuckles pounding on the ground.

In the cafe, coats of paints layered up on the cafe table.

Linda grabbed him. 'What's wrong Neon, Neon?'

Neon felt lacerations all over his face and inside his body.

'Neon 23, what the fuck?'

'It's fucking equations, sir, they are all over the fucking place, they are completing, balancing, we have to keep moving, we have to break.'

Neon kicked the table, knocking it flying. Tommy Bones stood staring at him, his arrow face so sharp, Spodge, an ice cool blade and finally Linda, a collection of jagged metal scalpels pressing towards him. She reached her hand out, but it was covered with cactus spikes. The very touch of death.

'That's the painting,' said Linda.

'What?'

'There, under the table.'

And true enough, the overturned table had dark blue inkblots with a luminous green tinge, an unmistakable Albert painting. Written in big letters was *The Starting Point*.

'Fuck.' Neon pushed out, moving across the Diner floor, marvelling, yet horrified by the violence of the corners on everything. He ignored the taunts of the Bugs, ripping open the door. The metallic clanging blistered his ears.

The air was cold, but only for an instant. As soon as it knew it was him, it poured acid on his skin. Alarms sounds surrounded him like angry saws. Crow Street was a disease, a virus being injected into his eyes. He looked to his graffiti for solace, but the colour had been hijacked. The blue was cold, efficient, taking his breath with it as it pulled him over rusting city coral, the red poured out taking his mind, his skin, his tendons, muscles, the very peelings of his eyes, and the yellow, hot mustardy yellow gagged him while precise orange sliced open his skull. He turned, running past the glaring portrait of Linda. Feelings of déjà vu hounding him.

Everything screamed, ALBERT!

As Neon reached the corner where the Bugs had been massacred, he stopped. A net of mockery was waiting for him around the corner that he would *inevitably* turn.

'Bastard. You're coming for me, I'm coming for you.'

Intrinsic Thought-blots

16

The night retreated and the urban mass turned its silver stare towards Sindin Hill. Victor met the stare with disdain and then returned to rubbing his thumb over the chequered grip of his gun. He placed the gun barrel to his temple. The hollow feel of the round steel quickened his pulse, but he didn't pull the trigger.

Killing himself would make no difference, for *he* would never die.

Another fucking conundrum. This one broadcast by the Fortis Tower, over east.

It all started last night. His head drawers had been so full of rage they spewed open all over his head. To ease the pressure, he'd poured rage into fires that burned over Eastside and assigned buildings to people. Neon was the preposterous Halifax Stadium, Liv the Cadillac Hotel, Emily the tombstone shaped Chrysler Tower, Linda wouldn't stay still no matter where he put her, and his father was the Fortis Telecom Tower.

Once he had strung them all out, the city had responded, working a clinical urbanology on his placements. Gangs with burning torches had lurched from fire points towards Halifax Stadium. From the hill he could hear the chanting and screaming—him too—like they were off to burn the mad scientist who had brought the curse down upon them. Halifax

Stadium lit up well, flames dancing to the *burn, burn*. Unfortunately, what they hunted had slipped inside of them. It was anger *of* the machine, *in* the machine, *because of* the machine. Neon was the air between the cogs, that which didn't move in a moving machine, shit, he was even more than *that*, he was the force that created the necessity for movement, that made other things move, not out of the way, no, it wasn't that easy. Neon was a triggering, a spasm, a reaction, a disease, a high level atomic aggression. He passed through, yet remained installed in everyone he encountered. Of course, even if burning the stadium called Neon changed nothing, it felt pretty damn good.

Victor smiled, spinning the gun in his hand, pointing it at the skyscrapers and making shooting noises. A creeping feeling started on the back of his head. The sense of being watched by those cold black spider eyes. He let it move across his scalp. *Father dearest...* the man was worse than Neon.

Neon worked with your father, betrayed you.

And Neon was worse than his father. Neon said he should avoid thinking—bit fucking convenient. Victor punched the earth beneath him, making a tin can roll down. The label was bleached out and the rusted bottom looked like a squashed face.

'So why don't I tell you of my shit? Did the city send you to speak to me? Got my diagnosis, have you? Ah, you're much too fucking quiet.' Victor whacked the can away.

But the image was in his head, starting to crawl, burrowing its way inward.

Rusty can man.

Illumination. 'Yeah, you wanna fucking come now. Come on

then.' Victor pulled his ears, bared his teeth, squeezed his eyes, his stomach twisted, sitting bones ached, heart thumped and nostrils flared. He pulled at the weeds beneath him and scoured the city vista. Skyscrapers became the chimneys of the bilious underground machines that had been cooking his emotions. Their vulturous smoke re-contaminated his lungs. The city was a ravenous crocodile, buildings perched on its gridline back. The city was a communication, an automated referral unit from the inside of a maniac's mind, a progressive grid of symbolic inference.

And he heard it.

'Fuck you, Neon!'

The sound fell on the hill, disturbing insects whose triggered excretions informed the air of developments. The air took the information, knitted it together and threw it back into another cycle.

Sirens, screams, trucks, cars, and trains made their sounds, but underneath it all was a hiss, a bed of clicks and crackles, that held every day noise like gravity held bodies. The air tasted like a telegraph pole. Victor bit at it, eating the visual landscape. He was a monster spreading out over the city, big gnarly building teeth, pink-brown river as a tongue, streets as veins and ring road face structure.

He shook his head, got off the ground and stumbled across the hill. The place was a mess—beer cans, plastic bags, condoms and cigarette butts everywhere. He pulled at his jaw, there was a few days stubble there, but it felt like someone else's hand was pulling someone else's jaw. He went back and sat watching the city. He had to see in the right way.

He stared and the city stared back. He felt synchronicity in his eye movements and the city's connection to him magnified, a thousand strings attached to a thousand streets. He felt the buzz of the city underneath the hill. He raised his arms up, stretching them out, feeling buildings crackle inside his elbows, across his chest and down the tough harbour of his jaw. He felt the heartbeat clacking of the D-train as it nosed across the city. Heard the scrape of the meat-slicing wheels as they tilted around corners.

Standing up, he felt the city rise with him. He was the fabric, and the structure of everything was connected to the urbanology inside him. His head crawled with buildings and tenements, layers upon layer built and rebuilt, formed, transformed, mutated, created, merged, destroyed and rising without restriction. Circling forever and forever circling, there were a million fucking streets and he was on every single one.

'Time to get some fucking answers.'

He expected Bugs everywhere. Their smell was here, Bark Bugs, the little fastidious murderers, and larger ones, Cockroaches and Earwigs, the generals of the game, but there were none around, just neat piles of rubble amongst haphazardly smashed up cars.

He ran his hand over a car, it was dimpled all over, the paint beaten off and the steel beneath rusted like it was already years old. The seats inside were shredded into little strips. The rubble behind the car was laid out in the shape of a car shadow. All around, rubble piles extended out from streetlights, mirrored panelled benches and piled up in perpendicular shapes below buildings. Everything had a complete shadow replica.

The Bugs were bragging, mimicking the primitive cause and effect of the city.

Up ahead at the street corner was a small gathering. The characters were un-Bug, yet also un-human.

Moving closer, he saw three women in long, shawl-like dresses. Huddled in deep discussion, they had their backs to him and swayed together like underwater plants. Their voices were just beyond his hearing. As he got closer, pressure started building in his ears and his mouth began watering.

'Salivic celluloid,' one said, amidst grated laughter.

A bubble expanded around his head.

'This one is only for you.' And a squeal of laughter.

Victor felt like a tube was being pushed in through his ear right to the other side.

'Come down the velvet highway, Victor Scram.' Wild screams.

Victor felt nails on his face, clawing and pulling down his neck, slicing into the muscles and tendons, fingers groped his insides. He let it go. Just let it be, there was nothing else to do. The torment stopped, but a warm burning feeling remained all over his head.

'Is that it?' he said. He was standing in front of them, about fifteen feet away, on the street.

The women turned to face him.

Their forms were elusive, human-esque, but the watery movement presented a confusion of images—he saw strips of seaweed, but then they transformed into crimson feather boas, surrounding sharp chinned faces. He saw black holes for eyes and red pouting lips, he saw shark's teeth, lion claws and eagle talons, then soft hands and bodies smelling of cinnamon perfume. He had his throat removed, his eyes plucked out, and his carcass placed on a platter like a pig with an apple in his mouth. Then he felt a tug, the city fabric, clusters of buildings and black wires, pulling him back. Three black eyed girls stood against the wall. They were all Emily.

'You're afraid,' no particular mouth said.

Victor was about to say 'cheap words' but he stopped himself. He always did that, said things before considering if they were accurate. Maybe the words weren't cheap, maybe he was afraid, afraid to let go. Truly let go.

'Victor,' the Emily on the left said. 'It's time.' Her mouth movement did not seem to correspond to the words she said. Inside the mouth was an inky hole, which fizzed and became a television screen. A grainy black and white image showed chained up people being maimed by hooks and whips until little white puffs of air passed out of them. The air was gathered by giant bugs and placed onto a conveyor belt, and there they were shaped into small lips. These lips were then taken and placed around teeth picked from enamel clouds in the sky. Youthful, pink tongues were plucked from a cactus where they gestured like obscene stamen. All this was arranged into a grotesque parody of a face, which was stuffed onto a puppet-like body. The stumbling entities trundled out of a factory. The image faded.

Victor nodded at the woman. She smiled an Emily smile — the sides of her mouth climbing up her cheeks. She turned and walked to his left and down the street, looking back at him. He watched her body sway. Sweet Emily—dark hair and dripping angel eyes, a killer smile and rounded eyebrows. She intoned her head towards the other girls and Victor looked back.

'Victor,' said the second Emily.

The mention of Victor's name seemed to pull his breath out. This woman had a similar black, televisual mouth. It was like looking down a telescope at a rolling black ball. But it wasn't rolling, it was spinning. The image zoomed out and Victor saw there were many shiny black balls, all spinning, they were packed tight together, yet they all spun in perfect unison without infringing on each other. Victor moved out further from the image and it appeared that the balls were poles with rounded ends. They were immensely long, stretching to infinite ends. There was no noise, but the poles were so immense, so encompassing, that Victor's ears filled in the absent grind. He raced along the poles with his eyes, but he had to see faster than his brain, and his pupils became pulled out like melted plastic. As they extended, they pulled at the connection point of his brain to reality—the very core of him and nothingness. In his heart he knew these were exact particles of matter, the minutiae of existence. He tried to return to the street, but it wasn't the street he arrived back into. It was Neon's studio. He watched Neon dip a paintbrush into a pot of black paint, the brush came out with a long black curl of paint containing billions of black, spinning balls. Victor looked from them to Neon's burning eyes and manic grin. What the fuck?

And then Victor was standing in the street, staring at the woman. He felt like vomiting. The woman's face softened, the screen disappeared and it was Emily. She also walked to the left. The other Emily had gone. This Emily was chewing on her thumb, and looking at him with smiling, playful eyes. Her shoulders like the horizon, so perfectly placed.

'Victor,' said the last girl.

Victor turned. Same black mouth, but the words coiled out around Victor's head like a tentacle, pulling him forward. He wasn't sure if he had fallen over, but he could smell the road, the dust aggravating his nose, tar hard against his forehead. He stared at the shapes beneath him, in every little crevice and hole there were angles; a direction of momentum. Everything had arrived in a direction and no matter how final its placement it was in some infinitesimal way continuing in that direction. But then it wasn't the road beneath him, it was a face, and he was pushed tight against it. He smelt what the other nose smelt, a greasy man-smell. He stared at the eyes, his mouth was pushed tight and he felt stubble and he tried to move to rip his face away, but it was like his face was glued to it. He wanted to shout and the other face wanted to shout, a vicious pact. And every thought he had, he felt the other face had too. They were pushing and shaking. There was such a replication of movement that he slowed, letting it be. He was pressed against his own face. A door opened and he was back in Neon's studio with Linda doing his portrait, her hands like laser beams fusing him to his own image, bringing him face to face with himself. That was one thing, but *her* face, etched with a concentration like murder. She was glued to herself in everything she did — one hundred percent connected to every thought and action in a ferocious containment.

And then Victor was out. The last Emily standing before

225

him, like she was waiting.

'What?' he said, without really expecting an answer.

'Some people die, Victor,' she said.

'Yeah.' He locked eyes with her.

'And some people live.'

'Sure.'

'You're in-between. Your father put you on a path, but you never were so good at following instruction. That's the good bit. Bye.' She winked and vanished.

As the last ghostly wisp disappeared, he realised it was here that Emily had died.

A loud clang came from behind him like the city having trouble changing gears. It came from over Well Street and Delta. He turned and headed in that direction. There were more people on the street. Some were kicking rubble out of the way and opening up shops. One shopkeeper stood outside his shop door, a man in his fifties, dirty white t-shirt tightly circulating his large stomach, apron draped down in front. He was bald on top, short haircut on the sides, and his forehead was piled up with wrinkles. He stared at the street mess with a tough look of dismay and simmering anger.

Victor walked over to the sidewalk, stopping a couple of feet from him. 'Morning.'

The man turned towards him, wearily. 'Seems to be.'

'Bit of a mess, this.' Victor gestured to the street with an open hand.

'It's the plague.'

'The plague?'

226

'They let it happen.' The shopkeeper said with a faraway look.

'They?'

'They.' The shopkeeper threw his hands up. 'There is always someone else pulling your strings, someone meddling in the affairs of your life. That's what happens in the city, it's what you give up to live here.' And with that he turned and walked back into his shop.

Victor walked on, somewhat pleased by the shopkeeper. As he got closer to Delta station, he noticed Soul Bugs gathered under the bridge. He counted eight of them, Earwigs, hard looking bastards, with black eyes. They had adapted a new uniform, short black leather jackets with a large belt at the bottom pulling the jacket across diagonal breasted. They had tight fitting black trousers with turned up bottoms, and shiny, black boots. There was the impression that they were guards of the station, except they were only bothering people with looks. Victor slipped past and headed up the stairs of the station. There were no ticket inspectors and he walked out onto the platform. The electronic displays hummed but flashed incoherently. People hung on the platform with gray faces. They looked afraid, as if the city was under occupation.

The D-train wobbled its way down the track, driver's expression impassive as she passed. People got off with pale, silent faces. At the far end of the platform a bustling gang bundled off the train. They looked shiny and animated compared to everyone else; bright jackets, striped tops, dark shades and very obvious baseball bats.

They brushed past Victor, but kept turning to each other,

spinning around, walking forward, spinning around. They were nervous, but had core strength.

Victor followed.

They stopped at the top of the wide concrete stairs, still circulating around each other like a shoal of fish. They didn't appear to have a leader and Victor couldn't work out whether this was a strength or weakness.

After some hesitating they moved down the stairs, the other passengers not paying them much attention. When they got to the bottom they turned into the tunnel where the Soul Bugs were—everyone else turned the opposite direction.

Victor moved down behind them, counting nine. They were like a street baseball team, trousers with cuffed bottoms, baseball boots and cuffed waist jackets. But it was rag-tag, all different colours, worn, frayed, dusty, covered with many patches, but most with *Black Street Chuggers* somewhere.

As they entered the underpass, the Soul Bugs turned calmly to face them, as if they were waiting for a pre-arranged rumble. The Black Street Chuggers twirled their baseball bats. Their sunglasses were off and they looked nervous.

Victor sensed they were gonna take a pasting. He walked under the bridge to the left of them. 'What you planning here?'

The gang swung around. 'Clear out, man,' said the nearest one, a short dude, with a scar curling around his left eye.

The Bug's eyes were trained on Victor. He moved away from the gang and closer to the Bugs. They rippled back a little and turned to each other. One triangle faced Bug reluctantly stepped forward.

Victor turned back to the gang. 'Looks to me like you might

take a bit of pasting here. These are the Earwig variety, nasty beasts.' Victor moved towards the Bugs again and they pushed back a little further, in a V formation. The gang moved forward in a straight line, their collective eyes burning with an unmistakable *illumination*; more of Neon's street soldiers.

'Who you, man?' asked another gang member, tall and skinny with eyes like a flat fish.

'Victor Scram.'

The tall dude laughed. 'Yeah, me too.' He nodded his head at the other gang members. And then he sneered. 'Victor Scram ain't nothing but a myth.'

'What you talking about?'

'Victor, fucking Scram, shiiit, cartoon fucking superhero, his name inked all over the street. Gets the old men talking around their barrel fires, *Victor Scram'll come and save us*. Ain't no one gonna fucking—' The voice fell away.

The dark interior of the tunnel jarred against the bright street beyond. The light and dark were like clock faces smashing together. One spinning from Victor, one spinning at Victor; an adrenal synchronicity. His vision sharpened and he looked up into the dark, cobweb covered bridge arches.

'Victor Scram'll come and save us.' The words floated into the shadows.

Victor noticed damp stains speckled across the arches—big ones, small ones, spinning, star-like ones, like stained snowflakes. The cosmology of the pattern, the planning, the intricate layout of it, poured all over him, pulling his head wide. No one did designs like this, not nature and certainly not normal men. For a second he was back in his father's study, staring, trying to understand the speckled patterns. Now it made sense. It was the shape of all things, an intense study of origin. It was the pattern that told him who he was, what he was and why he was. Every instance of his life was created from this pattern and could be created with this pattern. As his eyes followed it down, written above the arch at the exit was *Intrinsic Thought-blots of the UnderCity*. Victor laughed. Everything was reversed, it wasn't *what* he saw, but what he *wanted* to see. The city was here for the taking, his taking.

'…ain't no one gonna save us, man,' the tall man's voice continued. 'Cos we don't need saving, see? Got the new mind, the new fucking thinking.'

The tall man was one pinprick of information, a connecting node in the streets of Victor's mind.

'Cancel the fucking myth,' said Victor. He took his gun out, creaked his neck and shook his arms out. 'And turn your fucking head-lights on.'

Eyes clicked on him, ultra-intensity, *illumination* reading.

Victor felt himself glow as their awareness dawned.

'Shit, man,' said the scarred eye one. 'What the fuck you made of?'

'Well, it ain't nothing nice. Now let's get these Bugs sorted.'

After they had laid waste to the Bugs, Victor convinced the Gang to head to the Diner. They took the D-train to Garelt, exiting onto an empty platform. The gang went to check out the graffiti, while Victor stood at the spot his father had died. The air smelt of burnt electrics. He crouched and stared down at the railway lines, imagining his father's exploding head. Vomit rose into his mouth, but he didn't stop, he let the image flood down his mental circuit, down the streets of his mind, over bridges, into rivers, overflowing out of his veins into the sewers. He impaled himself, his body gripped in a spasmodic episode of septic information. Down the steel tracks his eyes flowed. The tracks were clean, harshly polished with the entrails of a father's expectations.

Victor's hand touched the ground and feeling a sticky wetness, he saw his fingers were red. He turned, following the trail to graffiti on the wall behind. A face glistened. An unmistakable Neon—sharp black curves, grinning mouth, intense eyes and greedy nostrils.

The graffiti had been rushed, paint still dripping, but this took nothing away from the glaring presence. The teeth were huge, grinding industrial slabs consuming all that lay before them. The grind filled Victor's ears and metallic saliva slid down his throat. Neon was reconstructing, managing, malnourishing, tormenting, teasing and cajoling the human structure to peel off the wall. The cheeks bulged as if they could erupt into laughter. The whites of the eyes were deep pools, pulling him in, but once inside the soft white swirl, down came the black eyelid, all heavy and spiked. In the dark were damp stains—big ones, small ones, spinning, star-like ones. It mimicked and it mocked, challenging the past with a red, raw present.

Victor was one up on Neon and now Neon was coming back. Below was written, *Duelling Prophets of an Everlasting Power*. Neon was outside the remit, he had shifted gear and he wasn't gonna stop there. Of course, nor the fuck was Victor.

The Black Street Chuggers were talking excitedly about the graffiti in the underpass.

The underpass reeked of sleaze. Stretched faces leered on the walls, mouths extended, as if caught in the slow motion of speaking. Lewd body shapes revealed every nuance that had created them; the background, the father, the mother, the environment, the noise in the air at birth, at conception; electronic, spatial and caustic. Fantasy and desire intermingled in the juice of sex, the raw and the profane slamming against walls. The city was having her legs spread—sky scraping erections eased past pubic hair street signs and entered vaginal junctions, bridges cupped breast shaped arches and shop front stockings adorned shapely street thighs, the viewers' glassy eyes mirrored the frantic images as rivers of cum flowed beneath their feet.

Shit, a vision stopping at nothing. Maybe that was why Victor liked Neon. Neon wasn't afraid to make the final move. Damn. Was he starting to *like* Neon?

'Hey,' he shouted to the Black Street Chuggers as they exited. 'Welcome to Crow Street.'

Before them lay another fantastic assembly of graffiti. It swarmed over burnt out cars, over rubble, broken glass and trash; a new skin for the disintegrating city.

The gang came out, slowing as they reached the street. Then they stood stock still.

Victor felt proud. It was the visual vomit of internal guerrilla warfare. This was where he belonged and who he belonged with.

232

The Diner, down on the left, bulged with mausoleum-like status. The sidewalk outside had a semicircle of cleared rubble. Further down, at the end of the street, some new people were hanging, but Victor couldn't pick up their details. Across from them, was an unmistakable Linda painting that threatened everything around it as if it was loaded. A few more of her paintings were around the Diner. They were of her face, but not vainly so, more like watchdogs to the Neon works.

One of the street corner people started moving up the street. The Black Street Chuggers eyed it too, standing strong, heads up. The figure moved around the rubble with ease. Victor still couldn't make it, but it had the Bug uniform, leather jacket and pressed trousers. What he noticed was a sound. The thwacking sound that had freaked Neon.

The scar eyed, Black Street Chugger, Tino, went to move forward.

Victor put up his hand.

'What up, man?'

'Let it come, we gotta learn what they're doing, where it wants to go.'

Tino stopped.

The Bug passed the Diner on the opposite side of the street, twitching its head as the Diner door clanged open.

Tommy Bones jazzed his way out and stared at the Bug. There was no reaching for a Bug Box, though. Tommy started waving his arms, doing a crazy dance. The Bug shook its head, waving its arms back. It was like Tommy was trying to conjure something.

'What the fuck, man?' asked Tino.

233

'Don't know, don't know.' Victor started walking down, heading in a diagonal towards Tommy. He noticed the Ambulance of Unforgiven Screams move across the end of the street, heading over to Jefferson. Tommy was still waving his arms around which seemed to be annoying the Bug.

'Nice dancing, Tommy.'

'The fuck, SCRAM MAN!' Tommy's face lit up. 'Oh the shit, man. Where the fuck? SCRAM MAN!' He started moving like he wanted to hug Victor, but didn't.

'How you been, Tommy?'

'Been heavy shit without you, man. Neon done and he gone.'

'Gone?' Victor felt a pang of shock. 'Where?'

'Don't know? Out, voody doos, fucking seizure in the mainframe, prayers and the single shotgun blast to the fucking ether, man.'

'Fucking hell, what the fuck, Tommy?'

Tommy shuffled like a tap dancer. 'Eh... he went out, never came back in.'

Linda appeared in the doorway. Face sparkling, eyes like beacons and a sweet smile. 'Victor. I think we need you now.'

'Yep, I knew you would.' It was good to see her, even if she was more Neonified than the Neon.

They went into the Diner and Linda and Tommy ran through the details of what had been happening. From what Victor could make out they were all living in different fucking universes. It didn't bother him.

The Kage and Raucous had formed a collective of Gangs.

The Black Street Chuggers melted in with them and they all scarpered off, leaving him with Linda.

'This is like polite warfare.' Victor said, eyeing the Bugs on the other side.

'You sure?'

Linda was walking through him. He didn't mind. After the Emily prophecy, he felt he knew Linda as much as she could ever know him. But even without that, her eyes were a film, rolling with the greens and blues of youth, eager flowing waters that had met with the brown trudge of the city, which was, in turn, softened and silkified by her beauty. She was torn and troubled, but succeeding and going further.

Victor gulped his coffee.

The Diner no longer resembled the place Victor had first stumbled into. All the corners had been shaken loose. It wasn't just the tables and surrounding chairs that Neon had graffitied. The whole place seemed brighter, dirty still, but oiled and functioning. The Bug side was dour, but a new dour—efficient, no surprises, strong and relentless.

'So, where's Neon?'

Linda's eyes flickered with an angry concern. 'He's out there. Out there somewhere, evolving. Can you imagine, like *that man* needs to evolve. Albert is pushing him and he's gonna push back.' Her eyes welled with tears, which she quickly blinked away.

Victor could have sworn her tears were made of paint.

'You know, I'm not so sure your father was all things great.'

'All things? How about any things? I was wrong to fire off. I never even cared about the man. It was just the sense of being

235

overlooked.'

'Overlooked is more your father's territory than Neon's.'

'You're right there. The way I see it, you gotta act and Neon will act, that's for sure. He doesn't have a choice.'

'You got a choice, Victor?'

'Not the choosing type.'

'But you're the God of the City.'

Victor laughed. 'Now you're talking like Neon.'

'But its true, isn't it? Everything in the city centres on you.' She raised her eyebrows and smiled a dazzling smile.

'What?'

'With you it's so easy, it's clear. I mean, you're a madman, but—'

'What?'

'Nah, you know... shit.' Linda chuckled. 'Who's gonna love you, Victor?' The words floated out of her mouth like fat butterflies and flew down into the coffee.

Victor took a slug and butterflies took off inside his head.

Multicoloured paints poured out of Linda's eyes. In the flow, Victor saw images of himself unravelling with repeated charm, *person to know, person to go*. It was the perfect invitation to explore self and reason, but it wasn't his way, he didn't have that luxury. His streets were cold and hard and too many people looked to him. Linda was the razor sharp instant, he was the cars going past, whispered words passed between anxious ears, *Victor Scram, Victor Scram*. His choices concerned other people.

Linda laughed and leaned back. 'Well, what else are we gonna do while we wait?'

'Don't wait, get out there, stir the pot. Nothing's going to get Neon returning like someone painting better than him.'

'Oh yeah, like I'm waiting for Neon. What about you?'

'Think I better find the man myself.'

'See you at the starting line.'

Victor sat alone. The Bug heads across the Diner were bobbing up and down, like someone was yanking their chain.

'Victor?'

He turned to see Liv's rounded, red lips, moistening as she stood at the dividing line.

'Busy?' she said.

He got up to admire the lips but her vacuous eyes filled him with repulsion. Of all the paths people chose, she chose to shut down and be regimented by hate. 'Piss off, Liv.'

'Don't you fucking dare.'

Victor scowled. She really did have poison coming out of her. 'You're rotting Liv. There's only so long you can sit with death.'

'It's coming down on you too. Mr fucking Dickhead.'

'Bring it down, Liv. Bring what you got.'

'It's already here, asshole.' Her mouth twisted, like slugs were being wrung out. 'You see those ones, out there.' She jerked her head towards the street corner. 'Yeah, well, Daddy is fucking come to sort you assholes out. And you and Neon, you're number fucking one on the list.'

Her pure hatred almost made her attractive to Victor again. Her commitment was impressive; pure and vital. Just everything he wasn't.

'Yeah, see you later Liv, unless the worms finish with you before then.'

Victor walked down West Lafayette and over onto East and Black. It was obvious Neon had been out this way—his graffiti intermittently appeared on walls. The paintings were casual throwaways though, not his usual headfucks.

They led to the Central Train Station.

Victor marvelled at the three epically pillared arches that formed the front section and held up a hulk of office buildings behind. On either side, enormous towers pulled back like giant shoulders. The central building was maybe twenty storeys tall. The top storey was twice the height of the others, with boastful balustrades all around. But behind the splendour, the windows were all smashed and the detailed facade was crumbling and dropping off. Demise poured from windows, gushed down the marble steps and surged towards him. Dreams squealed, vision squalled, power and greed begged for forgiveness, but there was none. Here, the old empire was going to be turned on its head.

Father Almighty

17

On Shelley Street, Bug pheromonal trails hidden under the odours of musty rubble and gasoline attempted to hijack Linda's head. The street's resident rat population undulated through the intricate maze of rubble—connecting, changing, infecting and perfecting. She slotted the shapes into her mind map, completing the *multi-neurological mosaic*. In all the graffiti faces she had painted, she remained, watching the stifling congeal that lurked in the city. It was concentrated right here, number 46 Shelley Street, a vast, but anonymous, office building.

Standing before the entrance, she noted the dull tarnish of the aluminium frames surrounding the smashed front doors. The entrance had lost all reflective material, which was a pity, because she was being followed. All the way over here, she had seen the *Ambulance of Unforgiven Screams* passing intermittently at junctions behind her. She wasn't so worried, the streets were so covered with debris it would be a while before they got through.

Her immediate concern was what was in this building. The high ceilinged entrance hall was derelict and empty. There were bare chalkboard walls with holes in them, separating the outer hall from the inner. On the floor were thick, dusty electrical cables, mangled aluminium door frames and red and white warning tape which was ripped and stretched. The direction of the mess indicated that something had dragged itself inside leaving the stink of death in the air.

Her boots crunched on the ground as she stepped through the smashed doors, but the sound didn't travel far in the heavy atmosphere. She took out her spray can, composed herself and looked for the right part of the wall to announce her presence. There were some minor tags, but most of the walls were clear. She picked the outer hall, central wall. One moment of calm and then she depressed the nozzle; the hiss deafening, a million bells ringing in the decay.

'You sure you want to do that?' a deep, male voice said from behind her.

'Who's asking?' Linda wasn't too surprised. She projected her senses but strangely she had little to go on—a man.

'*The* Man.'

'And one sharp muthafucker at that.' Linda turned to face the iron headed ambulance man. His face was surrounded by her sense queries, as if they just didn't have the password to get into his head. 'And why wouldn't I want to do this?' She held the can sideways in her hand, finger still on the nozzle, noticing with wry humour that Spodge was behind him with a raised gun.

'You again?' the man said, directing his voice behind to Spodge.

'How you doing, Spodge?' said Linda. 'Still following?'

'Well you fooking crazy, always in wrong place.'

Linda raised her head to Spodge, noticing the bigger man exiting the Ambulance outside the building.

'Meet Arthur, Arthur Sven,' said Iron Head.

'Stay the fook back, Arthur Sven.'

Arthur Sven stood calmly behind Spodge. Pendulums of weight seemed to hang from his cheeks. He was heavy, like the ambulance.

'We gotta talk,' said Iron Head. His face was ravaged with age, but Linda got the feeling it wasn't an age that people experienced here. The two men were fish out of water, the ambulance their land submarine.

'Don't bother reading us,' said Iron Head. 'We know your kind.'

'Flatter yourself. What do you want?'

'You want to come in the ambulance?'

'Can't say that I do.'

He turned and looked at Arthur Sven. 'Necessary?'

'Not sure,' said Arthur. 'She ain't no Neon, but she sure as hell ain't no angel. You wanna put that gun down?' he asked Spodge.

Linda watched with fascination as Spodge turned to Arthur. They immediately bounced off each other. Between them, concentric circles fell in a myriad of patterns; horizontal, vertical, diagonal, fractals, inside each other and out. It was attraction between two hearts of similar velocity. Neither smiled, but deep down there was immense happiness.

Spodge lowered the gun.

Linda had the two men in her line of vision.

Iron Head jerked his head towards the inside of the building. 'That's not a battle you want to start on your own. We need to talk about Neon. Turns out, he's too much.'

'Hah, that's a surprise.' Linda laughed.

'Not in the way you might think. Albert underestimated him. It's the holes, you see. They're in everyone. Well, most.'

'Holes?'

'Go look in the ambulance.' Iron Head looked to Arthur, who nodded and moved back.

Spodge moved over towards Linda watching both men, gun at the ready. 'You go, Linda, I cover you.'

'What you think, Spodge?'

'I think these men are important, but don't know if I like why.'

Linda sensed that the city was listening closely to what they were saying. She stepped out through the broken building doors and moved towards the ambulance. A smoking manhole cover served warning that there was a vast cavern underneath them.

One of the back ambulance doors was open. The ambulance emitted such a quietness it slowed Linda's thoughts, making her feel normal. She felt the air on her face, sweat drying on her body, her clothes too tight, a stone in her boot and itchy hair. She needed a wash, her jacket was ripped, her jeans filthy. Where had all the home comforts gone, the smell of soap, warm water and food?

A cold tug came from the ambulance. Arthur Sven's face was impassive; no explanation or sympathy. Inside was a child on a bed with an oxygen mask on his face. Somewhere deep inside, a cold drop of water landed on a very intimate part of Linda. Her throat tightened. Eyes rushed forward, but they fell. Image gathering was useless. It was her ears, her nose, her sense of thought that was required. This was a place of missing pieces and this child was missing from someone. Neon.

Linda climbed in, oblivious to anything else. She crouched by the bed and held a small pale hand. The nails were colourless, the hairs on the arm feebly standing up. Arthur Sven stepped in behind her, sat at the top of the bed and placed his hands around the child's head.

'What?' Linda asked, struggling with the presence of the child.

'We hold blacked out memories, try to get them unravelled.'

'Why?'

'It's essential for them to finish their process. Without that, scars of black fester are left hiding in the subways of pity. They seek re-entry into the minds of passersby, igniting only vengeance and horror.'

Linda felt trapped, she thought of Victor. 'Like I helped with Victor, you want me to help Neon?'

'It won't be that easy,' said Iron Head, from the ambulance door.

Spodge stood with him, somehow appeased, her ball bearing eyes steady.

Iron Head got in, and gestured for Spodge to follow him. 'It's better in here, no one hears.'

Spodge clambered up, gun out of sight. She moved to the back, watching Arthur Sven who was watching her.

Iron Head sat on the bed opposite the child and Linda remained crouched on the floor.

'Victor,' began Iron Head, 'was willing. Victor is open, inclusive. Neon, he cuts through, slices, shatters, there is no

243

other part of him; nothing gets left behind. It's impressive, it's incisive, but when nothing gets left behind, there's no you, no me and none of this guy.' He pointed to the kid. 'We can't deal with people like Neon. There is no point of entry, no doubt, no hesitation. He lives tomorrow, and that really pisses off today.'

Linda thought of the hulking mass in the building outside.

'What happened to Neon?'

'What happened to him? Arthur?'

Arthur shook his head. 'What makes anyone step beyond themselves? One essential sliver pulled from inside, a heart mutilated by life's twisted fate.' A bead of smoke puffed out of his eyes, rising towards the ceiling in a column.

Linda followed the white tendril. On the ceiling was a circular cloud of white and dark gray clouds, like a mock-up of a storm. There was an eye in the middle and flashes behind. Linda found herself robbed of her extra sensory abilities and realised she was paralysed. Fear ignited deep inside her but her aversion was pulled into the storm. Sound became distorted, the air so heavy it sucked in sounds, even the light was sluggish. Everything slowed down, time itself elongating apart. Her body struggled, veins and heart trying to adjust to the new conditions. She realised that the flashes in the clouds were millions of arms and legs flaying and kicking. The clouds were made up of squeezed air that escaped when scared little hands clenched into fists. The child's hand that she was holding, squeezed hers. She rose through the darkest clouds and out into a cold autumnal day. A house, an art nouveau spire top, and a man whose back was familiar, so familiar. A woman shouted at him from the doorstep, a beautiful woman, strong cheekbones, sharp mouth and a face of stern anger and resentment. The man turned around—it was Victor's father—and walked away. The woman went back into the house. Inside, gleaming, dark polished wood floors, cold, exquisite metal sculptures, paintings hung all the way up the open stairs, faces, bodies, twisted, tugged, graphically conjured, sharp aesthetic bohemian figures painted on doors, staring and daring. A multicoloured light shone through stained glass windows, beaming colour that lit up the tears on the woman's face.

'Karl?'

A small boy came down the stairs, perhaps seven. Neon. Happy face, open and bright, tumble down hair and clothes covered in paint.

'Karl, I'm sorry.' She knelt down to him, placed a gloved hand on his cheek.

The child looked at her, bright blue eyes probing.

'That man was your father. Father almighty... aren't they all. Karl, no one should be a performing monkey in a cage for anyone, no matter how talented. Never listen, my son. Be the one that breaks them all. Be free, and hopefully one day your pain will subside and in the clearing you will see more than has ever been seen. My beautiful son, in life there are holes, we step into them and then one day we step out again. I love you.' And she turned, pushing open a door to a beamed living room, walked to the centre, stepped onto a chair, placed a noose around her neck and dropped off.

The child screamed.

Linda screamed as blackness swooped over her towards the child.

245

'Linda. Linda.' Spodge's voice came out of the darkness.

'Oh my god. Did you see it?'

'I felt it.'

'What on earth? What are these people doing, why? What the fuck?'

Iron Head sighed. 'Albert was Neon's father. He put Neon in place as he later put Victor in place. But Margaret, Neon's mother.' He blew out. 'She outflanked Albert, she outflanked him with her own death.'

'Why is it so important? These are fucking children.'

'They are playing a higher game than us. A different world, a different way. They know what they are doing, they make decisions, they make impacts, smarting, outsmarting, creating cycles of life that are extraordinary, but terrifying. We knew Albert planned ahead, but this threw us. This throws everything into question... and then Neon...'

'How will he understand that?'

Even Spodge looked shocked.

'What do you expect me to do with this?' said Linda.

'Well, you got Victor Scram and Neon, that's a lot of stuff. But you're Linda Kalom, that's a lot of stuff on its own. We won't deny we thought you were going to impede. But this is all beyond what we knew. Albert played everyone. All hail his genius, but Neon plays faster still, and you, you play like nothing we ever saw.'

'And Victor?'

'Victor, he lets you two do what you do. Without Victor there's nothing. The city would have eaten all of you long ago.'

'What are you gonna do?'

'We'll keep going, keep gathering,' said Iron Head. 'There isn't much time left.'

Linda felt they were talking about her.

Linda and Spodge watched the ambulance trundle off down the street.

'Holy shit. You gonna tell Neon?'

'I don't really know, Spodge. It can't even be that straightforward, can it? What the hell was wrong with Albert? And Neon's mother? I'm almost impressed, but I'm scared, I'm shocked. I didn't even know lives were lived like that. Cold, brilliant, even fucking exciting.'

'I think Albert was sick, crazed in the mind.'

'Shit, wasn't the world a simpler place a couple of weeks ago? Do we really need to do this? I'm afraid I might never sleep again, never think straight. That I have to go into the darkest hole on my own. It's just too much.'

Spodge placed her hand on Linda's shoulder. 'You don't have to go anywhere alone.'

Spodge's eyes were ball bearings rolling with perfect steady momentum. They said *I go with you, all of me, without hesitation.*

'Thanks, Spodge.'

'You're the one, Linda. You're the only one who can make this okay. Neon cuts through, but he won't cut through you.'

The road streaked beneath them as Spodge expertly weaved the motorcycle through the dusky streets. Linda leaned on Spodge's back, letting her mind drift away from the rushing images. Victor and Neon... time and logic were running out—theirs and hers—if she was going to catch them, she was going to have to die a hell of a lot faster.

Her bee droned inside. The bee wasn't about questions, it was about one flower at a time. For a moment there was an incredible silence—the sacred prayer of a bee. Passing buildings swayed and shimmered, their strict architectural shapes bending and forming into giant urban flowers. First the dahlia, deep crimson flows of brain petals pouring out knowledge and wisdom, her bee dropped within, selecting and inspiring; then moving onto the fennel plant, outer space telegraphs of yellow comets shooting out of her soul; to the fanfare of angelica, feeding into the encryption and entanglement of life symbolism, a touch of the hilarity and abundance of the snapdragon and the whole bouquet mixed in the harsh cathedral of the foxglove. At the end of the row loomed a majestic, but wilting, sunflower.

They had reached Central Train Station.

Spodge skidded to a halt near the main entrance and they stepped off, dwarfed by huge Romanesque pillars. The pillars were covered with graffiti—hastily drawn skulls, numbers, names, dates and times—like someone had documented the day progress got disconnected.

Linda went in, trying to ignore the musty smell of piss and fabric rot. Greasy pillars showed where bodies had pushed past, but all were gone now and the beige marble ticket hall was like an ancient tomb.

Neon's presence cut through the walls, the very atmosphere

dissected by his movement. He was sick and wounded, but viral and effective.

Linda strode through the ticket hall armed with all the person she was. Her mind map projected out in front of her in clear blue digitals as she moved. She was goddess, sick herself, and that was how she was going to reach him. She would leave it all behind, every separation of herself from the instant of moment.

Spodge was nowhere to be seen, but that was okay, she would be doing what was needed. Linda reached the arched entrance to the main hall. As her eyes adjusted she saw a vast empty concourse—dusty marble floor with stained ivory pillars curving up into an immense chest cavity. Neon was in the middle, running around and gesturing to the ceiling. He looked like he was dancing, but Linda knew otherwise. She dropped her life away as she walked, every step another death and correspondingly new spectrums appeared before her. Neon was working with the elements of environment, plucking chemicals out of the air. She could see he was angry and frustrated. He kept reaching up again and again, throwing down formulas, then grimacing and starting again.

He ignored her. Completely.

She moved around what was laid out on the ground. It was like an alchemical junk yard—twisted metal mutations with slimy concoctions dripping from them.

'Neon?'

'What?' He didn't stop nor look around.

'What you doing there, sweetie?'

Neon stopped. 'What?'

Linda smiled. Between them snakes of union hissed across the rubble-scattered floor. In trenches, soldiers gathered — warfare, ceasefire, peacetime, warfare and then stalemate. Each of their dead things nodding their heads.

'Why the concoctions?'

Neon's eyes dripped with the same acids as his creations, tears from conclusions that didn't satisfy.

This was not the Neon Linda knew. This was a man looking ahead and finding it occupied.

'Who have you seen? Why is there a gap in your head?' he said.

'Why is your head tied in knots?'

'It's not, they're not mine, they're not my fucking knots.'

'Whose are they?'

'Fucking Albert. He played us all. Expected, so fucking expected. Who the fuck was that man?' Neon shook his head, trashing his hands around.

Linda swallowed hard. 'Well...'

'I see, know something do we? Outsmarted the Neon, eh?'

'It's not a game.'

'Oh but it is, isn't it? You've come with knowledge, secret pieces, I don't see them and you know what, *I* don't fucking care.'

'What if it's something important to you?'

'The I, the you, put it together, you're left with another. Someone else, I'm not interested.'

'Look, I found out —'

'Don't say anything. You found out something and you want me to bend towards you, to lend an ear. Gonna put a

250

piece back in, are you?'

'Why are you so hateful?'

'I'm not. There is no I, there is this, nothing else.'

'Yeah, but there are reasons.'

'Reasons, oh reason, reason me fucking blue, reason this fucking head.' He grabbed his hair, eyes flashing. 'Reason to be fucking bothered with reasons and words and shite. There's not a reason on this fucking planet that will step in my way.'

'Listen.'

'No. Talk to me like you are fucking here, Linda. Go on, just try it.'

'Damn you, Neon.' A tender part of Linda exploded out, blasting against the sides of the vast hall. She tasted the icy water that dripped down the walls, tarnished as it slid across dirty bricks. Tarnished by fucking association, her too.

'Last step, Linda.'

'Last step? Bullshit, Neon. I don't step *from* you and I don't step *because* of you.'

'Course you don't. What would be the point in that? Isolation, Linda. The tribunal of the soul. You're alone with the stinging accusation of self, flattered by thought, plumped by understanding and waiting for the crucifixion.'

'Crucifixion?'

'CRUX OF FICTION.'

'I'm not interested. You're playing games.' In a click, Linda moved outside herself, cruising on the feelers of her senses. The molecular makeup of her nervous system spilled out into the room. Neon's words merged into her cells, changing her makeup, connecting her to the environment. She let it happen, didn't respond or react. But this was her environment too.

She walked to a section of wall—Neon muttering and dancing to himself behind her—and let herself flow out with the paint from her spray cans. Layers and layers of self appeared; external features, but deeply inlaid in each was the map of her inner system, her codified response to stimuli, all the secrets of her single person. She mapped the environment feeds—air moisture, floor vibrations and listened to the song of the vaulted ceiling.

She saw how many strings were attached to Neon. How *he* was manipulating the environment around him. Everything he did, every thought, movement, gesture, breath, even his drops of sweat, fell in pre-destined places to have an effect.

She began dismantling the picture she had drawn, separating the pieces in her head and shattering the mosaic. Another picture instantly appeared beside her in the next columned square. *She* had created *another*. With her death mask firmly in place and her bee working overtime, Linda began to place parts of herself around the building; two, four, eight, the paintings flashed onto walls. She was able to watch from every angle, crawling around the upper floors of the building and amplifying her presence. One face became twenty, she became her creation and her creations became unhinged.

She walked out into the ticket hall. To her left was the ticket counter. She slid her hands across the cold beige marble. It demanded its role—stern, immovable and traditional. She got onto the counter, crawling on her hands and knees, she was inflamed, wanton, bastardised as person, ripped from the sky and stuffed into a hungry body. Her limbs seized the opportunity; muscles, sinews and nerve endings pushing, burning, relishing the reckless power coursing through them. She knelt, body spasming, hands locked in mock prayer.

'New destination please...'

Tills gaped with open mouths and smashed screens stared like empty eye sockets. Blue digital readouts appeared, sparkling against the ancient walls. There were street names— West Lafayette, Shelley, East and Black. Her mind waited in those streets. The street names appeared in a circular pattern, but in an outer circle were her mother, brother, her home town, and in another layer, the Neon appeared, again and again, layers and layers of the name, Neon. Different aspects coloured each name—his hair, his heart, his feet, and underneath these, his teeth, his gums, and further; his eyes, his retina, eyeball tendon, she sailed in on an eyelash, irritating him, making him rub his eye, pushing further into the sea of tears. And who are *you*, Dr Neon, Karl Long prior to the demented infusion?

'Fuck off!' Neon shouted from the main hall.

Linda shook her head, leapt of the counter and stormed in. The inner hall was bathed in a golden glow.

'What are you doing?' demanded Neon.

Linda felt her hands extend and her shoulders drop back. She felt aggression stream all over her body, tingling and banging on extremity ends. Her feet gripped the ground like octopi, her hands wanted to grab somebody, one body, him, Neon. Her eyelids drooped, her mouth sneered, eyebrows perched, jaw clenched. Neon stood, likewise positioned, one shoulder thrust forward, legs spread apart. There was a thousand drums playing, crackles in the spasmodic electricity

253

between them. Linda clenched her bottom teeth against her top ones, her tongue pushing hard like a limb, her eyes began to water—sweat, mascara, tears dripped as her temples throbbed.

She had his attention now, a thousand locks with a thousand keys. And she saw him twitch in the extremities of ultra violet; aggression and arousal desorbing from his controlled mental state. She moved to the left, he to the right. Giant paintbrushes shot through the air like spears, but they fell harmlessly to the ground in front of her.

'How archaic,' said Linda.

Neon's face twisted, contorted like it was transforming itself; melting and reforming.

Linda felt herself pulled forward, pulled right up to his face and pushed against his flesh. She read his sweat and instantaneous panic blisters erupted inside her eyes. She felt his teeth against hers, kissing but more, mingling, pulling her teeth out, mixing them up, deforming, reforming and placing his teeth in amongst hers. They bit together, saliva spreading like butter over her neck as he tore at her flesh. Linda threw herself to the side, Neon moved with a speed that wasn't human. Linda felt a pain in her spine like her spinal fluid was boiling, she moved herself further, separated her personalities, standing behind Neon, to the side of him.

Neon threw his head back and laughed. 'What is it with you, you just keep fucking moving. I just don't get that.'

Linda saw his face, for that moment, human, a friendly smile playing on his lips that softened his face, his nose slightly rounded, cheeks inflated with the freshness of youth. That young child.

'You impress me, Linda.'

'Stop what you are doing.'

'Stop?' Neon shook his head. 'What is stop? I don't know what you mean. Nothing stops. I don't...' He gestured around the building like it was a beautiful sweeping landscape. 'It grows, it continues. Like the matador's bull, it knows no other way. We are seized, you more than me. But that ain't where it's gonna stop.' Neon had a grin that seemed to shoot off his face, a string from inner to outer. He walked over to her.

Linda thought of the storm in the *Ambulance of Unforgiven Screams*.

'What? What is that?' asked Neon. 'That thing you just did?'

'I didn't do anything.' Linda felt tense, secretive.

'You did.' Neon touched her cheek.

It was the soft touch that Linda remembered from the studio, it surprised her again. He was tight, his body sinewy, his eyes ablaze with mania, but part of him cared, cared about her flesh and feelings. She placed her hand on his neck, felt his carotid pulse. It was a rhythm, part musical, part primal heartbeat.

'Come, my world is yours. Let us travel together,' he said.

'You don't even know...' Linda saw the roof of the vast chamber light up with constellations in blue digital readout. New stars from star systems she did not know.

Neon looked up. 'Remember when I first met you and I said, what happens when the stars reach the viewer who stares at them too long?'

'Yeah.'

'Let's find out.'

God of the City

18

Neon surveyed the ceiling with wonder. Linda was connecting things he never would. There was something in what she was doing, something more than the smoothness of her moves, more than the curves of her mind, that made him want her. It was flow and it was now. She had more genetic peak than anyone he had ever met. He didn't even think he could paint her, she seduced all his parts. She drew his suggestion before he could even reach for a paintbrush. *Help me*, part of him wanted to say, *please help me do this...* but another part warned him, suggested that he should kill her, take her out of the picture.

'*Neon 23?*'

'*Yes, sir?*'

'*What the hell is happening?*'

'*We like this.*'

'*Well, stop fucking liking and start analysing.*'

'*Of course, well you opened there, you became a person and she laid her electric map on top of yours and that was one hell of a fucking match and then as you manipulated the map, she moved in tandem with you and you merged like a mutation, interestingly because of the match with desire and genetic realignment, it went cellular immediately. You are changed irrevocably, as is she.*'

'*Bullshit,*' said Neon.

'No, it's true.'

'I know it is true, the point is, it's distraction. We must stay separate to hit full tilt.'

'Yes, but—'

'Are you weak, 23? Are you looking to pass the job onto another?'

'Due respect, sir, there ain't many of us left. I mean, we're all dying here. You too.'

Linda's face. A face he saw reflected everywhere, on the walls, in his head, a multiple representation of persuasion. He could see a mesh over her features and if he concentrated, he could move into a tiny square, even smaller than a skin pore, they made cells look like cities. There was no one more perfect for the job.

The air cracked. Something was moving that shouldn't be, a grinding of two stones being forced across each other. After the stellar vision of Linda, this was low down, brutal.

'23? What have we got?'

'It's like the city has gotten up and started walking.'

'Am I disturbing?' Victor said.

'And it's talking.'

Neon swung around. 'Victor Scram, if it isn't the living breathing... where the fuck you been?'

'Being doing a little bit of that thinking, Neon.'

'That little thing, yes, that I know. I know it well.' Neon walked over. 'Work out who you are?'

'God of the fucking city, some might say.'

'Yes you are, and a liar, corrupter, manipulator.'

'*Me?*'

'Genetically so. Still touchy about your father?'

'Makes you nervous, does he?'

'Just wanna know where you lie.'

'Don't like the man. In fact, I think he's funny and small. A little man with big plans.'

'Set us all off though, didn't he?' said Neon.

'That he did. But hey, you don't do what you're told and I don't do what I'm told and Linda, no one is gonna even start on her. So you know what, Neon, I'm sorry. I, Victor Scram, am sorry. I got a little cross, you know.'

'Yeah, you did get cross there, Victor, and you went and burnt that building, the old Halifax Stadium.'

'You saw that.'

'Oh yeah, clinical urbanology. I was very impressed. For one of those old fashioned guys, you developing some new licks.'

'Well, before you destroy everything. I'm gonna get some.'

'It ain't me, she's the dangerous one.'

'Nice of you to say. Hey, Victor. What took you so long?'

'Been checking the perimeter, huge Bug activity out there.'

Neon looked to the north wall where tunnels led down to the train platforms. He sniffed the air. There was a strong musty, copper smell coming out.

He resisted the urge to race over.

'Forgot to say, got this for you,' said Linda, waving a small cloth at Neon.

The unmistakeable sprinkling of ink blots on a square of cloth—Albert's work.

'But I guess you already saw it at the Diner.'

Neon came over, wary as to how he would be expected to

react. 'Nothing would be happening without a reason.' Neon kept his thoughts to the periphery.

'Neon 23, what have we got here? I need someone to go into Albert's equation, and I'm not risking it.'

'Neon 12, sir. Ready for the job.'

'Right, get in. I want information, but do not return to my head. I do not want his fucking programming going on. Remain outside and find a way.'

Neon watched Linda. He could see her nostrils flaring and accessing information, but her eyes were on him. Superb shades of brown and green, scattered with the casual blend of nature's ingenious bouquet. Charm, she oozed it. The thought of isolating himself with just one person turned him on more than he could have ever imagined.

'Why not?' said 23.

'Quiet.'

Linda stretched out Albert's fabric. 'What is it then?'

'It's caution. Albert was a master of display and distraction.' Neon felt like burning the cloth. Stopping it right here.

A hollow rumble came from the train tracks. They all looked at each other.

Neon smelt information. It was Neon 12 laying out a communication. The odour of stewed carrots to begin with, over to fries, then taking a trip down to tequila, and finally down to coffee. Neon nodded, inhaling the warm biscuit of coconut, then the stale fibres of a downtown rug in a destitute block. The fibre in the rug let air molecules settle, conserve their energy, consolidate, then sprung them out the window and down to a overgrown lot filled with discarded cars and their remnants, a biography of human secretions were spread over misshapen concrete lumps, broken bricks, glass, rusted metal and dried out grass. Neon kept the information at the point where it connected to the mind. At that point, there was a highway junction where mental thoughts and nervous system reactions met. He delicately threaded the smells under his reaction network. Placed them on the thymus table that had been disconnected from the mainframe. He shuffled the smells, the order was not the important piece of information. The experience of each of them produced a reaction, these reactions were transformed into colours by the optical segment. As the wind of thought travelled over the colour surface, a tune was created.

'Shit. That's pure Albert there, 23. A complete retelling of the human experience.'

'It's not any human experience, sir, it's ours.'

'Yes, it is, but it's slightly wrong, Mr fucking mimic ain't got the right key to enter our lock. Fucking obsessed madman.'

'And we are?'

'Oh we're obsessed alright. But, and this may shock you, 23.'

'Ok.'

'We're more human.'

'Even though we may obliterate everything human?'

'Now, 23, that's a little strong, we seek only the sparkling lights, the neon, the new, that is all. We don't dictate, we capture, we don't steal, impose, nor corrupt, we evoke.'

'Yet we need what he has done.'

'Well, he has done what he has done. And in the scheme, in the quantum floral, it matches what we do. But he never had the fucking *imagination, 23. He really didn't. To mimic is one thing, yet it differs greatly from the capture, from the true, the evocation...'*

'We're hearing the melancholia there, sir.'

'Well, it's true, isn't it? At the peak of exhilaration is always annihilation.'

'I hear that sir, but if that tune was ours, look at what is coming for Victor.'

'Well, well, well, the whole of the city feed network stolen from the master.'

A red human shaped figure emerged from one of the tunnels to the platforms. It seemed to be made up of thousands of lines and it stank of damp copper.

'What the fuck.' Victor hooked his gun out.

Linda stared, eyes widening.

Neon moved over a bit closer, knocking his pointless sculptures out of the way as he moved. The figure stood in the entranceway about thirty feet away. A long whistling sound came out of the figure.

'What the fuck is that?' asked Victor.

'Ask your father.' Neon stood still.

'He's dead.'

'Ask your father.' Neon gestured towards the figure.

'You are shitting me.'

'That's not a person,' said Linda.

'No, but it's what informs one. The ultimate environment feed. It's all there, Victor. Everything you have been prepared for. You're the reverse of the environment feed process. You, Victor, fucking, Scram, seriously, did your father have any fucking idea!'

Linda laughed. 'God of the City.'

'Maybe I'll say no.'

'Yes,' said Neon. 'And you could, but the Bugs will jump into the seat. And of course, don't doubt that they're not waiting outside to fight for it.'

'Now that I'll enjoy. It's the expectation that rankles, and Emily.'

'Tell me about it. I don't think Albert counted on humanity, I don't think he knew what it meant for Emily to die. He could second guess human existence, but understand why you would put flowers on a grave, something else entirely.'

Victor clapped Neon on the shoulder and headed over towards the figure.

Linda stood stark still.

She was a million pieces of person swarming over Neon's innards, taking hold of all he had forgotten to hide. She poured into his eyes. Gripping him in a way he couldn't but like.

'It's time we started to work,' she said.

'Thought you'd never ask.'

With Victor on one side and Linda on the other they exited Central Station and headed down to Spodge who stood on the scorched lawn outside with the other Kage. Below, on the concrete walkway, was *the Army,* Victor's rag-tag collection of street gangs. Neon liked the modernity of the Black Street Chuggers. Their faceless leadership was a perfect foil to the Bugs.

There was an urge within himself to return to the studio. Some part wanting to retreat and hide.

'Neon 23, do we have any memories left?'

'No sir, everything is gone now. Thing with memories though, they seem to really engrain themselves, seal themselves in sinuous slumber.'

'Nice. Check again. We don't want any hesitations.'

'Yes, sir.'

Neon turned to Central Station, taking in the punctured windows. He thought of what became of glass when it was broken, how dangerous it became. Was that him?

Spodge was watching.

Neon nodded at her. Her approach took no prisoners either, but perhaps she made less mistakes.

She looked away quickly.

Neon went over. 'Spodge?' She had a black hole in her head.

'Neon.'

'Who you been seeing?' Fuck, it annoyed him. The roof was taken off the world, but some fucker had put a lead box in there. Neon laughed. 'Been in an ambulance, Spodge.'

'Don't know what you saying.'

Neon saw the tenderness of her bronzed skin. Saw her as a real person—hurtable. 'Well I guess I know where your loyalty lies then.'

'Don't do that.'

'Don't do what?'

'You fooking know.'

'What you been told?'

Spodge gave a reluctant smile. The little girl inside her pleased at being found out.

Feelings washed out of him without his consideration.

263

'Don't worry, Spodge.' He put his arm around her and hugged her into his chest. He felt her lighten and fall against him like a giant teardrop.

Neon took a deep breath. There wasn't much moisture in the air. The city was drying out. They—the gangs before him with their movements and words—were the only lubrication. These were the brave people—ones who took care of their thoughts. He kissed the top of Spodge's head, let her go and headed back towards Central Station.

In the foliage underneath the windows, rattlesnakes shook their maracas, thousands of them. He disregarded them, stepping straight into the bushes. Spiders crawled all over his legs, pulling him downwards. Fear was trying to gain control. He laughed, it would take a fucking sadder day than this to stop him. He flared up his cans—purples, blues, and the red. The colours grew, creating an effigy of vibration and getting Linda's attention. He could feel her breath on his neck from forty yards. Then she was beside him, her feet in a swamp crawling with leeches. She cared not. She began to paint, not with him, but she wasn't going to be left out.

Behind, the gangs began to stir. Inside, the Mantis started to openly prowl.

'Neon 23, what's our situation?'

'Well, let's see, we're nearly all dead and the Mantis is one mean muthafucker.'

'That's okay, have no fear, just pluck the fucking juice from it and carry on regardless.'

'We got issues here.'

'Yeah?'

'There is only six of us left, 13, 178, 26, 165, 54 and me. Can you feel death?'

'Yes, it's a chamber, and when you enter you are left outside.'

'One last request?'

'Of course.'

'Let us get to Linda?'

'Easy on that, 23.'

Linda was laying down colours like she was tearing strips off the building. Her hair hung in front of her face like fallen trees in an ancient rainforest, sheltering and creating new biospheres. It took him back to the jungle, to where it all started.

'Neon?'

Victor's voice pulled Neon out of his reverie.

'What about this?'

Neon turned around.

The street was swarming with Soul Bugs, hundreds of them advancing in a military formation.

'Welcome to godhood.'

He pushed Linda's hand—got a glare—and walked over to Victor. 'Okay then, now we're getting started.' Neon's hands felt good, just itching to lay out some Bug. 'Linda?' he looked across at her as she sauntered over. 'Shall we begin a master class?'

'Sure.'

'Tommy?' Neon shouted over to Tommy Bones who was gesturing at Johnny and Spodge. 'How's those moves going?'

'Well now, Doctor...' Tommy came over, fresh and glistening like a morning spew. 'So, here's the situation, man. So we was twisting and listening, like in the mainframe where sound wave machines cascade. Super charged, with the scre-scre-scream and we heard the gong of wrong.' Tommy made frenzied movements with his arms.

'Johnny!' Victor shouted.

'Course, man.' Johnny trundled over.

'What the fuck?'

'Well, see, it's implication.'

'Yeah?' said Neon. 'And the implication is?'

'Well...' Johnny looked around. 'You nothing new, man.'

Victor stepped in. 'What?'

'You gotta hear it, Scram, man. I mean in the ultimate interface, and it seems almost wrong, but the Neon is nothing new. Impressive, but...'

Neon felt irritation spike inside. He ignored it, for now. 'It's true,' he said. 'Now, don't be angry, cos really, I ain't got that much fucking time. So spit out the thinking, young Kage kids.'

'Now don't be talking down to us, man.' said Johnny. 'Cos, we seen the walls and we seen what falls, and we seen wheels turning, and buildings burning and fires that join fires, and wires that melt and become irrelevant, but you didn't make this happen.'

'I see, so I'm accused of not causing everything.'

'We looked to you, man,' said Tommy.

'Doing a bit of fucking looking, were you?'

'Easy,' said Linda. 'They're kids.'

'Yes, but not just kids, they're not little kindergarteners mimicking their abc and 1, 2 fucking 3. These little pharma-cultural investigators have left the confines, have charted the rusty rain and become distracted. You can't investigate the unimaginable.'

'You're not making sense. You're going fucking loopy and there is a swarming army of Bugs over there. Look. This is not the time,' said Linda.

The Bugs were about a hundred yards away and the conflict was getting them excited.

'You're right. She *is* right, Tommy. You picked *this* moment, when I had picked *my* moment and now we're all stuck here at the intercourse, fucking with time.'

'Yeah, man, but it don't compute.'

'It don't compute, course, it don't compute. You want me to conjure, you want me to be a magician? Creative perhaps? You think I get the fucking opportunity, do you? Think I get the luxury?'

'Easy, Neon.'

'No, there is no fucking easy, Victor. Easy to fit in, to slide down worn roads. But no, be the Neon for a moment. See the world, and see it again, and see it one more fucking time, see it till your eyes burn black holes through your head. See it until every insight is tortured out of the thoughts. Awww, you realised that I don't create for you. Your little fucking heads did a fucking recognition. Nothing, Kage, nothing of any fucking importance. What the hell are you doing on this side of the road? Get lost, but don't go away. Don't be those curly brained sheep. In your narcotic famed interiors, don't be looking, don't see.'

'I don't know what you're saying.' Johnny looked troubled.

Tommy Bones was pacing like he needed a piss.

'You can do, but do alone. Not tethered with question, not with consideration. Be the frazzled, inflamed little heads that you are, but go into that fireless night, where singular thoughts hide and independent events dictate. Do not look at me. I see with eyes of death and no other viewing is required. You're the creators. You made that Bug Box.'

'And why did they freak you out, man?'

'*Why?* What's inside the box, Johnny?'

'It's stuff, man.'

'What's inside the box, Johnny?'

'Don't be fucking, man!'

'Johnny?' said Tommy Bones. 'What the box, man?'

Everyone stared.

'Nothing.'

'What?'

'Nothing.'

'Neon, stop.'

'Open it, open that box.'

Johnny cowered, looking crestfallen.

'Leave him, Neon.' said Linda.

'No,' said Neon. 'You don't understand. This is the essence, the ultimate in mastery.'

Johnny raised his head slightly.

'Lift your head, Johnny. You lift your head. You wanna know what killed me about your box?'

'Yeah?'

'The fucking knife edge of doing something new. That hesitant fracture from nothing to never before. What *is* in the box?'

Johnny opened the box. Linda, Tommy, Spodge, the Chuggers and Victor gathered around. Inside was a small computer fan, some crumpled bits of paper, half a brick, a luminous green joint and some hair. Nothing was connected to the lid and its flashing lights.

'Johnny?' said Tommy. 'Shatters on the insight, man.'

'No!' said Neon. 'Do not fear or defame, do not judge these things. For here' — he pushed everyone aside and stood by Johnny — 'is the new mind. To place innocuous objects in a box, who would have thought it? More important, who the fuck would have done it? Put something anywhere, put a peanut in the road, put a plastic cowboy on the moon. Who would dare do that, a madman, a fool, perhaps a genius? No one need know anything. I mean these Kage kids, they're free from all this fucking knowing, they're discarded in the undergrowth, re-emerging with the ultimate nothing.'

'The exact nought-etude, that's beautiful, man,' said Tommy. 'Cream of the stellar blue.'

'Too fucking right, Tommy. The naught is sought after. You look at them.'

They all turned and stared at the mass of Soul Bugs, teeming, gleaming, twitching and squealing.

'They want the nothing, they seek it, they seek to turn and fill it, poisoning the pockets of the mind's night.'

Spodge walked over. 'Hey Neon, can you talk a little fooking faster? We got serious fooking problem heading up here.'

'You know what the Neon speaks, Spodge?' said Tommy.

'*Know* ? Course I fooking know. Out of the inky darkness we came, and at the end, we fooking go back in. While we are here, we ignore it. It calls to us, but most refuse to hear it. Some hear it by accident, they are pulled apart, broken on the wheel, others seek it, aggravate and abuse it. But this man.' She pointed at Neon. 'He plays tunes on strings of the stuff. You don't think. You just need to be and then listen to that.' She pointed to her heart.

Yeah, she knows, thought Neon. That one knows it all.

Spodge put her hand on Johnny's shoulder. He stopped frowning. They stood, face to face. Neon watched with admiration. She was tuning him in, fixing his frequency.

Tommy raised his eyes to Neon. 'So who are you?'

'I'm a poet, a rascal, an adventurer. I'm in the right place, knowing where it will occur and watching. I'm aware of occurrence. I stand and play as events unfold, I have exquisite timing, that's all. You're the changers. I have done nothing. All slight of eye.'

Neon felt a swell in his chest, like he had just picked up a web connection to everyone. He saw the gang stringing out like feelers, absorbing the information of the advancing disease. Linda stood on his right, Victor behind him. 'You take this on, Victor?' But as Neon turned, he realised that the connection was only passing through him. It came from Victor.

'All hail the God of the City!'

'Anything left to be godly over?'

Neon walked off with Linda.

'You said that all gods had to die?'

'I didn't say that.'

'Well, you thought it.'

'That I did. But that is only our gods. Victor's gonna outlive all of them, us included.' They headed away from the warring din, over to West Street, cut down West Lafayette and arrived on Shelley Street. Everyone had retreated and the streets had the feel of a ghost town.

'About earlier,' said Linda.

'Yeah, I didn't see that.' They stared but neither entered beyond the eyes. It was like they had merged on another level, two sides of one brain.

'Stay here,' said Linda

'There is no here, it's all gone, we're just trailing through the wake.'

Neon looked at her shawl. He hadn't noticed it before; shiny, black lace fabric, with small bells hung around it. Now that he noticed, he could hear a slight tinkling. Wool, lace and underneath, flesh; the soft adventure. For a moment, Linda was a woman. Just a woman. A beautiful fugitive. Her eyes promised boldness. They expanded consciousness, stripped him naked and terrorised every part of him.

'Stop that,' he said. 'The city trembles with fear.'

'You're resisting.'

'I'm not. I. Am. Not. Now come on, if we don't get stirring, we're never gonna get the keys to the fucking kingdom.'

The Battle

The Battle

19

On the street below, the Bugs were organised into relevant groups—pinchers, stingers, grabbers, crushers, burrowers, projectors, and the brutes. Victor's motley collection of fighters were less organised—sluggers, shooters, blades, techno heads and bat wielders—intense, impatient, and most definitely, insane. In the oily Bug pheromone laced air, the fighters' faces were draining of colour and voices were cracked and minimal.

'You okay, Tommy?'

Tommy was fidgeting more than usual. 'It's hard to take on the Neon, man.' His lower jaw twitched.

'The man is maniac, Tommy. That's what he has to be. No other reason.'

'You're big, Scram, man. You gonna turn out to be something else?'

'You don't get let down by me, yeah? You get that? We stand shoulder to shoulder, Tommy, man by man.' Victor pointed to the Bugs below. 'You wanna let those fuckers take our city?'

'No, man.'

'When you think of it, we couldn't be anything other than the people we are, Tommy.'

Tommy nodded. 'Sure.'

'You know I've seen kids spraying the name of the Kage.

They hear what you say, Tommy. Shit, they possibly even understand you.'

Tommy's head rose, shoulders dropping down. He was nodding hard, his whole body starting to move. 'You wanna scale this, man?' He held out the luminous green joint to Victor. 'Called the Scram-daliser, Johnny build it in special honour you, man.'

Victor took the joint. The smoke coming off it went through a rainbow of colours at the heat and then turned racing green as it drifted out. Victor flipped his gun out and, holding it by the barrel, offered it to Tommy. 'You take this, Tommy.'

'The gun, man?' Tommy nodded with a grin. 'But, what you?'

'Nah, you take it. It's good on the close encounters. Think this one is gonna be something else for me.'

Tommy smiled wide and started waving the gun around.

Victor took a drag on the joint and electric water shot around his head. Every compartment of his brain took a piece, drank it and passed it on.

Holy shit.

In the centre of his head was the red, copper smelling figure created by his father in the train station. What his father had committed murder for; there was no other word for it, suicide was passive, his father's death was active.

'I am the person, of the person, that you want to be,' said the creation.

'Are you now?'

The smell of copper pulled up the memory of blood streaming down the railway tracks. It was horror, but more—

timing. His father didn't live a life so exactly, so grotesquely, in order just to throw himself randomly in front of a train. The memory played and Victor watched, but he didn't look at the obvious, he smelt the air, he touched the tracks, listened to the hiss, crackle and screech. All that surrounded the moment, all that informed, fed, directed and expected—but at the moment before impact it all stopped, ever so briefly.

Bang! Wrong man on the tracks.

The city did a double take. In the looking between in front and behind, the city got fascinated by its own immense feed system. It gazed just a millisecond too long... all the while, blood streaked down the rail tracks—breaking triggers and reversing the dictator's caress.

Now the blood had returned as a sculpture, millions of information gathering journeys around the city, layered into *the person, of the person, that he wanted to be*.

He was tempted to say *fuck off*, but the creation knew him well. The rhythmic twists and turns of the D-train were already clacking in his head; stations, streets, alleys, buildings and people shot by—all waiting, all hungry. *He* was the D-train transgressor, the one who could move over tracks mid-ride, wean truth from oily city sleepers, bang with the death heads in greasy girder wastelands, hunt on the night rails of insurrection and persuasion and sink shots with devils and romancers of plenty. All the while, doling out one word, *Scram*, that castle amidst the rot 'n trash.

The creation began to break apart into individual dots. Each dot infinite, isolated and complete. Information plugs tar-coated his mind, sky scrapers erected in his mouth, spiking his thoughts up into the heights. His eyes were pulled like a canopy across the sky above the city. And then it all exploded — intense equations scrabbling around, biting his insides, eating him, completing him, leaving him behind. He was everything and nothing. One big monster, one bad mutha.

'Fuck, Scram, man. We got Bugs,' said Tommy.

Victor felt his eye sockets suck back in, jaws snap, teeth pull together with steel cables. His hands became iron fists, arm muscles tearing and ripping hard against resistance. 'HEY!'

The collective looked up. Faces turning away from inner contemplation.

Victor leapt up to where a statue had been toppled.

'Before you, there.' He pointed down at the Bugs. 'There you see the Soul Bug, the haters, the plague. Today, the city is for the taking. They think they deserve it. They, the humble servants of dictate and instruction, want to be the new controllers. Do we sit and wait? Do we turn our heads and hope they go away? No. We make a stand, a stand beyond person. I stand for nothing alone, you stand for nothing, but together, together, we become a hammer to break the chains of slavery. This is the powerful time, a time when what you do might fucking matter. Inside each of you there burns a fire. A fire that does not want to die. That does not want to lie down and listen to instruction. So let's fucking burn. Come fight with me, brothers and sisters and together we'll defeat the filth that has crawled into our city and filled its veins with disease. Today we stand, and forever, we live. WHO'S WITH ME?'

A roar went up. Faces animated and angered — the hairy, bristled, beautiful, ugly, scarred, blacks, whites, tans, greys and all in-betweens—their bloodshot eyes maddened by freedom.

Tommy Bones started making his moves, snaking luminous ropes stringing out from him to others. There was a Neon-esque tinge to it, hearts beating too fast, minds over-stimulated. Tommy moved forward, everyone looking at him. His features and moves were frantic, like something was trying to break out of him. Gang members started to move, like their muscles were retching. For a grim second, Victor thought everyone would dance, but it wasn't dance. It was breaking apart and mattering. These heroes were mutating right before him. He could feel them coming out of his shoulders, his back and his head. They were breaking their connection to the environment, making their choice.

Music started playing—industrial beats coming out of the station and the decaying buildings around them. Victor stayed perched on his platform as the gangs moved forward.

The Bugs had an effective strategy. They drove forward in formation, weakest first, sacrifice at will.

Raucous and the Headlong Brigade piled forward. They were blunt and good at it. But as they got deeper into the Bugs, Bug pheromones laced the air, lacerating Raucous, his face twisting and contorting with pain.

Victor found he could feel what everyone felt. There was a mesh coming out of him and going through everyone—steel lines of connected thought. The Bug attacks hit the mesh with small silver hammers. Then the hammers grew larger and the steel lines became strained. This pulled at each person's veins, tendons, bones, glandular and nervous systems. Everyone was getting stretched to their limits. It was an all out assault on

276

what it meant to be human. Lacerations of resentment travelling up the spine and encircling the mind with barbed wire.

Raucous and his gang continued forward, driven by pure will. They were impenetrable in the one place that couldn't be breached—belief in each other.

The Bugs regrouped and laid down new seductions for the mind.

Raucous' rugged face contorted. In his hand was a baseball bat, but he wasn't using it. It had become a prop, something he didn't understand. A Bug had noticed as well—Earwig, leather clad and incisive. It advanced on Raucous, trying to further prise into his mind. Victor leapt off his pedestal and ran down into the melee. The Bugs scarpered as he moved through them but not far enough for his liking. They had something behind them. Victor stopped, watching them lining up, they had a desperation he hadn't seen before. All around him, his people were being lacerated, doubts being plunged like daggers to the heart. It tugged into him through the mesh. He was used to pain, but he sure didn't like to lose a fight.

In-between the squares of the mesh were inky pools, you couldn't see them, they were behind the teeth, inside the stomach, deeply embedded between the ears. They created moments, but didn't appear. That was the true battle ground—otherness.

Bugs advanced around him, the woodlouse, *Armadillidium*, the ant, *Formicidae*, and the termite, *Blattodea*, all effective burrowers into nothing. They would plug the mesh—after they had plugged the people—with hate and sorrow.

277

Victor started laying them out, fists like pile drivers, one, two, three... but that wasn't it. It got him nowhere. He stopped in front of an earwig troop. They eyed each other. They invaded and he let them right into his gut. They crawled all over him producing what they produced—the sticky grime plugs of death that had killed Emily. It didn't matter. A Bombardier Beetle grabbed him, he felt the hands on his throat. He let it happen, felt the air in his throat constrict, felt the blackness of oxygen starvation. But he wasn't there, he was in the Bug's head watching himself—a suicide bomber implant.

The Bug twisted and turned, unsure, confused, plagued from within.

All things to be and being all things.

The devil mesh tourniquet tightened with every turn. Victor saw them all, Emily, Neon, Linda, smiling, nodding, it was tomorrow and yesterday, a bucket of fire instead of a head, cheap circus trick for thoughts, the ones where you lose yourself. Gunpowder, luminous green joints, half bricks, these were the gods of the new city. Madness on parade.

The Bugs hated it, it cursed their conformity, reversed all their impact and caused them to implode. But still more came, evolving faster.

Victor found his way to Raucous. 'You okay?'

Raucous was in a cloud of his own failings.

'Come on, man. What the hell are these Bugs setting off in you?'

Raucous' eyes flickered, but they were still far away.

It was a fucking disaster. Victor thought about getting Neon, but that didn't seem an option.

Spodge was standing by a car wreck, the road around her cracked into octagonal shapes. The city was drying, humans floundering everywhere. The Bugs offered an oily promise— survival and then slavery of all living things.

'Scram,' Tommy called out, but it wasn't a person's name. It was the question. What could be done?

'SCRAM!'

The sound travelled through smashed windows of the buildings around them and across rubble strewn floors. It bounced off street lights, bus stops and shop fronts, replacing the noise of living. It travelled across humanistic implements— conveyor belts, tin can apartments, plastic wrapped food, the pointless but inevitable production of restless impiety, the primal force that had brought them together—attraction of facts, unknown meanings, flesh, illusion and bastardary. People didn't know what to do with them, but they took part, were part of it, and somewhere out there were isolated towers in mutilated wastelands where maidens and crones, scientists and alchemists, further people, further minds, probed, pushed, placed eyes above mouths that puckered, shouted, teeth biting, giving out fucking hell and getting it back. Impaled thoughts, and knives stuck in thoughts, and thoughts as knives, fingers, hands, arms forming from shadows, from the sticky in-between, one last thought for everyone—bliss and exit.

Bugs started to get laid out. They couldn't take the pace. They got left behind with all the questions, the human aspect— the fuck knows why, but do it anyway.

The Bugs squealed a tear in the fabric of the city.

The ground rumbled, tremors travelling up through Victor's

feet and lacerating his body. He dropped down, plummeting into the innards. He felt what people wanted. The desire and formation of thought bound into construction. The scream of person, crushed and encased in programming. From far beneath, a hidden city gushed through him and everyone around. A raging torrent engulfed them, breaking the sticky tentacles of slavery. Victor cared deeply, but it wasn't him, he was just one point in a city of a million dots.

Slowly ebbing back into his head, Victor relaxed his jaw and sucked in a breath, realising that he had stopped breathing. The Bugs had disappeared. The street was strewn with fallen men and women—faces rewritten with horrific grimace.

'Scram, man.' Tommy raced over, his eyes glassy.

He gave Victor a big hug and Victor let him.

'Good to see you, Tommy.'

'Oh shit, man.' Tommy gestured at the fallen comrades. His hands pressed to the sides of his head.

'Pity they don't disappear like the Bugs.'

'No, man, my eyes a filament to not forget.'

'You what?'

Johnny Ease stumbled over. 'The walls, man. We need to remember, to chronicle.'

Tommy grinned a big toothed smile.

Victor nodded. The air smelt cleaner. He felt big, as they said. Yet somehow, not as big as before.

Tommy and Johnny headed over to the nearest building and started graffitiing. Their movements were jagged, different to Neon, they didn't seem to have the same presence of intent—

recorders not instigators.

Something caught Victor's eye. A bit fucking late for the ambulance.

Spodge moved over beside him, with a look of expectancy.

'Someone you know, Spodge?'

'Maybe so, Mr Scram, just maybe.'

The Ambulance pulled up past them, the back doors crashed open and the two men jumped out.

The inside of the ambulance flickered like a candle in the darks of Victor's mind.

Spodge and Arthur moved off together.

Iron Head remained. 'Your father would be proud.'

Victor nodded. 'I don't know if he did pride.'

'He did in the early days.' Iron Head rubbed his eyes.

Victor saw sadness on a hard face.

'He laid everything out, himself included,' said Iron Head.

'Maybe not a bad thing.'

'Yeah, you say that, but you picked it up. It's the men that you are. It's what keeps you together, and all of them.' Iron Head nodded over at the rag-tag collective that was left. 'You got the birth of something true going on there. Good luck with that.'

'Doesn't sound like you'll be hanging around to see it?'

'Nope. You're the underneath, but we're underneath, underneath.'

'That's fair enough. You got something for me?' Victor glanced at the ambulance.

Iron Head smiled and looked Victor in the eye. 'You're all done. What's in the ambulance is for Neon.'

'Got an address?'

'No, you?'

Victor had no answer for that one.

The street beneath them shook and the smell of scorched plastic filled the air.

Everyone's heads lifted.

There was a snap and the ground began crack open.

Victor blinked, but as he opened his eyes, a force blasted against him so hard that particles in him scarpered. Voices turned into slow motion roars and the cracking street became an incremental collection of flashes.

As reality caught up and everything returned to normal speed, a huge black stinger came out of the ground. It streaked through the air at lightning speed and impaled Arthur Sven through the back.

Spodge reacted, a knife instantly appearing in her hand, and she slashed up, cleanly cutting the stinger off where it entered Arthur's huge frame. He slumped to the ground.

'FUCK!' screamed Iron Head.

Victor ran over towards Spodge, grabbing Raucous' baseball bat from the ground. But the creature was gone. Spodge was on the ground holding Arthur's head, the black spike still sticking out of his chest. Tears streamed down her face, uninterrupted rivers, but no shudder or sound. She looked straight at Victor and he felt a wallop but held her gaze, letting her feelings flow without inhibition.

Iron Head walked over to them. 'I have to leave. This isn't finished yet, something far worse is coming.' He looked at Arthur. 'But without him...'

'I'm sorry, man,' said Victor.

'There aren't many cut from his cloth and I have one delivery to make.'

'Let me take it,' said Spodge.

'What?' asked Iron Head.

'I take it, but not like the old way.' She pointed to her motorcycle. 'On the back.'

Iron Head placed his hand over his mouth. He looked at the ambulance. Looked at Spodge. 'Do you really? That's one important cargo.'

'I fooking know.'

He sighed. 'Do it. If Arthur liked what you are made of, that's enough for me.'

Spodge shot away, her bike nosing and weaving through the debris. From the back, small hands tightly gripped her waist. The little ambulance kid was stronger than he looked.

Victor turned back to the gang standing behind him. The Black Street Chuggers were placing rubble over the bodies of the fallen and small mounds littered the street. The Kage had covered a large part of the wall with words and pictures. Tommy was quick with his spikes and ragged turquoise and luminous green. Johnny Ease was laying in the details with shade and shadow, and the Lady Fox was curling the forms together, bringing out the meaning with voluptuous form. The three moved like techno-lizards, watching and recording a psychedelic tapestry for the future.

'Shit,' said Victor seeing a gathering of Bugs coming down the street led by Liv. 'Fuckin woman.'

Liv separated from the Bugs and came alone.

Her makeup had run, eyes like boats on a black river.

'One last try, Liv?'

'No.'

'What do you want?'

'I want it to stop.'

Victor smirked. He wasn't angry with her, she was just a tragedy. 'You made your choice.'

'I didn't though, did I? I didn't choose. I just let it happen.' Her eyes welled with tears.

Victor moved closer. He didn't want tears. 'You gave it all away. You helped them.'

'I know. But I can take it back.'

'Why *did* you end up becoming the enemy?'

'Never found a friend I could trust. Enemies, those you can rely on.'

'That's not a sustainable future there, Liv.' Something about her made him want to collect up her pieces and stick them in a jar. She was fractured and should be broken but was living through pure will.

She moved towards him.

Victor flexed, ready for a knife, a gun. The eyes held him, they were believable, open, they spat, they snarled, they seduced, they looked deathly tired and they looked totally at him.

He knew where she was.

She wrapped her arms around him and laid her head on his chest. All tension evaporated as her slender frame sunk softly onto him.

He hugged her, his arms sealing together in a perfect fit. That surprised him. Her hair smelt like bitter blackcurrant and her neck of musty honey. The fabric of her dress smelt of burnt chocolate dipped in body sweat and city chalkiness. He smelt down past orange peel armpits to her exquisite hands, now smeared with inky mascara, wheat-smelling snot and the sharp glue of broken nails. Her breath was long and deep, lifting her slender ribcage and stomach. Victor smelt her fig-like belly button, sweet jasmine and tang ammonia between her legs, knee folds of lemony grease, dirty vanilla ankles, shit... she was pure fiction, yet somehow perfect.

Iron Head came over. 'Love or hate?'

'Probably both,' said Victor

'Good luck with that.'

Liv detached, stood back, almost apologetic, but tough. She nodded at the Bugs. 'They are clods of death, tarred with life, *my life*, all the super shitty bits.' She watched them hatefully. 'The beauty is, if you don't think about death, it doesn't exist. Puff, they can all disappear, which is fine. But if they disappear, all that shit returns to me and I don't want to go through that a second time.'

'The black hole is looking for a black hole.' Iron Head looked at his ambulance then turned to Victor. 'If I was looking for someone to hear a million screams continually, would I pick her?'

Victor looked at Liv. 'Every time. But who do *you* pick, Liv?'

'I pick you, Mr Scram.'

A flash, a blast of wind, a scream of Bug and the back doors of the Ambulance closed with a resounding thump. It trundled down the street with Liv and Iron Head inside.

An eerie silence remained.

'Who drives that thing?' said Tommy.

'We all do.'

Over East Side, the pixelated blur Victor had seen from the hill, hung so heavy it had started to block out the sun.

'Finish up now,' he shouted to the Kage. 'We might have passed Level One, but you better crank up some fucking mega moves for Level Two.'

Infectual Insanity

20

'Number 46, Shelley Street. I've been here before.'

'Yeah, you're so clever, Linda. Been in?'

'Nope.'

Linda saw in Neon's gaze the blueprint to the comedy that led them here. This was where the humour was going to end, where the ball was going to be potted, the ball that was rolling into her eyes and all the way down into her heart.

'Thinking of walking away, Linda?'

'Only when I've finished.'

'Something else to learn?'

'No.'

'So why then?

'I'm here to stop something.'

'Anything to do with me?'

'Flatter yourself.' Behind him, the interior of number 46 looked like a cheap film set; presence had moved out of buildings and into people and that left the city purposeless.

'What do you want to do in there?'

Neon raised his eyebrows. 'I want to break the last rule.'

'Sleeping with me?'

'You're all bad, Linda. And you're twice as good as that.'

'Is that so?'

They walked through the smashed aluminium doors, across

the unfinished floor of the lobby and into a windowless concrete corridor. The corridor tilted downward and quite quickly the air pressure built. Down and down they walked, beyond where miners went, down past the explorers, down beyond the dreams of engineers, past fears, consideration, down into the intestine of the city.

They arrived at a cavern. It was dark yet everything was known like there was a light flickering on and off at incredible speed. The walls dripped with grease and at their base were white and scaly ostrich sized eggs covered in feathers and slime. Around these, nest like, were munitions, bullet belts, truncheons, discarded guns and pornography.

Neon hummed beside her, as if he had been walking down this corridor all his life. She put her hand on the back of his head, fitted her fingers at the base of the skull. There was an urge to push them through, to squeeze his brain, explore the folds with her fingers, pinch, pull and bite into it.

'Who builds a building with downward pointing corridors?' she said.

'You tell me.'

In the darkness beyond them hung nothing—terror as absence.

Neon whistled.

The darkness infiltrated Linda's nostrils and eyes, quicksand surrounded her heart and silence slid through her ears like knives. Everyone she had ever known was dead. There was nowhere left to move. Yet it was just a basement—cold concrete walls, black puddles and rounded concrete pillars. She and Neon stood alone, cold, hungry, perched on one side of ultimate madness.

Neon put his hand on her cheek and looked into her eyes. 'There is a subtle beauty in the horror. Such freedom, eh? It's all so clever. To think we would come here, uninvited, yes, but how very intelligent of our design to give us the perfect entry into the engine room.'

'We're nowhere. We're in an empty basement.'

'Yes. How cold your fear is.'

A bed appeared in the middle of the room. An enormous bed. A body thrashed around in it. Reaching out in every direction, blind, defenceless and agitated. It was her.

'Your story, the one you told me when you first painted me. All to here.'

'Ain't that the funny part,' said Neon.

The slime on the walls slid down, snakes of it moving thickly across the floor.

'What's funny?' said Linda.

'That you think it's my story, when it's actually yours.'

The snakes began to form spikes along their spines, jellylike but infinitely penetrating.

'You're Victor's brother. When you were seven, your mother committed suicide in front of you to break the expectation chain.'

'Of course, well... ain't that sweet. Lacerations of trauma in order to create genius.'

'So modest.'

The snakes were forming together, each spiny back becoming the upper and lower jaws of a great mouth.

'Just words,' said Neon.

Fluorescent lights droned, but it was dark, so dark.

The bed was warm, soft, it spoke to her, told her about hidden places and pliable embraces, about mouths kissing and hands roaming around bodies, it told her about flowers, how they swayed in order to attract attention, how the wind was a fallacy, an explanation for the dance of life. The bed spoke further, it reminded her of who she had been, that small doll in a world far from here. 'So, Neon...' but every word became a tooth in a black jellylike jaw. She dropped into the congealed gardens of her entrails, placed desire in the pond and watched the bedspread dampen with tears and blood. The eggs at the base of the walls were her creations, threatened by the filthy ravages around them. On the bedspread was a pattern—small spiky flowers, yellow, hits of orange on the edge of the petals, there were snakes inside, the burrowing kind, the borrowing kind. Her forehead bulged, the black jelly mass was forming inside her. It plunged along her veins, arteries and sealed her eyes. It was repugnant, yet somehow it was the secret edge to everything that existed. It was vision, drips of it coming from the inside, a carnival of thought racing to the equator of awareness.

Neon laughed. 'I knew who you were all along. I teased you for the longest time, knew all about your mounds, your half eaten fruit, I elongated the garden of paradise... and you're insane, and you're insane.'

Fingers trailed down through her eye, the jelly structure, the spiked silhouette of a cut from above, incision.

'I am the doctor, you know.'

There had never been space in her head for two before. It all ached as they plunged into the sting sac of the Queen bee.

'You're just the examiner, I'm the source,' said Linda.

'Careful what you wish for, honey bee.' The underfloor thundered, concrete giving up its solid form. 'There are others who would beg to differ.'

'Let's make them beg then,' she said.

'How your cheek is rounded, you're a floral delight, bolder than a million dreams. I couldn't do it without you.'

'Yeah, carry on.'

'Your mouth, like a trumpet.'

'Oh, nice.'

'A herald, a blossom of person, the melody, the art of presentation, of elation, perfect pieces of the end in you, Linda Kalom.'

'Is there now.'

'One kiss.'

'One.'

'Only one.'

And as lips sealed, tomb lids dropped, the nuclear devices of the world became aware, hearts blackened and souls trembled in the long division of existence. For it had long being known that he would come, that he would enter as virus and implement the destruction of all kind.

The kiss was made of steel.

The inner bowels of the city erupted with a bilious gas. It shot past Linda in minutia, angry grasps passed through her eyelashes, ferocious instigators of pain, they shot over her eyeballs, past her ears, searing, scorching and squealing. Thoughts blackened, screamed and raged about fear, horror and the system dying, but she was anchored by the kiss, sealed in the instant of person, non person. She felt Neon's blood boil, his adrenals pass boiling point—infectual insanity. She moved, he followed, she dreamed, he cajoled, she danced, he laughed, but it was not funny, for through the part of her that was ripped out and pulled upward, she saw the city; ferocious insurrection, looting, fire and heinous crime erupting. And in the quiet places by the river, off flattened rocks, armless creatures slithered into the water, sickening chemical blots appeared on the horizon, the illusion of thought was dying.

They ran.

It followed.

The Loneliest Man

21

Spodge screeched up on her bike, a kid glued to her back. The Ambulance and Gangs followed led by Victor, Tommy Bones, Johnny and the Lady Fox.

'Spodge, how you going?' said Neon.

'Delivery for you.'

'Not for me, Spodge.' Neon smiled at the kid, liking the look in his eye. Lost in the wraps of Spodge's leather jacket the kid looked like a crow—shadows growing under the features. 'It's you he needs.'

'Sure.' Spodge's eyes shone.

A roar came from behind him.

'*Sir, what the fuck have we done?*'

'*Well... you ever get tired, 23?*'

'*It's hard to know what else there is.*'

'*I've maybe not treated you so well.*'

'*I've always found you to be a true gent.*'

'*Really?*'

'*No, sir. You're a complete scoundrel, the worst, but the very best at it. You played that one well.*'

'*We played that one well, can you feel the spite?*'

'*That Linda, oh...*'

'*Yes, we must escape her.*'

'*Escape, but she—*'

'But nothing, nothing at all.'

'Of course. It's cruel though.'

'Anything else is domesticated and pointless.'

'Will it mean anything if we're alone?'

'We're set for the stars, 23, mainlining the poisons of matter, boating across the thinking plan, the violent squall of a genetic sea, we're pushing off, arriving, we're destined, we're the vomit, the chasm, the willing but hapless organism, the sought after and from, the liberation man, the incineration man, the ought to be, the—be more than the one that went before. Thought is an octopus and all of this is a vicious tapestry, we will seduce the serpent from the seams, we will unfurl, uncurl, unfathom the spectacular, steal through, rip down the curtain of fools, and in the shredding, circumvent the destiny of the one who was cursed the most, then we will be gone. The loneliest man in the world was the first one.'

'Neon.'

'Victor Scram, alive to fight another day.'

Victor completed everything that was broken—the windows, the cars, the crumbling buildings and the people. He was supposed to let it fall apart, but he never did listen. A lifetime of Albert placing instructions in the city and a son who didn't listen to a fucking word. A pair of sons. Served the stupid shit right.

'...out there.' Victor waved his hand around.

'What?'

'Weren't you listening?'

'Funnily enough, no.'

'...Neon!'

'What?'

'You just keep staring.'

'Spiders in the soul.'

'Know the feeling. You gone and pissed everyone off.'

'Why so?'

'I dunno, perhaps unleashing hell might be part of it.'

Neon turned around. There was a whirlwind outside Number 46, and out of it creatures were crawling, bug-like, but worse, deeper, darker, further, blacker.

He turned back to the angry crowd gathered around Victor.

'You think that's my fault?'

'Yeah, man. People are dying,' said a man with a scar over his eye like an accusing finger.

'What is with these people, 23?'

'Loss, abjection, they're still wanting to enter the raffle for the meaning of life. Peel the ticket, take the chance.'

'Do they even care where they were going? Still hitting out, looking for reasons. Maybe we should just look through this guy, incinerate him. Then we'll just kick back and check out the cool girls with fancy arses.'

'Neon?' said Victor.

'Yeah?'

'What you up to?'

'Not that much. It ain't me, Victor. Think of it. Do you see any bugs around me? Always around you, around the Kage. Did you see me destroy the city? Did you see me do anything but paint other people?'

'You just came out of that building.'

'Yeah, with who?'

'You blaming me, Neon?' said Linda

'I ain't blaming. You're the changers. I have done nothing. I know who you are. I see you all. *That* is behind me, but it's in front of you.'

The crowd hesitated.

'You expect me to believe that?' said Victor.

'Expect? I don't expect anything of you, Victor Scram, you're the exodus of expectation. We're the end of the line, you and me.'

'I'm not you.'

'Oh you're all me. You're missing the bit there. I see you, click. If I didn't see you, you wouldn't matter.'

'You're a ridiculous contradiction.'

'Yes, touché and all that stuff.'

'People died, Neon. Raucous, most of his gang.'

'I know and it's very important that I get on, because even though there is great attraction in finding me as the cause of everything, cause is just a symptom swinging on the branches of pain. We are our own monsters.'

'That's just words, Neon. These people aren't dealing in words.'

'I apologise, it's no time to be selfish. I'll give you one from the road.' Neon jumped back. With a flash, a piece of street curled up like a roll of paper. 'Why, what is this before me, is the world unravelling? Oh no, that man is mad, he's a little fucking loony, oh no, the world is unravelling, everything we believed in is dying, oh my aching heart, and I was hoping to get a house, to have a pool, maybe a small dog, little smooch to hold at night. God forbid, what is this I see before me? I have *nothing* here before me.'

'Are you finished yet?' said Victor.

'No. I'm just about to start.'

Victor waved the crowd away. 'Listen Neon, you're a bit of a fucking cuckoo, but I've always liked you, even when I didn't like you in the slightest.'

'You're big there, Victor.'

'Now, I don't care what the hell you've done. That thing down there. Sure as hell, I'm gonna do my best to annihilate it in a moment. But just knowing what the fuck is going on would be good.'

Oh the truth, yeah, a nice street. And Liv, I see over there, sex as well perhaps?'

'Yeah, that too.'

'She'll try and kill you.'

'I don't even care about that. It's not so important to me, second chance and all that.'

'Yeah, Albert, or dad, parented in a really fucked up way,' said Neon.

'Dad?'

'Sure, yeah, mine too.'

'Shit, ain't that the turn up. Anyway, we're all here clanging on the mainframe, as Tommy would put it, and I can see that you're not a casual observer.'

'Neon 23?'

'Yes, sir.'

'Isn't it funny, that here, at the end of self-ness, self is still curious as to what Victor sees?'

'He's only gonna see what he feels. He's an emotion driven creature. A fighter, a lover, a winner and loser. The finest one of them

all.'

'He's changed though.'

'Sure, now he is a monster of the most immense order. The neural networks inside him are almost infinite. A nest for humanity.'

'Yeah, and all that isn't. But I guess he's good for the job.'

'He's a selfless beast, must run in the genes.'

'Not mine.'

'Really? Just cause you don't want the glory of response fed network, doesn't exclude the fact that you're taking the last cut for everyone.'

'I'm thinking there may be a way.'

'It has to be Linda.'

'Of course it has to be Linda.'

'But how, how can we do it? Can we embellish the lavish, can we caress the tigress thigh, spread the fleshy moon, shuffling sighs and cries —'

'Calm the fuck down, 23.'

'Yessir.'

'We have the plan. The plan is the same. Just one extra speck of dust in the harmony.'

'Neon? Neon?'

'Yes. Trust, Victor. That is all I ask. We came this far together. You go that way.' He pointed towards number 46. 'And I go that way.' He pointed in the opposite direction. 'We're the best of them, Victor. Must have had good mothers.'

'Will we meet again?'

'I know my road, and if you get to the end of yours, well shit, let's grab a beer, bruv.'

The Blood of Human Nature   22

Victor turned to the crowd. 'Alright boys and girls, let the Neon get on with his world. Move him along.'

Linda watched Neon like a hawk as he moved off.

'I guess you're tied in with him?' said Victor.

'One way or another. I think we've been tied together way too long. How you feeling?'

'Need some action.'

'You do, do you?'

'Not—'

'Yeah, yeah, you and Liv. Can't say I approve.'

'We're not fucking married.'

'Nah, you're further along than that. She's a lot of person.'

'What do you know of that?' Victor raised his head at the mass outside 46 Shelley Street.

Linda nodded. 'I'm not entirely convinced it's complete. It's part of me in the main, little bit of others. I'll tell you what.' She turned to Victor and looked straight into his eyes.

A pour of liquid took off the top of his head. Oily tendrils massaged his brain. It was fleshy but from a deep, sea creature world. Victor let it happen, moved away from the pleasure and emerged in the Diner. Simple layout, one table at which he was seated on a red faux leather bench, a small counter where Linda stood, and a black background.

'Jeans and t-shirt,' said Linda. 'No fancy clothes for me to wear?'

'You got no top on.'

Linda laughed and her top reappeared. 'Now, Mr Scram, here is the news. I know who I am, don't interrupt, I know that isn't genius. But...' She sat opposite Victor and poured a bead of multicoloured paint onto the table from a coffee pot. She ran it horizontal till it crossed the whole table. She then poured four round circles at the corners of the table, putting the coffee pot in one. Pointing at the remaining three circles. 'You, me, Neon.'

The Victor circle hovered upward and expanded larger. The Neon and Linda ones, moved up, turned sideways and began to spin at a rapid speed.

The hairs at the back of Victor's neck began to rise. The blackness around them felt febrile like a nesting ground.

The two spinning circles shot through the Victor circle, and stopped above it, still spinning.

Linda had what looked like an oar sized paintbrush with a thick, pale wood handle and a tear drop shaped head. She plunged it into the dark, stirred, brushed and jabbed it.

The Neon and Linda circles were spinning so fast, smoke came off them. The Victor circle hummed, vibrating like it was the top of a pool of water.

The table snapped in half.

Victor fell back, rolling off the bench as it too snapped shut like a pair of vicious jaws, squeezing the faux leather until red liquid poured onto the floor.

Beside them, suspended in the darkness, hung a painting — two large slashes of entwining paint, red and white, and a dancer at the bottom.

'A Neon?'

'Yep. *The Blood of Human Nature*.'

'Fitting. He planned this?'

'He saw it could happen.'

'An innocent man.'

Linda smiled laconically and walked over towards Victor, large paintbrush in hand.

The red liquid had formed into a snakelike creature and was moving intently towards him.

'So the blood of human nature comes from a bench?'

'From anything it wants to be from. Blood has red cells and white cells. There's the red, you're the white, the defender.'

'And you're the dancer.'

'Ta-da.'

'Okay. What does it want?

'It wants Neon.'

'What's he doing?'

'He's trying to kill it.'

'Not too surprising. And what do I need to know?'

'That it can only get into the city through you.'

The street was as he left it.

Linda smiled, almost apologetically, and moved off after Neon. 'Be the best, Victor.'

Tommy ambled over. He was shaking the gun in his hand, staring at it. 'Scram, man, it seems that the night has leaked into my head.'

'Ain't that the truth.'

301

Powerful confusions surrounded them. Tino stared incomprehensibly at his baseball bat. It was the outline, that which defined. It was becoming more important than the objects.

Liv stood stock still, eyes on Victor.

Spodge, with the kid on her knee, had her head cocked, listening, watching and smelling.

'The internal cliff, man,' said Johnny.

Victor turned his shoulders and the image of the city moved a millisecond late—*it* sat between them waiting, its tongue a flickering blindness.

'Scram?' said Tommy.

But it wasn't about that anymore. The script for this one hadn't been written. Black salamander creatures moved around at the end of the street. They had no interest in a fight, they didn't need to, every movement they made connected with the pupil, connected with the mind, the heart, all the organs. Victor squared up—it was a two way street after all. He put his hand on his chin, pulled his mouth open. They moved forward, snaking over, *yes babies, come to papa.*

Liv squinted and winked. This was not news to her. 'Got a plan, Mr Scram?'

'Nope.' As he shook his head, all the drawers flew open, spectral horrors swooped down, Emily, Emily, Emily, Neon... Whirlpools formed in his mouth, telegraph poles erected either side of him, wires stringing between his ears, sparking with cracking wavelengths. Contaminated voices squealed, fugitives played in city parks, children picked up sticks, saying bang, bang with those implements of wonder and fascination. Pool balls cracked, bottles smashed and petrol bombs flamed. The city was tight, the night secretive and snortable. Brown crumbling buildings became weapons, their intentions loaded—spikes, daggers and dungeons. Fires illuminated starving people, citizens of plague town where charcoal graffiti crawled low with the cockroaches. Lost causes waited in the corners, screams of the previous law bearer, now hermetically depraved. What lurked behind was hulking forward, out of shop doorways, through alleyways, over rat greased rust it swarmed, ravenous for the form of the outside.

Capitulation engulfed everyone.

'Shit. Run,' shouted Victor.

They ran, eyes corroded by the vision eaters.

Victor kicked open the door of the Diner. The Diner was intact in all its smoky yellow sanctity. People piled in and sat down. Everyone watched, curious of roles. Coffee scalded the thinking as waitresses sat on the counter, new, carefree ones with wide mouths and shapely legs. Listern scowled. The Bugs had gone and gang members filled their side, graffitiing tables and slashing the red faux benches. They threw empty cans, cups, sugar bowls and ketchup bottles at the back mirrors. They kicked toilet doors off and, as the cherry stools spun, music came from somewhere; one great party scene of the troubled soul.

Victor stood at the door with everyone in behind him. The Ambulance waited out on the street, doors closed, lights off. The street was empty, the quietness suspicious.

'Scram, man,' said Tommy.

'Stay here, Tommy.'

'No way, man.'

'Yeah, I'll be back.'

'We're coming man,' said Johnny. 'We got the box, man. The new box.'

Tommy nodded, pointing at a crudely bent cardboard box, with forks and knives stuck into it.

'Any chance this one is called, *we're all fucked*?'

'It's called, we got your fucking back, man.'

Victor nodded. They meant it. That was good. The street outside went to fuck knows where, so why not have the lost men for company.

They slipped out, the door not clanging behind them but damply thudding. Neon's graffiti looked old; a forgotten force. The new definition crawled around it, prodding, investigating and mocking. Tommy flung the box towards that side of the street. It thudded against boarded up windows and a Linda painting flared like it had been startled. There was an audible hiss. Tommy pulled at his hair. 'Crackles of the tubular envy, Johnny.'

'Yeah, man, what we been waiting for.'

Johnny went to move forward. Victor held out his hand.

'Now, Mr Scram, we do know that thee the man, but you gotta understand something here.'

'I do... what's that?'

'That we been waiting, man. Ever since you unplugged it all, ever since the stars been chuggin' way up in the blue, we been seeking the ultimate mainframe. Now that's it, man, and we gonna stick some connection in there. The Tommy Fucking Bones is getting his frazzle, man.'

'Chuck the tunes in the perpendicular incendiary, man.'
Tommy bared his teeth at the darkness.

'You guys are superstars of the flat line. But that thing is coming to me.'

'Oh we know. Its connection to you is the ultimate, nothing in flesh, mind or machine needs to be that together. It's gonna lay you out, Scram, man. Torture as an introduction, prolonged slivers of extraction as the main, more deathly than—'

'Got the picture, Johnny.'

Graffiti started peeling off the cube building opposite. The images fell to the street, quickly discarded by the wind.

Victor's face became 300 feet tall. His tongue expanded into a fleshy, saturated ball, eyes burned to charcoal, teeth flopped out, walloping his chin on exit, breaking his toes on the way down, his knee caps were pulled, twisted, snapped, thighs sliced, bones snapped, cock, arse, sliced, quartered, discarded, balls stolen, stomach frozen, exploded, razor shrapnel lacerating lungs, arms casually tugged away—stripping down the human.

Victor remained at peace. It was a family game after all.

The Beast skulked. This was just the introduction.

Liberty

23

Linda pushed Neon against a pebble dash wall, grabbing his chin to make him look at her. His eyes were blank holes. She smelt him, violently, but it was only the wall she smelt. She closed her eyes, ripped his body open, spreading him all over the street. There was no life in his form. She stormed into where his thoughts had been, but it was dry and empty. She came out and stared at buildings around her. There were scents everywhere, but she only wanted one. One molecule of vital Neon—a drop of sweat, paint, an odour left on the street, a breath lingering in her hair.

From streets away there came an enormous grinding scream. *Good luck, Victor.*

She focussed on the noise surrounding her. The crackling of rusting cars, the hiss of microscopic dust dropping from the dying buildings, the swish of air moving over the hairs of her nose, sweat drying on her forehead, dripping in her armpits, between her legs, her eye lashes slapping together, nails growing, hair grating, teeth squeaking, lips... And there he was—a tiny speck of saliva drying on her lip. She touched her finger to it, pinning it down in case it tried to completely evaporate.

Perfect.

'Don't go after him,' said a large shopkeeper, standing

outside a shop.

'What do you know of it?'

'I know that when he disappeared, the city became a better place.'

'That's cause he took your shit with him.'

Her bee leapt from its pedestal and swooped down, greedily seeking pollen. It could have it all. They rocketed forward, green garden turning from darkness to burning sunshine.

It took a while to adjust to the brightness of the vast desert. Hills were sparsely placed, populated with tufts of grass, cacti and rough bushes. Every rock and bush, every colouring of brown, yellow and grey, was exactly designed. This was one personal desert, she thought as a familiar sun soaked into her body.

Perched up a hill about fifty feet away, Neon stood—dirty ragged man stark against a brilliant blue sky.

Linda sat on a rock, took off her boots and flung them away. She ripped her tights away from her feet and then rose and gingerly began climbing the hill.

'Hotter than hell, ain't it?' said Neon. He smiled, eyes aflame, and bit his upper lip. 'Took your time.'

'Idiot.' Linda felt like hitting him, but maintained her composure. 'Rumour has it, I should have walked away.'

'This is what gets done.' Neon's face twitched.

Linda eyed him.

He stood stock still, grinning at her.

Spreading her toes out, she felt the sharp ground beneath her feet. Behind Neon, down the hill, were his sculptures. 'You're bringing them through?'

'Hole's getting ripped open now.'

'Ripped open by a creature that will destroy everything?'

'Ain't gonna destroy Victor Scram.'

'Nah, you're gonna do that.'

'Me? And what you doing here, Linda? Just a girlfriend, are you?'

Her head and body vibrated like they were made up of separate pieces. Gunshots came from out in the desert. Bang. Bang. She held Neon's image so that he didn't disappear. Had to hold it all, the hills, the tufts, the cacti.

Her chest inflated like a hot air balloon, eyes became vast blue pools, the sides of her jaw elongated down and individual thoughts expanded into eternities. She was waking up in a waking up... her feet burned in the sand, she knelt down, pushing sand over her fingers, smelling the toil of her years, watched the cacti, remembered wolves prowling at night in the cinema of the mind, felt her heart thumping in the sky. This was her land, all of it was inside *her* head.

'There was only ever going to be one. One person who would see unhindered,' said Neon.

'You're an intruder.'

'I'm unhinged, if that's what you mean. Let's not waste time.'

In an instant, they were down the hill and beside a shiny sculpture.

'Your great work,' said Linda.

'Pieces of the dazzle.'

The metal of the sculpture shone so bright it scorched inside her head and blanked out her thoughts. She retreated and reappraised.

She *was* standing in a dried lakebed, cracked hexagonal mud beneath her feet. She ran through her inner body system, established what connected to what. The presence of the sculpture made her body patterns collapse, it threatened everything. Linda moved, the sculpture moved. It dismantled her perception of body parts. Linda fought back. She reassembled her feet, felt the hot dust on her toes. She constructed the joining of her ankles, felt the flapping shards of her tights tickle her flesh. She turned them into wings, shot herself up into the air. She created, the sculpture dismantled — mind, limbs, and head. Linda stopped creating. It wasn't important.

And there was Neon's smile, his glistening sparkling eyes. Linda changed direction, evaded him, and his smile dropped an octave. She returned to her body and smiled. 'Impressive.'

'This is Neon 23.'

Linda saw another Neon, not with her eyes, somewhere deeper.

'*It's an honour.*'

'And who are you?'

'*I'm inside, like yours. I'm the last. We always wanted to meet you.*'

Linda smelt lotus, geranium, and lavender.

'He wants to walk in your garden before he goes.'

Linda nodded. She felt a lifting of her spirit, like eternity had just doubled.

'This,' Neon pointed to the shiny sculpture, 'is Liberty.'

The mixture of metal and textile was like a mini junkyard.

She wanted to say it was clumsy, that the eyes were just large light bulbs, but on their surface, dust was shaped into an intricate labyrinth. Hot desert air whistled tiny tunes through the labyrinth paths and she followed them, ending up in an inky darkness. Her heart fell in slow motion, raw pink lit up from a light below, and down there, glistening, was the immense spike of a bee sting.

Placing her hand on her chest, she thought of breath and water and imagined sitting down eating food and talking with friends. This experiment had gone too far. She had plummeted too fast, was no longer a person, she was an idea, a configuration, a summation of forces, she was beyond herself; a tragedy of individual.

The sculpture laughed at her, revealing teeth of crudely shaped rubble. The blunt, rounded teeth were like muscled torsos crouching from another grind together. The gums glistened, but not with moisture, they were tenements and from within, broken nails scratched at broken windows, cuticles getting cut on spider web fractures. Faces peered with stale lips, eyes limp and teary. And then there were the brave ones, those that rode on a roughly hewn tongue, the grime teasers, bodies ripped and rotting, corpses with eyes of seduction, their curled fingers grappling with decency, undoing straps and molesting the last hope.

'Why call it Liberty when everyone it embodies is trapped?'

He looked at her.

She saw *the him* looking, that blink of hesitation, almost stupidly childlike. She wanted to slap him, but was pulled back into the sculpture and its immense inner swamp of electrical cables—blues, greens, browns, yellows and black. *This is a ridiculous creation.* Connections were strewn like confetti. It was all words, computers, ballerinas and body parts. It was strobe lights, music and dancing. It was laughter and people screaming down alleyways. It was gunslingers, Bugs crawling under streets, wars and reckless people. It was hills, trees, lips pushing against each other, snaky limbs and lovers, overgrown car lots, sewer systems, memories and expectation. It was body systems strung up on wires and imprinted in minds. Everything Neon did was here. The paintings in his studio were etched on the bone joints, the sculpture head was tilted because Neon's characters overfilled the brain—dangerous dancers with razor hands, feet and eyes. It was what he stole, what he was given, and where he had taken it—cellulose and celluloid electrical binds, woven together with the secret of bird flight, all spinning on a nervous system, roulette spine.

It poured into her. She let colours become dreams, let crows carry off thoughts and drop them into oceans of emotion. She saw eagles wrap talons around urges, saw hippopotami overturn boats filled with desire. Within and without, society crumbled and reformed in an architectural epilepsy. Evolution raged in both directions, seething at the interference.

'Why?'

'Curiosity, ambition, the simple connection between human and nature and what would happen if you spliced the two and took a joyride. It's a simple voodoo. Give over your mind and we'll all be happy.'

'I don't think so.'

'You don't? You came all the way here to say, *nah, don't want*

311

to do that. I'd much prefer to go back to what I already know.'

'It's my head? Get out.'

'If you want me out, why am I still here?'

'Because I will capture your true face.'

'You're infected with creation. The origin did that, they trapped us in it.'

'And what are you proposing?'

'Something infinitely sharper, the shadow of the shadow. All set free.'

He touched her face, crimson tears of family rolled out of her eyes. There was nobody here except them and that stranger, the duke of darkness riding on the back of society. And of course, a bee and a praying mantis—two badass muthafuckers.

'You untie me, bitch,' said the sculpture.

'Did you use Liv's mouth?'

'Give it away, Linda.'

'You're playing, Neon. You're twiddling your thumbs, waiting for more than this.'

'Waiting for you, babe.'

'Yeah? You're waiting for something just over my shoulder a lot more.'

'You're the most extraordinary person I ever met. You're beyond it all.'

'I'm destroyed.'

'Who else could run a blade across the veins of humanity?'

'We're just kids, Neon, real people. You're tied into madness.'

'Not yet, truly. Don't you want to take the ferry ride across the velvet dune, surf the breath into the corporeal spiral, climb beyond, sever all ties...'

'We'll be dead.'

'The differentiation of completion is annihilation.'

'I care to live.'

'You don't though. The tools to kill are in your eyes, not mine.'

He was right. Because the truth was, she had it in her. She always had. All her life it had waited for one chance to make a lasting contribution, one paint stroke, one kiss, one word, one final ation. 'Can't we just be people?'

'No, we tried that, it didn't work.'

A painting floated passed them—Neon lying on a studio floor bleeding, Linda painting with a bloodied knife beside her.

'That never happened.'

'Every eventuality we create is possible, is lived, is rejected.'

'This is no different.'

'Oh, but it is. I'm the pattern, you're the seamstress and Victor will give you the thread.'

'Bastard.'

'Yes I am.'

Her stomach bent, mouth watered, eyes teared; buzzing, so much buzzing, tearing, waves crashing, resignation unfolding... *I see some music... there is someone up ahead...* unlock, unload, present and repent. A thousand flowers, a thousand hours, a thousand heart beats whipping the life force of the sculpture mind.

'All of you, but just once.'

An Erotic Funeral

24

A faint pixelated image of Victor, face locked in grimace, was visible on the graffiti wall opposite the Diner. The positioning implied it was burned there by the exposure of the Diner door opening. Snap.

Neon pushed the Diner door open. Inside was a new chaos—gang members new and old, but no Victor or Kage. He closed the door and returned to the street.

'Where is he, 23?'

'This is murky stuff, sir. How can we see?'

'Let the bloody Mantis tune us in. This is his time.'

Buildings revealed revolving epicentres, their all possible directions loomed, lurked and nuzzled the epidermis of dark space. It let them.

'I always wanted a bigger world,' said Neon

Cars sat smug in their decrepit state, happy that they had no further to go. Forgotten people strolled past in trails of yesterday's stimuli. Closer to the graffiti wall, a million dots of person lay splattered around—Victor's theatre of inevitability had played itself out.

'Neon?' said Linda.

He turned.

'Fuck, your eyes.'

'Damn, Linda. Ssssshhhh.'

'Why?' The word hopped out, bounded around. She smiled; sharp lines from her eyes probing the murky night.

The beast was everywhere. It touched his shoulder, curled in the shadows of Linda's throat and slipped along in the gutter setting off the tick-tock in the rusty clockwork of building shadows.

'Where's Victor?' said Linda.

The question elbowed past Neon's ears and punched his mind. 'Close.'

Linda laughed, sharp lines snaking down.

'What?' said Neon.

'Listen.'

Victor stood in front of them.

'Interesting,' said Neon. 'I would say Victor Scram, but I don't believe that would be the right name.'

Victor's face was bloated, eyes glazed over and, from between pouting lips, small puffy clouds appeared.

'And what do we have here?' Linda walked close.

The Victor turned unsteadily.

Linda smiled.

'23?'

'This is it.'

'Is what?'

'The crux of externality. We will no longer be ourselves, we shall be the occurrence of everything else.'

Neon's chest tightened. 'Free it, Linda. Let it out.'

'Yes, baby. All for you, honey pie. Sweet cakes.'

'Shut the fuck up. Be serious!'

'Nope, not now. It's all happening, Neon. This is the

moment in-between. I do believe we're already over the finish line.' She winked.

Neon's head wobbled. Thought was being reversed by stimulation, caress and invitation. He was dying in both directions, before injury and after injury and Linda's eyelashes were the main weapons. *She* was dirty, knee deep in dark pools of street, but she was wise in the lavish, a personality controller and epicentre of all that was desirable. She was love, pleasant caring, yet cruel torturer; she was captivating, insanity creating, she was sexual, a caress, deep love that flowed over the tops of razorblades, oozing sentiment, squalling with the creeping catcalls of cabaret vultures. She fed on the him, creosoting his soul, terrifying, but all good, the deep bellow of heartfelt, trouser belt, canon shot, goddess of the day and night, she was the flower that bloomed in order to die, a waterfall of elaborate coffin screams.

Shit... he was getting lost in an erotic funeral. Move the leg over, temple the lavish, incinerate breasts in semen inferno. Intention, not such an innocent saliva, was proffered by her soft lips pouting in all possible directions. 'You're using a strange science there, Linda.'

She laughed. 'Should be easy for you and your urchin nature to understand.'

He shook his head.

'23?'

'24.'

'*I don't have a 24, Mr Mantis.*'

'*No you don't.*'

Linda grabbed his hand. She fell, he caught, she cried, mad

316

lady, no better way. Tears of yellow flowed across the sidewalk, orange opened its hands, purple suggested an elopement, sister blue cooled his eyes, mother black slowed his heart and sure footed green lit up the gallows with an electric flashlight.

The executioner scrubbed their heads.

Spodge sat on the sidewalk with her back against the Diner. She waved, her other arm around the Neon child who was tapping little nooses that hung in the air.

More gang members arrived, took up seats beside Spodge and watched. There was nothing left to fight. The arrival of origin had left everyone nonplussed, disappointed and normal.

'I would have liked to have delivered more,' Neon shouted.

Their heads didn't rise.

The Diner sagged. For such a shithole it had given a lot.

Spodge shrugged at Neon.

He could see she couldn't move easily. None of the crowd could, they were as good as painted, everything was. A fire burning down by the street corner flickered out strips of fabric—yellow, orange and red, harmlessly flapping in the wind. Something had occurred, some ingredient had evaporated. Yet the small Neon child who sat with Spodge was moving without restriction...

'It's you?' Neon shouted. 'You designed this.'

'Have I..?' He smiled a strange little smile, halfway between daydream and malice. Blood had started to fill his pale cheeks from the bottom.

'Did we decide on a plan, is it between us?' asked Neon.

The kid knocked a noose, which knocked a noose, Neon watched them ripple towards him.

Victor's tongue lolled and he cried out in pain, a roar from deep within the bowels.

All went dark.

'There's nothing here,' said Neon.

'How cold your fear is,' said Linda.

'Turing the tables are you now?'

'Yes, I am. I'm the key.'

'You're not.'

'So why am I here?'

'You get an answer to that question, let me know what you find.'

'I don't believe you have a fucking clue what you're doing.'

'That's just rude, etched in truth, but essentially rude.'

'So what then?'

The Neon child stood up.

Neon felt nooses slap against his face. The air smelt of damp twine and petroleum.

'Shit, Neon. It's everywhere.' Linda looked exhausted. Black bags under her eyes, freckles in the gray skin around her mouth, or perhaps it was dirt.

The Victor beside her was a blimp, an inflated mess.

'My paintings never made this much sense.'

The kid Neon walked towards him. Swaggered.

'Bit of a bad ass, are you?' said Neon.

'I'm you.'

'Bit of me, in fact, just one piece.'

The kid's eyes were puddle factories, messengers from a dark heart.

'What's the plan, kid?'

'I hoped you'd know.'

'Nah, that ain't true. I never hoped for anything, never fucking once,' said Neon.

'Peaceful life?'

'Never wanted one.'

'Peaceful mind?'

'Never expected it, never requested it. You got a lotta questions for a little 'un.'

'Had a lot of time to think in the dark place.'

'How *was* that?'

'It was a limitless vacuum, a sucking, timeless tribunal of continuous poison, but that's just on the outside, the shallow bit. On the inside it was a visionary excursion in prolonged self-torture.'

'Sounds useful.'

'Oh yes. You don't remember the decision, because I took that memory with me. I knew, all that time that we had decided to do this.'

'Course you would. How did that sit with you, fella, did it make you cross? Was it circumstance that angered you, or was it something else, something more personal?'

'Limitless poison. Think about that, think about what *you* would do with something like that.'

A drum started, metal squalled, Deathwatch beetles emerged from the shadows—tick, tick, tick.

'And I thought the city was clockwork,' said Neon.

'It is in the secret places,' said the kid. 'All over the city are invisible handles, switches, connecting points. Every day and night people press them, punch them, kick them, flick them

319

with eyelashes, brush them with lips. All around, Mr Older Neon, all around.'

'Yes. Secret code, is it?'

'Listen, Neon,' said Linda. 'I know you and the little fella got a lot of catching up to do, but there is a sense of impending doom here.'

'Yes, yes. But no. I see nothing of doom. I have thought this through, Linda.'

'You haven't planned a fucking sausage, Neon,' said Victor, deflated and normal looking.

'Victor Scram, alive and well *again*.'

'Where the fuck is that thing?'

'Ah, it's around somewhere reproducing.'

'Reproducing?'

'Yes, red blood cells can't reproduce, white can. The originator had no ability to be in this world. It isn't possible. You get fathers and mothers, oh yeah, you don't get origin. There is no need, it doesn't exist once creation has been implemented.'

'But it's here?'

'Oh, we brought it back. Little bit of self reflection for it.'

'And it wants to kill us, you mainly.'

'Sure, I am infinitely killable. It is very exciting really, at last to be narrowed down to the one that can die. Who am I? Bang, there you are.'

'You're getting close there, old fella,' said the little 'un.

The window of the Diner smashed, its silver tears cascading down onto the gang members beneath. A manhole cover shot up, walloping a car on landing and the Kage popped out of the ground.

'The men... and the woman,' said Neon.

Johnny, Tommy and the Lady Fox shuffled over.

Johnny cleared his throat but not his eyes. 'We have connected to the sense flow, of what there could be, but do not know, we... of the mind that went before, all you, and we... of a kind, you cannot know, we, alien species in this pot of shit city, glad versions of males, and bad clad females, and hail, this man, Neon, for he is the electric blue, he that actually could do.'

Linda glowed. She was enjoying this.

Neon nodded. It was nice, there was no doubt. All friends together. It made sense to kill them all. Or did even he, at last, care too much?

Linda brushed her hair back from her face. Her hand was a lizard, her face fur, her mouth a mind. She was decent, capable, but earthy, the soil that held them all so long.

Neon turned to the kid. 'Handles, you say.'

'Yes, the city is filled with them.'

'Show me.'

The kid smiled. 'I will not.'

Tommy Bones wheeled over. 'A little Neon, man. We could get rid of the old one.'

'You're free now, Tommy. Take your spaceshit out of orbit, break the sync, the flavour of life is repugnant. You should no longer wish to hear a-rat-a-tat-tat.'

Tommy looked up, eyes floating in the chemical swirl of vision-drenched narcotic thought.

Neon smiled. 'It's an inevitable conclusion not to do so, but you must always further yourself, you will never find what you seek as long as your feet can touch the bottom.'

'Are you killing me?'

'No, Tommy. You've been dead for a while now. It is of no concern, it was a very dramatic journey and to be here now, with this visual presentation, most impressive. Clinging is a very Bug-like tendency. Solid leverage, open up the transmission—stars, acceleration, onwards to the immaculate beyond.'

'Johnny? Foxy?' said Tommy.

'Yeah, man. Turning, returning, returning,' said Johnny.

They headed down the street, jazzing, wiling, turning and returning. Of course they weren't dead, but they were dead to what was going to happen here.

'There goes the Kage.' Victor nodded, then looked confused. 'I don't believe I have a head.'

'Ah, Victor, you lost your head long ago. Course, how could you remember without a head?'

'Puts me at a distinct disadvantage.'

'I wouldn't say that, you never used it so well.'

Victor of course did have a head, just not like his old ones. He was lucky, he had completed the journey to his world, he had succeeded.

'You better head off, Victor.'

'Nice pun. Don't know if I want to leave you guys.'

'You already have. There is nothing left here.' And there wasn't. Streets were a distant memory, Diners, cars, buildings, they were a sentimental viewing, a possible, but not very fucking likely. This was a chattering transit village between what was and will be. He and Linda were criminals, the accused, the intended victims. Bugs waited inside them. Everything was decided, inevitable really. *'You can't fuck with who you are, isn't that so, Linda.'*

'I don't think you should be in here, this is a very private space.'

'Girl, you look so pretty, it's nice that you decided to put shells in your hair.'

'Yes, it's my mermaid look. I've decided that being a little girl was the only possible reason why it all happened. I don't think I ever got over being that free, you know. It really kinda pisses me off, this memory based interest in things.'

'Shall I kill it now?'

'You won't be doing that, Neon.'

'I won't, Mr Mantis, of course not, cause the inevitable conclusion of all this is the suicide gene. I will only be able to kill myself, am I correct?'

'You could be, but really, I'll take care of that for you.'

'Of course, you'd like that, wouldn't you. I'm not knocking the sensory extraordinaire, I certainly needed you. I think though, you are exaggerated. You've been inside too long.'

'Not much longer.'

Saliva poured out down Neon's chin. He wiped it. Blood. Eye veins split open, blood pouring into his eyes. No one cares, no one cares.

Beast moves forward, humanity drags backwards.

The beast moved down a tunnel where once the street had been. White scaly, nervous system like creature, bleached slug body, tapeworm face—an expected horror.

Linda's spray can dropped without making a noise.

Spodge tried to run over but there was nowhere to put her

feet.

Somewhere behind Neon's eye slithered a snake, not creature, but raw stimuli made flesh, the sinewy secretion mass of human creation.

He crawled in with it.

The Beast stood next to the Mantis. *'You will be judged.'*

'You can't judge me,' said Neon.

'I'm what you're made of, you're mine.'

'I am something other.'

'You're confusing the viewer as a separate entity.'

'You're confusing the entity as something I give a fuck about.'

'Shall we test your theory?'

A buzzing sounded and a bee joined the terrible two.

'And you would leave me there?' said Linda.

'Of course not, shall I introduce?'

'I'm sure we've met. Missed out on getting your Bugboy over, did you?'

'You.'

'You've got a good rep there, Linda. They want to judge us.'

'They would, they're curious as to why you're not scared, fear is their prerequisite.'

'I was thinking it was because of my genius.'

'Of course, vision, mania, talent and a kind heart.'

'Aw, still trying to stop me?'

'No, it's all okay, but here is where I stop. I have a life that I want and if it's not what you want, then we part'

'Shit, Linda. All this way to say that?'

'I wouldn't want you to underestimate how real it is.'

Shit, she had one pair of soft wings, something that came

from above, not flying, just not falling, and flowers for eyes, the arc of the petal that pulling feeling—dew drop surf to the heart.

'You're a thief, Linda. You stole everything I didn't want to be and you held it safe inside that madness of yours. Can't you see why we are here? We kill it.'

'And you die, because whatever part of you that comes from it will be extinguished.'

'I don't care.'

'Neon!'

'I care for you, I do.'

'Do you want to be like Albert, like your mother?'

'I am not the inevitable progression from those.'

'Are you sure? We broke the binds, Neon, you are other, I am other, we have it all to explore. There is no rush. What they are, what they expect, it isn't the way.'

'You're scared, Neon.'

'You mean, you are, if I am nothing but you.'

Neon turned to Linda. I'm sure at times I will not be the person you want.'

'You're rarely the person I want. But I don't want a person. I just want to be stood beside, to have someone hear what I hear, see what I see, dream where I am and escape every day with me.'

'Sure, why not.'

'Really?'

There was a clanking, a flash of light and a blast of desert wind. A scream moved from the inner to the outer of both Neon and Linda's lips.

'Try me, you bastards,' said Neon's sculpture.

'And what are you?' said the Beast.

'I'm Liberty. A little touch of indiscipline, a smattering of tragedy, infantile you might say, belonging to none, not him, not her and definitely not you.'

'Mantis, take care of her, it, or whatever that aberration is.'

'No, you filthy fiend,' said Liberty. 'The Mantis is compromised on every level of my appearance. I can mirror the tilt of his ocular pass, his definition, I can reside behind his eyes, can dream in his essence at will. You can't touch me, bastard, I erode the fabric of your control and every time you know me, a piece of you disappears. I am the cream of maniac, the seclusion of self and the scribe of the new city.'

The bee hummed, the mantis raised those praying arms, eyes furious and the Beast swelled, all shadow disappearing from its form, attempting to engulf what could not be engulfed.

Neon and Linda stood on the street. But they did not truly exist on it, for all they were formed of was to be annihilated.

'So we're done now,' said Linda.

'We sure did something. *And* we let it go. Nice that.'

Slowly, up the drainpipe of their brains, gas rose, form became ineffective as transformation placed its feet on the ledge. There had been flesh and there had been thought, there had been people waiting in a city, Diner waitresses swinging their legs, there had been a man who could raise the consciousness of the city with a single movement and there were kids out there, broken ones who no longer needed to be fixed, there was a girl who had a dream and in that dream a man came alive and he too had a dream and that dream led to other dreams and those two dreamers just could not stop, they laughed at the ladders they used to climb through the stars and tripped each other as they ran away from beasts that swore to kill them. They had no knowledge any more of the other parts they had left behind, their two slumped bodies being picked off an empty street and placed carefully in the back of that old, rusty ambulance.